The White Witch of Rosehall

The White Witch of Rosehall

A very striking and curious story, founded on fact, of the West Indies of the early nineteenth century. The descriptions of island life and scenery and of obeah magic are particularly well done.

The author was for some forty years editor of *The Gleaner*, the leading daily paper of the West Indies, and his influence on Jamaican thought and life was immeasurable. He was awarded the C.M.G. for his literary work; of his books, *The White Witch of Rosehall* is probably the best known. His style may be best summed up by quoting from a letter written to him by Somerset Maugham: 'I enjoyed your two books; they are full of life and character ... They are also, a trait not too common in modern fiction, extremely readable.'

By the same author

PSYCHE
MORGAN'S DAUGHTER
THE CUP AND THE LIP

The White Witch of Rosehall

Herbert G. de Lisser

MACMILLAN
CARIBBEAN

Macmillan Education
Between Towns Road, Oxford, OX4 3PP
A division of Macmillan Publishers Limited
Companies and representatives throughout the world

www.macmillan-caribbean.com

ISBN-13: 978-1-4050-8592-2

First published 1929 by Earnest Benn Limited
Published by MACMILLAN EDUCATION LTD 1982
Reprinted 1983, 1984, 1986, 1988, 1991, 1995

Typeset by EXPO Holdings, Malaysia
Cover design by John Barker
Cover illustration by Judy Ann MacMillan

Printed and bound in Malaysia

2011 2010 2009 2008 2007
10 9 8 7 6 5 4 3 2 1

Contents

CHAPTER 1

The New Book-keeper

ROBERT RUTHERFORD reined in his horse at the stone and iron gates that opened into the estate; half a mile away, on an eminence that commanded a wide, sweeping view of canelands, hills and sea, stood a building, the fame of whose magnificence he had heard when in the town of Montego Bay, some ten miles to westward.

White in the golden light of the sun it stood, the Great House of Rosehall. It dominated the landscape; it imposed itself upon the gaze of all who might pass along the road that ran in front of the property; it indicated opulence. Young Rutherford knew that it represented the pride and arrogance of the planter caste which still ruled Jamaica, and whose word, on its own plantations, carried all the authority and sanction of an arbitrary will scarcely curbed by laws passed in recent years for the protection of the bondsmen. Behind him, a few paces from the outer edge of the road, rolled and glittered a vast expanse of sea, all blue and purple, with snowy breakers rolling lazily to the shore. Above him stretched a vault of azure flecked with clouds. It was eight o'clock in the morning. The month was December; the year, 1831.

The cane, full grown, flowed up to within a short distance of the Great House, a spreading carpet of vivid greens. In the midst of it, to his right, he saw the sugar works, from the chimneys of which floated and wavered in the breeze long columns of grey smoke. To the left he spied a building on rising ground which he guessed to be the overseer's house; and on this side also, well within sight of the building, he saw a village of huts embowered in greenery. He had been long enough in Jamaica to recognize in this the slaves' quarters.

He twitched his reins and the horse moved forward.

As he slowly trotted up the long path leading southwards he noted the slaves, clothed in coarse blue osnaburg, busy cutting canes in the fields, women as well as men armed with scythes and machetes, and hacking at the roots of the slender green-topped plants. Wagons drawn by oxen and by mules stood in the paths, several feet wide, which divided field from field; in these wagons the workers heaped the canes they cut, and as he passed he saw some of these vehicles moving on their journey towards the sugar mills, with a creaking and groaning of axles and amidst shouts from sable drivers who ran alongside of them cracking ox-thonged whips four yards long and calling to the cattle by name. He saw other men armed with whips also which they brandished menacingly, though not at the oxen and the mules. These were the slave-drivers, sturdy fellows whose duty it was to see that the slaves did not loiter or slacken at their work; yet in spite of them some of the labourers lifted curious eyes to gaze for a moment at the strange white man who seemed to be going up to the Great House where lived the lady owner of these domains. The drivers glanced at him also, but asked no questions, for he was white and therefore one of the masters who gave commands and put questions, and was not there to be interrogated by such as they.

But before he had achieved half the distance to the house he perceived a white man riding towards him. This was the only other man on horseback discernible, a young man like himself, the estate book-keeper doubtless. The man cantered up, made a careless gesture of greeting, then inquired: 'You are Robert Rutherford?'

'Yes; you expected me?'

'The overseer told me last night that you would be here today; we expected you rather earlier, though; at daybreak, in fact. You are going to be told you are late, Rutherford.'

'I had to ride from the Bay; I shall be up in time tomorrow morning. You are my colleague?'

'Yes. My name is Burbridge, and I have been doing the work of two book-keepers for the past week. They cleared out the other man as soon as they thought you were nearly here. You see that house?' He pointed in the direction of the overseer's residence. 'That's where Mr Ashman, the busha,* lives, and I know he is there now. You had better go up there and report to him. I'll see you later.'

'One moment, Burbridge,' Rutherford stopped him. 'Give me a hint as to the situation here before I meet the boss, will you? Nice place this?'

'I have stayed with you too long as it is, old fellow,' replied Burbridge quickly. 'My job is waiting on me; all I am supposed to do – if I am even supposed to do that – is to give you directions where to find the busha. I don't want to be blamed, if I can help it. And look here, don't, like a good chap, repeat anything that I have said to you, will you?'

'Well, you haven't said anything,' smiled Rutherford, 'so I can't repeat it. This seems a strict sort of place, doesn't it?'

'You'll find out all about it for yourself,' answered the other man, who all the time had been closely scrutinizing

---

* An overseer.

Rutherford. 'You have never been in the West Indies before: I can see that.'

'No; I have come to learn planting and estate management.'

'Humph. Well, you'll learn. I must be off now.'

'Just a word. Shouldn't I go up and see the owner?'

'Mrs Palmer? You, a book-keeper, to call on her? She doesn't have much truck with the likes of us, Rutherford, unless – well, you'd better ride on and make your apologies to Mr Ashman for being late, and then he'll probably send you back to me to set you to work. I am senior book-keeper, you know. Where's your luggage?'

'Coming by ox-cart from Montego Bay. It will be here some time today.'

'See you later.'

Burbridge cantered off, but not before Rutherford had observed his keen glance in the direction of the Great House and the overseer's residence. Evidently the senior book-keeper was anxious lest anyone should have seen him wasting time. Rutherford smiled, a little amused. But he did not quite like the atmosphere of the place.

Yet he had heard of the hardships to which book-keepers on West Indian sugar estates were subjected as a rule. A sort of chief slave-driver, the book-keeper was in some way a slave himself. He had an inferior status, a poor salary, and (as he had heard) unlimited labour. But Rutherford's spirits were unruffled by all this, for he was here to learn, and schooling, he realized, meant discipline. He had seen Burbridge eyeing his clothes with a bewildered air; they were certainly much superior to those worn by the ordinary book-keeper or overseer. Burbridge himself was very poorly clad and seemed to think that any book-keeper who got himself up as though he were a person of means was either mad or looking for trouble. He was clearly puzzled as to how to place the new-comer.

Young Rutherford pursued his way in the direction indicated, and soon came to the steps of the overseer's house. Three or four savage dogs rushed out the instant they perceived him, barking and showing their teeth at him; then a black boy quickly descended the steps and ran up with the question: 'What massa want?'

'Mr Ashman; is he in?'

'Yes, massa; massa come in?'

Massa would; he leaped off his horse and followed the boy to the veranda, where he was bidden to wait. A moment afterwards a stern-looking man of about forty-five years of age emerged from the interior of the house jacketless, his soiled corduroy trousers thrust into the tops of knee-boots, a day's growth of beard on his chin, and an inquisitorial, imperious look in his eyes.

'Yes, sir, you want me? Will you come in? You name is —?'

'I am Rutherford, Mr Ashman – the new book-keeper.'

Mr Ashman figuratively stopped dead in his tracks; his manner of welcoming host giving place instantly to that of a plantation boss who was accustomed to being a despot.

'Oh! Why are you so late this morning?'

'I must apologize; I couldn't get away earlier.'

'What ship you came by? I didn't know one was expected yesterday or today.'

'I came a week ago.'

'Then why the hell didn't you report at once?'

'Because I was not to turn in before today; that was arranged when I left England. We made a quicker voyage than we had anticipated, and when I got to Montego Bay I found I had a week on my hands. I brought a letter of introduction to Mr McIntyre, the rector. I stayed with him.'

'Letter of introduction, eh? The rector, eh? Well, you are a stranger with a lot to learn. But book-keepers don't go about this country with letters of introduction, and many a man has lost his job for being an hour late. And jobs are not easily picked up here, let me tell you.'

'Perhaps not. Do you mean that I am to lose my job before I have even found it?'

'Damn my soul!' shouted the overseer, genuinely astonished, 'is this the way you are going to begin?'

'I expected a different sort of greeting,' said Rutherford quietly, but with a glint of anger in his eyes; he was striving to keep his temper under control. 'I am a book-keeper, yes; but I might be treated courteously. I have just arrived and you keep me standing on your veranda as if I were a nigger slave.'

'Perhaps,' retorted Mr Ashman, 'you would like to ride up to the Great House and be received in Mrs Palmer's drawing-room? Now look here, don't commence by playing the fool or you won't last on Rosehall, I can tell you. If it wasn't that you were engaged in England you would be going out of this estate now in double-quick time! You seem to be quite a high and mighty gentleman, but you have a lot to learn and you'd better see about learning it damn quick. Sam!'

'Yes, massa!' The boy made his appearance suddenly; he had been listening to the colloquy behind the door.

'Take this backra* to the book-keepers' quarters and show him his room. When you have been there and have had something to eat,' he continued, addressing Rutherford, 'Sam will take you to Burbridge, who is your senior, and who will tell

---

* A white man.

you what you have to do today – and tonight. And remember in future that the overseer of an estate in Jamaica is used to being respectfully spoken to by his book-keepers, and when you address me don't forget to say "sir". English airs and graces won't do here!'

Ashman turned on his heel and went inside; Rutherford silently walked down the steps, mounted his horse, and followed Sam, who ran in front towards the sugar works, some half a mile away. Quite evidently, thought Robert, a book-keeper did not count for much here; well, he had been given a very clear hint of that by the Rev. Mr McIntyre and his family. His father had not known of these conditions, or of a surety he had never suggested this job to him. Yet it would be worth his while to stick it through. After all, he would not be a book-keeper for more than a couple of years, if as long.

At twenty-five years of age one usually sees the world through the brightest of tinted glasses, especially if one is healthy, well-connected and not ill-endowed with means. On the island of Barbados was a sugar estate, one of the largest there, which belonged to Robert Rutherford's father. The older man had never himself been to the West Indies; the property had been left to him by an old uncle who had lived nearly all his life in Barbados and had had no legitimate children. Mr Rutherford never contemplated the possibility of his going to look after the estate himself; that was a task, he said, for a younger man, and Robert, his heir, was naturally and almost inevitably that man. But Robert knew nothing about planting or estate management; he was still young, he should acquire some experience in those arts. To send him out to Barbados at once would, Mr Rutherford conceived, be a great mistake. In the first place there was still in charge of it an attorney who, so far as could be gathered, was tolerably honest; he could continue to perform the necessary work of supervision for some time. But if Robert went out to him to learn the business, the fact that he was his father's son and the heir to the property might prevent the attorney from putting the boy through the mill, while overseers, book-keepers and the rest would naturally look up to the young man, flatter him and endeavour to spoil him; thus, with the best will in the world, Robert might learn very little. Mr Rutherford knew that his son was made of good stuff, but he did not want him to be exposed to sycophancy and coddling when he should be acquiring useful knowledge and experience by practical work. So it occurred to him that Robert should go to some other West Indian colony to acquire the knowledge he would need for the management of a sugar plantation, whether he should afterwards decide to reside permanently on his own in Barbados or to visit it at frequent intervals.

This view was placed before the younger Rutherford, and he fell in with it immediately. Robert was fond of his father, liked to please him, and thought it would be excellent fun if he, a future West Indian proprietor, should begin planter life in the humble office of book-keeper – for that was what, he was told, it was best to do. Of the duties of a book-keeper neither he nor his father had the slightest conception; but when a firm of West Indian sugar brokers in London, who had been approached by the elder Rutherford in the matter, informed the latter that they could secure for Robert a position on the Rosehall estate in Jamaica, the transaction was settled at once, although the post was worth only fifty pounds a year, with board and lodging. Robert Rutherford had all the money he was likely to need in Jamaica; the salary was of no consideration. But this was to be kept private, for the boy must win his spurs like any other young fellow. Mr Rutherford was quite enthusiastic about this.

He himself had never been called upon to begin on the lower rungs of the ladder, he had never worked hard in all his life. But he had a great admiration for those men who had carved out their own fortune, and he wanted Robert, in a manner of speaking, to stand in the ranks of such self-made heroes.

The Rev. John McIntyre, rector of St James's Church in the town of Montego Bay, had known Mr Rutherford years before at Oxford. To him was sent by Robert a letter telling of the Rutherford plans and enjoining secrecy, for the reasons given above. Mr McIntyre, knowing the local situation, did not at all approve of those plans, but said nothing. He liked the young man at once and, learning that he was not expected at Rosehall for a week, invited him to stay a week at the rectory, at the same time advising him not to make his arrival known to the Rosehall people before the day he was expected. He would not have thus invited an ordinary book-keeper; such a one could have no social status. And had Robert, the son of his old friend, been dependent on this job for a living and a future, Mr McIntyre would have counselled him to push on to Rosehall on the very day of his arrival, being aware that a book-keeper must not claim any leisure save that allowed to him by his employer. But he did not imagine that Robert would remain long at Rosehall, or in Jamaica; and he hoped that even if the boy chose to stay in the colony it would not be as a member of the Rosehall staff. That was the one estate of all others that he would have warned his old friend against had his opinion been asked in advance. As it was, he thought it wisest to say nothing; Robert must decide for himself now that he had come out to the colony. He was a man and must work out his own salvation.

Robert Rutherford, twenty-five years of age, tall, strongly built, with laughing grey eyes, a kindly, humorous mouth, straight nose and curly brown hair, was a handsome young man, even a distinguished-looking one. He was a graduate of his father's university, an athlete; not brilliant as a scholar, though he had taken his degree, he yet had done some reading and had travelled for a year in France and Italy after his graduation. The voyage out to Jamaica had tanned his hands and face but slightly; the clothes which he wore, and which he had been told would be required in his job, were tailor-made and of excellent quality; he looked exceedingly well in them and was fully aware of that. His hat was a good felt with wide brim, and he wore it with an air; his knee-boots were of the best leather. The grey horse that he rode was his own; he had bought it at a good price some days before. In spite of his curt and even rude greeting by the overseer this forenoon, therefore, he was feeling satisfied with the world and not dissatisfied with himself; he could not pretend that he appreciated the atmosphere of Rosehall, but on the other hand he was conscious of a sense of adventure, an anticipation of interesting and strange experiences, and he never doubted that he would be equal to any situation that might arise.

Robert did not consciously realize that, had he been an ordinary poor fellow endeavouring to make his way in the world, his feelings would probably have been very different; that instead of his present composure he would have been dreadfully depressed. He did not admit to himself (though the thought must have been somewhere at the back of his mind) that if the worst came anywhere near to the worst he could always shake the dust of this estate off his feet and fare forth to hunt for pastures new. What he did think was that, in spite of the apparent churlishness of people on this plantation, he would do his work cheerfully and to the best of his ability (which he felt was of a commendably high standard), and thus would please both the old man and himself. His mother (dead now these last five years) had always striven to please her husband and had always impressed upon her son the virtue of doing so too. Mr Rutherford had inspired both wife and son with a real and abiding affection for him, and he amply deserved it. Robert knew that if he quitted Jamaica altogether and frankly told his father that life in the West Indies was impossible, the older man would feel that his boy had honestly tried his utmost and was not to be blamed. Therefore he was determined to do his utmost.

CHAPTER 2

Robert Interferes

PRECEDED BY SAM, Robert came to the book-keepers' house, a low, unpainted wooden structure of three rooms, with a narrow veranda in front, situated near to the boiling-house of the estate from which issued pungent odours of steaming cane juice and continuous sounds of voices and movement. He entered the room indicated by Sam, and paused at his first step, revolted. A wooden bed unmade, with a mattress which had long since seen its best days, a couple of board-seated chairs, a small table, two bare shelves against the wall upon which had been placed the odds and ends of the former occupant: that was all the furniture of this room. It was clear that he was not expected to have a large supply of personal possessions, for there was no space where these could conveniently be stored. Comfort in this cubicle was out of the question; quite obviously it was considered unnecessary to a book-keeper. He noticed a door leading into the middle apartment, opened it and stepped into the room. Here was a somewhat larger table, two or three empty boxes and a few more shelves. Nothing more. Sam stood slightly behind him. 'And where does Mr Burbridge live?' he asked.

'In dat room, massa.' Sam threw wide an opposite door which also opened upon the middle apartment. Robert had a glimpse of male garments hanging from a nail, and of a feminine article of apparel fluttering close beside them. This was not altogether a bachelor's quarters, then; it seemed as though it were a *ménage* for two! But no married man could, with any wife of any sort of position and breeding, inhabit that one scantily furnished apartment, and half share the centre hall or whatever it might be called with a bachelor or another couple. 'This may be interesting but is not enticing,' thought Rutherford; but he remembered he had made up his mind to make the best of every circumstance.

The door of the outside entrance to Burbridge's den was suddenly flung open and Burbridge himself appeared; he walked over to where Robert was standing and said briefly to the waiting boy:

'Sam, go and call Psyche; she's somewhere in the trash-house.'

Sam ducked his head and sped away; Burbridge seated himself on one of the empty boxes and motioned Robert to take the other.

'Mr Ashman has just sent to tell me to put you to your job, Rutherford, till he can see about you himself,' said he, 'so I took the chance to come and have a little chat with you. Well, how do you like it so far?'

'So far,' answered Robert judicially, 'there has been nothing to like.'

'Don't say that to anybody else but me if you want to keep your job; for when you lose one in this country it is hell to get another.'

'Is that why you stick here?' inquired Rutherford curiously.

Burbridge did not answer; instead, he himself asked a question: 'When are you sending back the horse?'

'It is mine.'

'Yours! It's a damn fine horse, that. You mean that you have bought it?'

'Of course.'

'Then you won't want the one they provide for you on this property?'

'Perhaps not; I can't say. Two horses may not be too many.'

'Mr Ashman is the man to decide that, Rutherford, but I am wondering—'

'About what?'

'About why a man who can dress like you, and have a horse of his own like yours, should come to Jamaica for a book-keeper's job. It doesn't look natural. You don't mind my forwardness, do you? We have to work together and I am lonely as hell in this place, so I would like to start off being friends right away. When the two book-keepers on an estate are not friendly it is very hard for both of them.'

'I should very much like to be your friend, Burbridge,' cried Robert heartily. 'And I'll tell you at once that I am not exactly a pauper; I mean,' he corrected himself hastily, out of regard of the other man's feelings, 'I have some means and so can afford to buy a horse and any other little thing I may need.'

'Good for you,' commented Burbridge moodily. 'I have nothing but my pay, like most book-keepers, and that is never enough. I have to stick wherever I get employment, for if you leave two or three jobs the overseers and attorneys come to think you are no good, and then you're done for. You seem to be all right, so you don't need to worry so much.'

'You are English, of course?' questioned Robert.

'Like yourself, yes; only, you are a gentleman.'

'Let us hope we are both gentlemen,' said Robert, but he had already noticed Burbridge's broad accent; just as Burbridge had caught the tones of Robert's cultured voice and observed his easy, independent manner.

'Can't afford to be a gentleman,' said Burbridge with downright candour; 'gentlemen book-keepers don't last long here. I'll get Psyche to look after your room till you get a housekeeper, Rutherford. Psyche is a good girl, but you will have to get your own, for she has a lot to do for me, besides doing her ordinary work in the trash-house.'

'She's your servant?' But even as Robert asked the question he knew from something in Burbridge's attitude and from his praise of Psyche that the girl, whoever she was, was something more than a servant to his colleague. His eyes lifted themselves automatically and again he spied opposite to him, hanging from a nail in the wall, that fluttering female garment.

'She's my housekeeper and a very good girl. I think I hear her now.'

True enough, it was Psyche, a middle-sized, pleasant-looking damsel of about nineteen years of age, light chocolate in complexion, and therefore sambo, with bright black eyes and a merry smile. She wore a single robe that reached to the knees, but it was not coarse osnaburg such as Robert had seen on the women in the fields; it was of much better material and must, Robert concluded, have been purchased with Burbridge's money. Her head was tastefully covered with a large scarf looking like a chequerboard of bright diverse colours; her feet were bare. She had nothing of a slouching, timid demeanour; on the contrary, she flashed Robert a merry glance, bade him good day, then, touching Burbridge lightly on the shoulder, asked what he wanted.

'This is Mr Rutherford, Psyche, the other book-keeper,' explained Burbridge. 'He is going to live in the next room, like

Mr Fanbourg did, and I want you to fix it up for him till he gets somebody of his own to do it. It won't be too much for you?'

'No,' grinned Psyche, looking Robert over with an appraising and appreciative glance. 'An' it won't be long.'

'That's so,' agreed Robert. 'I suppose they allow a servant, don't they?'

'Yes, you are allowed a servant to do the necessary things,' said Burbridge, 'but not for all the time. She will have other work to do.'

'An' dem all is tief,' said Psyche decisively. 'Dem all rob you, except you is their sweetheart. But you will get a sweetheart, massa, specially as you is such a pretty gentleman. There is Millie, my cousin; she is just twenty and she have good ways and is pretty. You want to know her?'

'No, no, Psyche,' laughed Robert with real enjoyment. (The eagerness of Burbridge's lady to find for him a special helpmeet, and her unabashed frankness about it, affected his sense of humour keenly.) 'I think it would be much more proper for me to select my lady-love myself: don't you agree?'

'Yes,' agreed Psyche, 'for, after all, what I t'ink may suit you you mightn't like; you' taste may be different. But Millie really a good-looking girl and can work, an' she is a free girl, massa. I will bring her over to see you soon; dat will be no harm, for you needn't teck her if you don't like her. What you say?'

'Just as you please,' laughed Robert. 'There can be no objection to the lady calling on me, if that is a custom of the country. And of course I shall like her, though that does not mean that I shall take her. And here is something for you, Psyche.' He handed the girl a dollar, at the same time glancing at Burbridge to see how he would regard this gift. He noticed that it was by no means resented by Burbridge. As for Psyche, she crowed with delight. Robert perceived that the advent of Millie was likely to be hastened.

'I live here,' said Psyche, pointing to Burbridge's room, 'an' Millie could live dere,' and she pointed to Robert's room; 'an' bote of us could keep dis place nice and convenient, and we could be happy an' virtuous.'

Robert stared. Then he remembered that virtuousness must mean to Psyche something quite different from what it signified to persons with a better knowledge of the English language, though not necessarily with a higher appreciation of the value of virtue. That Psyche was convinced that she was living a highly virtuous life he did not doubt for a moment. As for Burbridge, Robert realized that virtue meant nothing to him; he would have said that it could not possibly have any part in the life of a book-keeper – which was indeed the universal view.

'That's all right, Psyche,' cut in Burbridge, speaking with real kindness and affection to the girl. 'You need not go back to the trash-house till you have fixed up Mr Rutherford's room; but don't be long or I will be blamed. We'd better be getting along now, Rutherford. You will see when your boxes come; we aren't going far from here.'

'I wi' bring Millie,' was the last word from Psyche; then the two men mounted their horses and went cantering off.

The sun was now high in the sky and beating fiercely down upon the countryside; the whole scene was lit up brilliantly by a hard yellow light, and the flashing blue of the sea to the north challenged the sapphire of the radiant overarching canopy that reached from the horizon to beyond the hills to the south, and spread away to east and west, forming, to the eye, an immense inverted bowl painted in flaming colour. The sea-breeze had waxed in strength. Here and there stood groups of slender coconut palms, towering skyward, their long fronds waving wildly and clashing as they waved. Like sentinels on guard over the fields, huge cieba trees lifted giant branches into the air. The atmosphere was permeated with the smell of sugar in the making and of new rum; from far and near came cries of human voices and the lowing of cattle; overhead floated, with scarcely a movement, large black birds, the John Crows, a species of vulture which were then the only scavengers of town and country.

Burbridge was interested in all this not at all; he was thirty years of age and for eight of those years he had been a book-keeper in Jamaica. Nothing was strange to him, nothing new, and little was pleasant. With Robert it was different; his reaction to these tropic scenes, to this exotic life, was keen; it intrigued and thrilled him; to him this was a holiday, and what went on around him might have been staged for his amusement. He felt exhilarated as he rode by Burbridge's side; in spite of the heat he enjoyed it all to the full. But even as he drew rein at the still-house, where the rum was made, there came to him a shock. He saw a stout black fellow lift a whip and bring it sharply down on the shoulders of a girl who was stooping to lift a bundle. The girl howled and crouched, but did not dare to move, for the whip hovered menacingly over her. Three or four women in the vicinity trembled violently, bent over their tasks with feverish intensity; the moment was one of tension. Then Robert remembered that he was a book-keeper, and, as such, the boss of the driver who seemed to be about, in a spirit of brutal enjoyment, to strike the girl again. 'Stop that and go and attend to some other business!' he shouted to the man peremptorily. The fellow started to give some explanation; he was evidently astonished. The girl turned appealingly to her unexpected protector. Burbridge said nothing. The driver hesitated; yet he still held the whip above the young woman. Angered by his attitude, Robert rode up to him and kicked the whip out of his hand, the man uttering an exclamation of pain as he did so. Then Robert and Burbridge passed into the still-house.

'What was that brute lashing the girl for?' asked Robert.

'Some neglect of duty, perhaps,' replied Burbridge; 'but I guess he was really taking it out on her for a private reason; possibly she wouldn't have him and he is showing her what she might expect for her rejection.'

'But these people are not allowed to flog without express permission from white men, are they? I thought that in these days only the white men on the estate could give a flogging order.'

'Practice and theory are sometimes different,' answered Burbridge dryly, 'and if you prevented these drivers from using the whip altogether you would soon have every slave raising the devil. There's plenty of flogging on Rosehall, Rutherford – more perhaps than on any other estate.'

'Are the slaves here worse?'

'They are pretty bad.'

'But a lady lives on the property. Mrs Palmer herself lives here, and she is a young woman, I have heard. Doesn't she take a personal interest in things? What about her influence?'

Burbridge looked at Robert with a curious smile.

'You had better find out all that for yourself,' he said.

CHAPTER 3

Experiences

IN TWENTY-FOUR HOURS Robert Rutherford had learnt a great deal. As he sat on his horse the morning after he entered upon his duties at Rosehall, watching a scene which he knew would shortly develop in a fashion revolting to his feelings, he concluded that a mere description of the position of a book-keeper, however detailed, could never have brought home to his mind the nature of that employment as his brief personal experience of it had done.

Robert was a man in splendid condition; but even he already felt horrified at the tax put upon an unfortunate book-keeper during crop time on a sugar estate. Yesterday he had picked up the rudiments of his work and had discovered that he would not have a single book to keep (all that sort of thing being done by the overseer), but that he was expected, after a day in the field, or in the boiling-house watching the sugar made, to spend every other night in the still-house where was kept the fermented spirit and in which it was poured into puncheons for shipment at a little port two or three miles away. Last night he had taken up his post of watchman in the still-house. There he had to remain from about nine until four o'clock in the morning. He had seen the rum drawn out of the huge vats in which it was stored, had seen the puncheons filled and sealed by the workers, had seen to it that they were carefully loaded on to the wagons that were to convey them away, and even during the intervals when there was little or nothing to do he had hardly dared to close his eyes for a few minutes' sleep. He had been warned against this; the slaves would steal at the slightest opportunity, he had been told, and he would be held responsible. He had observed, too, that the slaves, half a dozen men, watched him furtively, evidently hoping for some lapse on his part. Once he had pretended to fall asleep, and presently there was a movement on the part of two men towards a rum vat: one of these men had a bucket in his hand. Robert had stood up suddenly and the men had melted into the shadows. How one book-keeper could perform a night of watching in this still-house three times a week, and accomplish his ordinary work in the daytime, seemed to him a problem which he himself would hardly be able to solve. Yet Burbridge appeared to manage it, sheer necessity compelling.

On leaving the still-house with its reeking rum, Robert, fatigued though he was, had out of curiosity wandered over to the boiling-house where the sugar was being made. All night the estate had been in feverish activity. It was customary during the taking off of the crop for a good deal of night-work to be done, and on this his first night as a book-keeper at Rosehall a night-spell had been in full operation.

At four o'clock in the morning there was as yet no glimmer of light, no sign of the dawn which would break later on; but the gloom was pierced and illuminated by millions of burning stars which, in that clear atmosphere and at that period of the year, shone out with a wonderful golden brilliancy. By their aid, and with eyes accustomed to the surrounding darkness, he perceived the carts dragging their slow way towards the boiling-house in which the machinery was situated; he saw shadowy human forms moving about singly or in groups, heard the curt commands of headmen in charge of gangs, and the sharp crack of the whips with which they emphasized their orders. The men who were working then would retire shortly, and the day labourers would take their place. All night the toiling and the shouting had gone on. And at intervals there broke out sharp peals of raucous laughter. There were shrill women's voices intermingled with the harsher tones of the men, and some of these men and women passed him carelessly chewing the cane they had cut for themselves, and talking in a dialect he could not understand. He was to learn later that these people were each entitled to a small daily ration of sugar and rum, from which they drew some of the energy which enabled them to prosecute the arduous duties demanded of them. He was to learn also that, in spite of all vigilance, they stole far more than they were supposed to have and consumed immense quantities of juicy ripe cane.

When he entered it, the boiling-house seemed like a corner of Hades. A three-roller sugar mill was in operation, a mill with three huge steel cylinders or rollers, into one end of which the cane was thrust, while out of the other end the extracted juice poured in a steady yellow stream through an iron gutter into large open receptacles, somewhat like great hollow globes cut in halves, which simmered and bubbled over fires on a long brick fireplace raised about two feet from the level of the ground. The two mills on Rosehall were worked by wind power and by steam, as on this night, and now the furnace was going and the heat it generated was infernal.

The men and women were feeding the mill with cane and the furnace with fuel. The men were clothed, each in a pair of trousers only, their sweating black torsos and muscular arms glistening in the glare from the flames. Men were feeding the fires under the shallow cauldrons, or taches as they were called, and constantly the cry rose for 'wood, more wood!' With ladles whose handles were several feet long the attendants skimmed the boiling, pungent-sweet liquor from one tache to another, and the thick substance incessantly formed bubbles which burst as incessantly, flinging upwards a thick spray. The voice of the big negro headman, or foreman, who was in charge of the boiling-house that night, rapped out orders to the ladlers to 'skim light!' There was a continuous movement. There was a perpetual babbling of voices. What these commands meant, and why there should be such a tumult, in all that glare of flame and terrible heat, Robert could not for the life of him comprehend. He remained in the boiling-house for but a few minutes, noticing that no white man was in charge just then. The black headman was evidently a trusted and competent man. Not for an instant had he ceased his labour of supervision and harsh commanding because of the unexpected advent of the new book-keeper.

Robert was glad to escape into the open air once more, which was delightfully cool at this hour. He went straight to his quarters, flung wide the only window it possessed, a window made of wooden slats or blinds, which permitted curious persons to peer into the room unimpeded as soon as it was open. That there might be inquisitive eyes gazing upon him did not matter to him in the least just then; indeed, he never thought of it. Thoroughly exhausted he tossed off his clothes, threw himself on the indifferent bed, and fell sound asleep.

He was out of his room at eight o'clock. Burbridge had been up at daybreak and among the fields, he had had no night duties and therefore was expected to be at his work when the slaves should begin to take up their tasks. But he spared a moment to ride up and say a few words to Robert when the latter emerged after a very hasty breakfast; he told Robert what he was to do until further orders. The latter, still feeling an interest in what went on about him, despite his fatigue, had during the last hour been taking in the busy scene that was set out before his gaze. The cutting of the cane went merrily on, the loading of the carts, the unwearied shouting, just as he had seen and heard it yesterday. But now his more practised or more closely observant eyes noticed other things also. Under a great shade tree, a silk cotton, he saw little babies lying on heaps of trash or bits of spread cloth, with one or two women looking after them. There must have been twenty of these urchins, none of them more than two years old, most of them younger, and they lay on their backs and kicked their feet in the air, or rolled about, carefree with the irresponsible freedom of infancy. They were the children of women who were at work and who had brought them forth from their huts, according to custom, to where they might suckle them when necessary. Meanwhile the little ones were placed in the charge of a couple of women whose business it was to see that no harm came to them.

There were some other children also, ranging in years from five to nine, and these were by no means idle. They ran about collecting bits of trash, which could be used in the furnace, and picking up cane leaves and other edible substances for the feeding of the hogs and the cattle of the estate. This was the Piccaninny Gang, the gang of minors, very young, but nevertheless useful, and over them was put an elderly woman, armed with a switch, whose duty consisted in seeing that the piccaninnies did not fail to do something towards defraying the cost of their keep.

But Robert's attention had been diverted from the antics of the children by some preparations which he saw being made not far from where he was stationed. It was now nine o'clock;

he was feeling somewhat fagged, and these preparations, the nature of which he fully understood, could not tend to an enlivening of his spirits. Burbridge had hastily told him that morning that three of the slaves were to be punished for misdemeanours, and one of these was a woman, the same girl he had saved from a whipping the day before. The slave-driver had reported her case to Mr Ashman, giving his side of the story, and Mr Ashman had decided that the girl deserved punishment. Robert suspected that his interference had had much to do with this decision; he was to be taught a lesson. This was, in fact, to be a sort of ceremonial punishment. There were some twenty persons assembled to witness it, clearly the more obstinate of the bondspeople. Burbridge and Ashman were on the spot. Robert had not been summoned, but from where he was he could see what passed with a fair degree of distinctness.

The three culprits, backs exposed, were awaiting their punishment. But there was, as it seemed to Robert, a deliberate procrastination. Suddenly he glimpsed a figure on horseback approaching from the Great House and attended by another; the riding was rapid and in a very little while he perceived that the first rider was a woman, white, and at once he knew who it must be. 'Mrs Palmer,' he thought, and felt certain that at least there would be some palliation of the sentence of the unfortunate trio who stood in such abject attitudes anticipating their torture. The girl might even be spared. A woman surely would have some sympathy with her.

The riders arrived, and the first was respectfully greeted by Ashman and Burbridge. The slaves around simply grovelled at the sight of her. Her face could not be distinctly seen by Robert, but he observed that her figure was slight and girlish, her long riding habit sweeping down below her shoes, her feathered beaver placed jauntily on her head. Her right hand held a riding whip. She sat her horse perfectly. He guessed from their attitudes that the condemned persons were beseeching her for mercy.

He moved his horse a trifle nearer to the scene. No one paid any attention to him.

He saw the lady nod to Ashman, who gave a signal. One of the men was seized and tied to a post, and a heavy whip rose and fell with a resounding whack on his skin. The wretch screamed out in fear as well as agony, a piercing scream that must have been heard a quarter of a mile away; but that had not the slightest effect on the man who wielded the whip. Twenty times came down that terrible instrument; the full sentence was executed; and then came the other man's turn. Then it was the girl's. Robert, forgetting that he was only an employee on the estate, and that on his father's own property in Barbados a similar scene might at that very moment be taking place, dashed swiftly up to the group, though without quite knowing that he had done so or what he was going to say or do. He was given no opportunity to say or do anything. 'Go back and watch those slaves load the wagon, Rutherford!' sternly commanded the overseer. 'What do you mean by leaving them when you were not sent for?' The voice was arrogant, intolerably insolent, and, as Ashman ceased, Robert heard Mrs Palmer say: 'What is he doing here? He isn't needed.' She did not even glance at him. Her gaze was fixed on the trembling, weeping young woman, and Robert Rutherford realized that he could not possibly aid the girl and might even make her predicament worse if he dared to say a word. He noticed that the driver he had stopped from beating the girl the day before was the man in charge of the flogging. The man flashed an impudent, triumphant leer at him.

He turned his horse and rode back, revolted, to his station. As he moved away he shuddered, for a long, terrible cry broke from the girl's lips and continued until her flogging ceased, though only eight lashes were administered to her. She was flogged to her knees.

A wave of disgust swept through him. He was not squeamish; he lived in an age when labourers were treated harshly and callously; in England the men who worked in farm and field had a hard time of it: long hours, heavy labour, wretched remuneration; so that their position was sometimes contrasted with that of the West Indian slaves, to the advantage of the latter. And soldiers and sailors were unmercifully whipped for trivial offences; the use of the whip was believed to be indispensable if discipline was to be maintained. But he himself had never seen a human being flogged before, and a woman at that; and the circumstance that another woman, young, of good breeding, and presumably of ordinary humane feelings, should stand by and see such punishment inflicted startled and shocked him. He knew that slavery was doomed. Emancipation had already been decreed; in a few years there would not be a single slave in these islands, and the bondsmen, aware of it, were now muttering ominously and showing every inclination to disobey their masters and rise in their own behalf. He had noticed something of this spirit in the nearby town of Montego Bay; he had heard about it from the rector; but here on this estate of Rosehall the evil, reckless spirit of former days seemed to manifest itself; the danger that threatened was ignored; here he was back in the eighteenth century instead of being in the early nineteenth. And a woman was the mistress of this estate.

He had not seen the face of the mistress of Rosehall; only her figure. He had heard that she had looks to boast of, was beautiful; but he thought that her countenance must be hard, lined, cruel; that it must reflect a soul that delighted in suffering. Only a devil would willingly watch the agony of others as she had done, was the thought that ran in his mind.

The punishment over, the group broke up, Mrs Palmer, accompanied by the overseer and her negro attendant, riding off to some other part of the estate. She was evidently making an inspection. Burbridge went into the boiling-house; Robert again gave his attention to the task immediately before him. He perceived that the slaves around went about their work with a sullen, mordant air, now and them exchanging a remark with one another in an undertone; he had a feeling that they were dangerous, deadly, though held in strict subjection. He believed he understood now what was meant by a smouldering human volcano.

CHAPTER 4

Two Women

AN HOUR PASSED and then he saw the mistress of the plantation returning. The sun was cruel now in the open, unsheltered landscape, although this was the cooler time of the year; but Mrs Palmer did not seem to mind it. She rode easily with Ashman at her side. She was coming in Robert's direction, but he kept his eyes fixed on the slaves who, aware of who was approaching, redoubled their efforts and began heaping cane into the wagons standing by the path. Not so had they toiled all that afternoon. The man on horseback, big and strong though he was, had for them nothing of the terror which the slim woman who was nearing them so evidently exercised.

'Is this the new book-keeper?'

The question was asked in a clear, musical, carrying voice, a voice which, though not lifted, could yet be heard some distance away, a voice of rich quality and of decisive vibrant, exquisite tones. Robert lifted his head and stared in its direction.

It was as though an electric shock had passed though him. He found himself gazing into a pair of eyes which he thought the most wonderful he had ever seen. They were black and of a peculiar, penetrating brightness; they looked through you: gazing intently into them you became conscious of nothing else; they absorbed you. The brow above them, though partly hidden by the riding beaver, was broad and smooth, and smooth, glossy black hair covered the ears. The nose was slightly aquiline, suggesting strength of character, a disposition and a will and an ability to command; the mouth was small and full, the upper lip too full, the lower one a little blunt and hard. A fascinating mouth nevertheless, made for the luring of men; and under it was a rounded chin, well marked, definite, strong.

Her complexion was brilliant, her colouring indeed was part of the attractions of Annie Palmer and had not been affected by her rides in the sun of the West Indian tropics, probably because her horseback excursions were seldom taken in the bright sunlight. She sat upright on her horse; sitting thus, she appeared to be a mere girl, though her age was in reality thirty-one.

'Yes, he came in yesterday,' Robert heard the overseer say in answer to her question.

He was conscious that Annie Palmer was scrutinizing him closely, studying him feature by feature, as it were, sizing him up, calculating about him. She did so quite openly, in no way hesitating or abashed. She must have seen the impression her beauty made upon him, for she smiled a little smile of satisfaction and triumph, forgetting the book-keeper and thinking only of the man. Ashman noticed this by-play, and a dark expression gathered on his brow. Ashman today was cleanly shaved, and anyone could see, in spite of his coarse mouth and insolent eyes, that he too was a handsome man. He was well-built, muscular, a masterful man and a quickly angry one. Anger showed now in his glance, in fists clenched upon reins and whip. But Robert did not notice it. Mrs Palmer did.

'Mr Ashman,' she remarked casually, 'I will ride back to the house alone; you need not wait for me.'

'But you will go over to Palmyra this afternoon, won't you? There are some matters I should like you to see for yourself.'

'I am not sure I shall go today.'

'But you said you would, Mrs Palmer. We arranged it on Saturday.'

'And now I say I won't' – a note of imperiousness crept into her voice – 'and that settles it. You can go over to Palmyra yourself after you have finished what you have to do here today. I will go another day. I'll not keep you now any longer.' She moved her horse slightly, so as to put the overseer behind her.

He said nothing more, but stared one long moment at Robert. Not liking the man, and noticing the look, Robert returned the stare, and fancied that there was not only hate in it but also fear, distinctly fear. Yet why should an overseer be afraid of a mere book-keeper? That would be to reverse completely the established order of things.

Mr Ashman touched his hat and rode off. Mrs Palmer's face broke into a brilliant smile as, to the surprise of Robert, she put out her hand to shake his. 'Welcome to Rosehall,' she said gaily, 'though I wish you had come at some other time when I was not obliged to superintend the punishment of rebellious slaves.'

'Thanks,' he replied; but bewildered though he was, and fascinated, he could not help adding: 'how rebellious?'

'That is a long story, and I could not tell it to you here. You don't know the difficulties we are having now with our people. Unless we inspire them with a proper dread they may rise at any moment and cut our throats. You look incredulous! Wait until you have been here a month. I suppose you think me cruel?'

'It is not for me, your employee, to think you cruel or to think anything disrespectful about you,' said Robert humbly. 'That would be impertinence.'

'Not in you!'

Again he was surprised. They had just met, and, as mistress and book-keeper, their positions were such poles apart that it was very condescending for her even to take ordinary notice of him. The usual course would have been for her to fling him orders, if she had any to give, through the medium of the overseer. Yet here was she talking to him on friendly, on familiar terms, as an equal, as though they had the same social footing. And she was smiling that dazzling smile of hers – what beautiful teeth she had! – and looking at him with a soft, alluring look. He had expected in his youthful ardour to find strange adventures in Jamaica; but of a surety he had expected nothing whatever like this.

'What is your first name?' she asked, seeing that he made no comment on her last remark.

'Robert. My full name is Robert Waddington Rutherford.'

'A rather aristocratic appellation: I shall call you Robert. My name is Annie.'

'I know, Mrs Palmer.'

'My name is Annie,' she repeated, with playful insistence. 'It isn't a pretty name, is it?'

Robert Rutherford was not only young but a gallant gentleman. He forgot all about his book-keepership; it was the gallant and the fascinated youth who answered: 'Not by any means as pretty as its bearer.' He added, as she laughed delightedly: 'But what name could be?'

'Good, good!' she cried. 'I can see we are going to be excellent friends. But you are a flatterer, you know.'

'Rather one who perhaps speaks the truth too boldly, but only the truth.'

'Better and better! But you puzzled me, Robert. How is it that you came out here to be a nigger slave-driver? You don't look the part.' She eyed him swiftly up and down, noted that his appearance was rather that of a proprietor than an underling.

'I came out here to learn the planting business,' he replied immediately. He forgot entirely that his purpose was not to be advertised abroad, lest it should interfere with his gaining of elementary knowledge and experience. 'But the sun; surely you feel it, Mrs—'

'Annie,' she interrupted. 'Yes, I feel it, but I can stand it. Better than you, who are not used to it.' Her voice fell a tone or two: 'I thought, when I saw you a little while ago, that a man of your appearance was hardly cut out to be a book-keeper; you are very handsome, Robert.'

Abashed at this open compliment, Robert glanced round to see if it could possibly have been overheard; some of the slaves were quite near. She noticed his movement.

'They don't matter,' she said indifferently; 'we are practically alone here. They don't count; they have no feelings.'

There was supreme if unconscious contempt in her voice, in her look. The people about might have been sticks and stones so far as they affected her.

'It is very dull here,' she went on. 'I am glad you came. How does Ashman treat you?'

'He hasn't had time to treat me well or ill as yet: I have hardly had anything to do with him.'

'He will treat you properly; he must. You needn't be afraid of him.'

'Him?' queried Robert. 'I never had the slightest intention of fearing him. Why should I?'

'Others have feared him,' said Annie Palmer with a slight smile; 'he is a passionate man with a strong will.'

'But what has that got to do with me, Mrs Palmer?'

'Nothing – maybe. And yet it may have. But don't worry about him; you won't really be under him. I reside on this estate and at Palmyra – that is the estate behind this one – over the hills': she pointed southwards. 'I understand all about this planting business. You say you want to learn it? Well, you had better learn it directly under me, and then you will have very little to do with Ashman. What do you say to me for your "busha"?'

'It would be impossible for me to have a more charming one,' he cried, falling in with her mood, intoxicated with her beauty and her evident liking for him, flinging to the winds every shred of prudence that might have suggested a circumspect attitude in such strange and original circumstances. The West Indian *ethos* was already affecting him. He felt at once inclined to live gaily, riotously, dangerously today and let the morrow take care of itself.

'Or a more competent one,' she added, with peculiar intonation and laugh. 'Lord! How bored I have been for a long time. Not a soul worthwhile to talk to for weeks and months. A drear, drab existence – dull as hell! Don't be shocked; I spoke literally, not blasphemously. Hell must be a place of utter boredom, which is the worst torture a soul can have. Torment from flogging or burning could not be so dreadful. To be bored day after day, no change, no respite, only the perpetual repetition of the same thing until even madness would be welcome: that is the worst misery that a man or woman could have. And I have had something of that misery for some time here. Only last night I felt that it would be a positive relief to me to see the Rosehall Great House in flames. I actually felt that!'

'A dangerous feeling, Mrs—Annie. Don't you know that Nero burnt Rome down because he wished to see what a great conflagration was like? Perhaps Nero was bored, too.'

'Very likely. But of course I wouldn't burn my house; I haven't many palaces as Nero had. And then I think my boredom is over now. I came out here this morning to see some malcontent slaves punished and I found – you.'

'If I can amuse you, I am sure I shall be glad.'

'Your friendship can make life very different for me,' she answered softly. 'You will come up to the Great House to dinner tonight?'

'I promised Burbridge that we should dine together tonight,' he hesitated.

'He won't hold you to that promise, I am sure,' she said dryly. 'I suppose he has been talking to you a lot about me? Old hands always talk about the proprietors to new-comers, you know,' she went on, as if in explanation of her question.

'No; he has said nothing.'

She was piercing him with her eyes as he answered; she seemed convinced that he was speaking the truth.

'At half-past seven this evening, then,' she said; 'till then, good-bye.'

With eyes aglow with admiration, which had grown and deepened as they conversed, and which she had seen with intensifying gratification, he watched her go. He saw her halt at the boiling-house and send a message to someone in it. Presently, Burbridge came out, hat in hand, and she talked to him for a while. Then she turned, gaily waved her whip in Robert's direction, and cantered off towards the Great House. Burbridge waited until she reached it, then slowly came over to Robert. His manner was diffident, troubled. He spoke with constraint.

'Mrs Palmer says she has asked you up to dinner; you can knock off at five o'clock if you wish, Mr Rutherford.'

'Mr Rutherford! Burbridge, what the devil is the matter with you?' asked the young man.

'I meant nothing, Rutherford; I wish you luck.'

'Go on – you have something else to say.'

'No-o. I don't think so. I'll see you this afternoon at our diggings.'

'Now what's the matter with Burbridge?' thought Robert, who had not observed the searching glance with which the other man had scanned his face. Burbridge had seen in the exaltation in Robert's countenance, had heard in the new vibration of his voice, all that he wished to know. 'He's fallen in love with her at sight,' thought Burbridge. 'Well, he is not singular; but I like him. Let's hope for the best.'

And Robert: everything had changed for him in the last half-hour. She liked him; every word she had said, every look she had given him, was eloquent of that. Why, they had almost been making love to one another in the sight of all men, in the midst of open fields, and she had spoken of Ashman as one who might be dangerous. Did Ashman love her? That was very likely; very likely too that Burbridge did. Any man would; she was so extraordinarily lovely, so fascinating. Not an hour ago he had been regretting that he had come to Rosehall, now there was no place that he would exchange for it. What eyes she had, what wonderful eyes! And what lips. And she was lonely here and bored; and he was lonely too, and would be bored but for her. He was only a book-keeper? Tut, that was nonsense; he was a West Indian proprietor like herself, or would be some day; meanwhile his worldly fortunes were quite respectable. He could meet her as an equal; she had understood that from the first. She had known him for what he was. Burbridge wished him luck; well, he *was* very lucky. He could not have imagined, much less expected, this amazing good fortune, this swift transformation of his entire outlook.

He noticed just then that some women in the cane piece had almost entirely ceased work and were staring at him with what he regarded as a curious, impertinent air. He turned to them sternly and ordered them to resume their task. One laughed a little but they all became busy; yet he could see that they threw glances at him as they toiled, and talked amongst themselves, about him obviously. He was still young enough to blush at this, for he felt that it might be about the mistress and himself that all the slaves on the estate would soon be talking. Some of them had heard what had been said. Did they fully understand? Annie said that they had no feelings, spoke of them as if they did not matter. And indeed they did not matter; what they might think could have not the slightest sort of significance. Tonight he would be with her, see her face again, hear her wonderful voice. He had never seen eyes like hers before, eyes that seemed to draw and persuade and subdue you, eyes that commanded, eyes that looked into your very soul.

The long mournful howl of a conchshell* sounded just then, and the slaves threw down their implements of labour and hastened to their midday meal. Many of them, squatting on the ground, drew out of bundles they had with them cold plantains and roasted yams, with flavouring of salt herring, and began to munch these edibles with hearty appetite. Some hastily built a fire to the leeward of the cane pieces and proceeded to cook some raw food. They were now chattering freely. The punishment which some of them had witnessed in

---

* A shell of a very large conch, pierced at one end, used as a horn.

the forenoon did not affect their appreciation of this moment, and Robert, as he rode on to his room, reflected that they could not really be unhappy if they could take life like this, so boisterously and with so much laughter. They were not treated badly; his judgement had been far too hasty. Annie had to be firm, but she was as kind as she was beautiful. He had no doubt of that.

He reached the book-keepers' quarters and ran in for a snack. He found Psyche all excitement, portentous with importance. She bustled about, explained that Mr Burbridge was having his lunch in the boiling-house that day, placed the meal on the table in the middle apartment, then said:

'Millie come, massa.'

'Millie?' Robert was at a loss to understand her.

'Yes, me cousin; I bring her fo' you to look at her.'

'Oh; but – well, I do want someone to do my share of the work here; but Millie doesn't belong to this estate, I think you said.'

'No, massa, but dat don't make no difference, Millie!'

Out of Burbridge's room stepped the lady of that name. A tall girl of about twenty, of golden-brown complexion and long, slightly frizzed hair, Millie was much better-looking than her cousin, better clothed, and had an air which the other completely lacked. At a glance Robert noticed that her feet were shod, an unusual occurrence among girls who lived outside of the town of Montego Bay, and not common even there. Millie wore white, which was spotless; her straight nose and gleaming eyes were attractive; she carried herself with self-consciousness as a girl who had known admiration and had learned to estimate her charms at a high value.

'Good morning, Squire.'

Robert noticed that she did not say 'massa'.

'So you are Millie, eh?' he replied. 'But how did you get here so soon? You don't live on this estate?'

'No, Squire; but I come here nearly every day, an' me cousin tell me that you – you want to see me. I was here yesterday, too, an' I saw when you ride in. So I know you already, Squire.'

'And you want a job to look after my part of this house?'

'I think I could look after you well, Squire.'

'I don't need looking after, Millie; but the place does. I am told that I can be supplied with a servant here, but perhaps you would do much better.'

'A servant?' asked Millie. Her face was troubled, disappointment plainly expressed in it.

'A housekeeper,' corrected Psyche.

'A housekeeper?' echoed Millicent. 'You like me, Squire?'

'Of course I do; you seem quite a nice, tidy girl, but liking has hardly anything to do with our arrangement, has it? You are a free girl, aren't you? How much wages do you expect?'

'We don't need to talk 'bout wages now,' said Millicent hastily. 'I can read and write, an' I saw you yesterday, Squire, an' like you.' She paused, not wishing to say much in the presence of a third party, and without definite encouragement from the squire.

She glanced at Psyche, who had sense enough to perceive that Millicent wished her away for a while. So Psyche went outside, to get something, she said, and Millie stood with down-cast eyes waiting to hear what the squire would decide.

'You can have the job if you like,' said Robert indifferently. 'You will come every morning?'

'Don't I am to sleep here?'

'Where? There is no place that I can see.'

'Then you don't like me, Squire?

'What do you mean, my good girl? Must one have a personal liking for every dependent? Of course I like you! Are you satisfied?'

'But, but – but if I am not to live here, Squire, where am I to live?'

'I can't solve that problem for you, Millie; you had better think it out for yourself. Did you expect to live here?'

'Yes, if you like me an' I am your housekeeper. You would be my *husband*, don't you understan'?'

'By Jove!' cried Robert, startled but amused. 'I get your point of view now! But I didn't tell Psyche that, though it seems to be the custom here.'

'I am sorry,' sighed Millicent, with a full flash of her eyes at the handsome face of the young man who she proposed should be her 'husband'. 'Psyche didn't tell me everything. An', as I tell you, I saw you yesterday, an' I like you when I see you. A lot of young bushas on these estates want me, you know, but I don't have nothing to do with them. You are different.'

'You are very kind to say so, Millie,' answered Robert, feeling somewhat embarrassed, yet flattered nevertheless, 'but there has been a misunderstanding. You won't take the job of looking after my room and my meals, then?'

The girl thought for a moment. She came to a decision.

'Yes, I will take it. I can wash and sew and cook, an' I can read and write.'

'Your qualifications are excellent,' smiled Robert, who was too happy himself not to wish to make others happy also. 'As your cousin would say, you are very virtuous.'

'Yes, I am virtuous,' agreed Millie gravely, 'an' you will find me so if—'

'Sufficient unto the day is the virtue thereof,' interrupted the young man quickly. 'Well, you can take charge whenever you like.'

'All right, Squire, an' I will sleep in *this* room,' said Millie decisively, indicating the middle apartment.

CHAPTER 5

The Great House

THE FINEST PRIVATE RESIDENCE in Jamaica, the Great House of Rosehall loomed huge and imposing in the gloom of the early December evening. It stood three stories high, broad flights of hewn stone steps leading up to a wide portico from which one entered the living-rooms situated on the second floor. A boy was waiting for the expected visitor; Robert threw him his reins, quickly ascended the steps and found himself facing a magnificent pair of folding doors, four inches thick and of solid mahogany, which hung on great brass hinges and opened into a spacious and lofty reception-room dimly lighted now by a pair of silver candelabra. There was an instant suggestion of wealth about this room, even of magnificence. But what caught and held his eyes was the figure of the mistress of Rosehall, who stood by a table placed near the doors; as he entered she moved forward to meet him with eager, outstretched hand, and now, for the first time, he noticed how small she was.

She had looked a bigger woman when he had seen her on horseback that afternoon, clothed in her riding habit. Perhaps, because of his own splendid height, she seemed to him smaller than she actually was. But all the stronger because of her slimness and the apparent fragility of her form was the appeal she made to him; robed all in white, with throat and bosom exposed, she was daintily graceful in spite of the spreading crinoline which, in accordance with the fashion of the times, she wore. His heart pounded rapidly as he took her hand in his and felt the soft, unmistakable pressure of her fingers and heard her words of welcome.

He had changed from his working suit. Psyche had been put to work that afternoon and had ironed out his things, which had been sent from Montego Bay the day before. He was dressed now as though he had been bidden to a banquet; she noted this at once, and was pleased by his obvious desire to appear at his best in her sight.

'Sit here,' she said, pointing to a massive horsehair sofa, 'dinner will shortly be served.'

The sofa was to the right of the room, among the shadows; he placed himself by her side and she began to talk quickly, almost feverishly, as one labouring under some great suppressed excitement.

'This is where I live, where I have lived for many years,' she said, 'and I am all alone in this huge place; not a very cheerful life, is it?'

'I wonder why you do it,' he replied; 'Montego Bay is not far; there would be company there, society for you. And of course there is Spanish Town and Kingston.'

'All nearly as dull as is Rosehall or Palmyra,' she asserted. 'You don't know them. And the people – horrible! They are narrow, fussy, inquisitive, full of envy and bitterness, always talking about one another, and nothing good to say. Wait till you know them!'

'Then you prefer to live alone, hiding your beauty here?' he asked, though wondering at his audacity.

'Do you think I am so beautiful, then?'

'You know you are!'

'Thanks. You do say pretty things. Of course,' she hesitated a moment, then went on, 'I haven't always lived at Rosehall, and I haven't always lived here alone. My husbands—'

'Husbands?'

'Yes; I have been more than once married; I want to tell you about that. I want to tell you before anyone else does. You see, I believe we are going to be great friends, and I have no friends to speak of – none in fact. And I should like you to know how unfortunate and unhappy I have been. I have been married three times, Robert.'

'Three times!' He could not for his life have avoided the exclamation. It had been uttered before he was well aware of it.

'Yes, three times. And they are dead; my first husband died of apoplexy, the second one went mad, tried to stab me and actually succeeded, and then stabbed himself. The last one – he was my first husband's nephew – died of drink, and yet people in Montego Bay seem to think that I was responsible for his end! How could I prevent anyone from drinking himself to death? Do I look strong enough to keep the bottle from a determined man?' He knew that she smiled as she asked this question, though her face was not distinctly visible in the dim candle light.

'Not exactly,' he answered, smiling also. 'But you have been unlucky above the lot of women. And yet you don't look as if you have been married more than once. You are so young!'

'But I was married first at eighteen, and my husband lived only until I was twenty-one. The other two married me for my properties, I think; and the one who went mad died less than two years after I became his wife.'

'I don't think anyone could marry you thinking of anything but yourself,' he protested. 'What are your properties compared to yourself?'

'*You* say that,' she replied, 'but you are different; I can see that. I have been a widow now for three years, and I made up my mind never to marry again, to have nothing more to do with men: I had had enough of them, you understand. The one who was a drunkard used to beat me; he would strike me cruelly sometimes, and I could go to no one for protection. It was an awful life. After his death I resolved to shut myself up in my estates, this one, and Palmyra behind. I have not been to Montego Bay for two years.'

'What an existence!'

'You may well say so. Even during the day I rarely move about on the estates, though now and then, like today, I have to make an inspection. I had to be present at that flogging you witnessed: I hated to be there, though I could not show it, for weakness would be fatal in dealing with slaves. But I had to be present, for they would have been treated far more harshly than they were had I not been. That was why I was there.'

'I thought so; I was convinced of that.'

'But not at first?'

'No,' he admitted, 'not at first. I was shoc – surprised to see you watching such a scene. I understand better now.'

'I want you to understand, for later on you will hear that I love to witness the suffering of my slaves – a manifest lie! If people, white or black, deserve to suffer, then suffer they must; I don't see why they should be pitied. But if I look on while they are being punished it is through a sense of duty – and to prevent too much punishment. That girl today was only given eight lashes. I could have given her three times as many.'

'I am glad you didn't! It would have killed her.'

'Oh, no; it wouldn't. These people have skins as tough as their dispositions, and those are tougher than you will ever guess. But slaves are valuable now and they have to be pampered. Fifty years ago we could burn them alive for a serious offence; today we are afraid to whip them, and they grow more insolent every hour. But I wanted to talk to you about myself, not about my people. I was saying how for three years I have lived in this place, and the one behind it, a sort of woman hermit, visiting no one, being visited by no one, and traduced by many who have never even seen me.'

'They are base to treat you so,' he exclaimed indignantly. 'There is only one explanation: they envy you your beauty and your wealth.'

'It may be so,' she answered softly. 'But, of course, had I wished it, they would have come to Rosehall. There would have been plenty of men to come; some wanted to. I would not encourage them, desperately lonely though I was. I wished to have nothing to do with them: I believe I had almost come to hate men.'

'All men?' he queried, knowing what the answer would be, for had she not shown him favour?

'You know I couldn't say that now,' she laughed. 'I myself asked you up here today; I am with you now, telling you my miserable little troubles. If you were ungenerous you would say I was bold and forward, and pushing myself on you.'

'If I were a fool and an ingrate I might say that,' he cried, 'and even then I don't think I should dare. You are kind, very kind to me, an unknown stranger who is only your second book-keeper. Why should you be so, unless—'

'Unless what?' she asked, prompting him, for he had paused.

'Unless you have a kind heart,' he concluded.

'I don't know that I have. My kind heart was warped long ago. But I want to be nice to you, Robert, because I like you – an unwomanly avowal, perhaps, but I have long ceased to care about what is called womanly by women who rob other people's husbands and lovers and still think that they are virtuous and good! I like you, and I am tired of all this loneliness. I want you to help me; and you would not do it as Ashman does – for money. I want you to help me as a friend.'

'I know nothing about this country, I am afraid,' confessed Robert; 'and you know nothing about me, remember. We have met only within the last few hours.'

A rap sounded on the door to the rear of them, the door opened slowly and a girl's voice was heard:

'Dinner is on de table, missis.'

'Come,' she said, rising, and they went into the dining-room.

Somewhat smaller than the hall they had just left, it was nevertheless a large, lofty, handsome apartment, running the whole length of the right wing of the house. In the room, besides the sideboard and a score or so of highly polished chairs, there were two tables, one, a huge oblong mahogany piece; the other, a small circular table set for dinner, with a two-branched silver candelabrum in which tall wax candles burned with a steady flame.

They seated themselves, two barefoot slave girls attending them. The meal began with turtle soup, and one of the girls filled their glasses with madeira.

A glance from their mistress sent these waitresses some distance off, though their eyes were vigilant to watch the diners so as to anticipate their wants. The girls looked nervous, painfully anxious to make no mistake.

'You know nothing about Jamaica, yes,' Mrs Palmer took up the conversation where it had broken off. 'But it is not professional help that I want, it is advice, disinterested suggestions. You said to me today that you had come out to learn about planting. You are not a regular book-keeper; anyone can see that. Won't you tell me something about yourself?'

He told her briefly all that there was to know. He told her the truth.

'I might almost have guessed something of the sort,' was her comment; 'though if you were a mere book-keeper it would make no difference to me. You would still be you, don't you see; someone that could assist a poor, unfortunate woman who is badly in need of genuine friendship.'

A girl came forward to remove the soup plates, another filled the wine glasses; again they withdrew.

'I am at your service,' said Robert awkwardly. 'Tell me what you want me to do from time to time, and I will do my best.'

'You shouldn't live in such squalid quarters,' she said suddenly. 'Would you like to stay with Ashman, the overseer?'

She eyed him narrowly; she looked relieved when she saw distaste registered in his face.

'With the overseer? No, thanks! I shall be much happier where I am.'

'I understand. Ashman is not very pleasant to subordinates, though you are not going to be a subordinate of his. Would you like to live up here?'

'Here? But how could I! You and I together in this house? What would Ashman and Burbridge and your other white employees say?'

She made no effort to disguise the contempt in her eyes and voice. 'Do they matter?' she asked.

'But the people in Montego Bay? Your own class. When they knew, they would – well, you – you can guess what they would do, can't you?'

'Talk? But this isn't England; it is Jamaica; and we are miles and miles away from Montego Bay and anywhere else. Besides, what would there be to say? We are together now, aren't we? Where is the harm? Where would the harm be if you stayed here tonight, in one of these many rooms; what real difference would it make whether you slept in a room upstairs or in your own room in the book-keepers' house? What would the actual difference be?'

'None, actually; but—'

'It is what might seem, not what really was, that you are thinking of, isn't it? But you are independent and so am I. This is my property, and I am mistress here. I don't care now what is said about me; I have suffered too much to care. Are you less brave than I, Robert?'

'For your own sake—' he began, and she laughed.

'I can take very good care of my own self; had I not been able to do so, where do you think I should be now? But you can decide what you think best; only, remember that you can stay at the Great House if you wish, and here is the only place on Rosehall where you should stay. They say it is haunted,' she added abruptly. And again she watched him keenly.

'By ghosts? Of whom?'

'Of the men, the people who have died here. Another of their lies. I am a woman and I stay here alone.' She swallowed another glass of wine quickly; she had been keeping pace with him in his drinking.

'And you do not believe in ghosts, of course!'

'Do you?' she asked.

'Frankly, I don't know. Who knows if he doesn't? But you haven't answered me.'

'Ghosts, Robert? Spirits of the dead? Spirits of hell? Yes, I believe in them; I know that they exist; I have seen them!

Don't be startled; I am not raving; I tell you I have seen them. But Rosehall Great House itself is not haunted; no house can be haunted if there lives in it a man or a woman strong-minded enough to defy anyone, anything, that might wish to return from the grave to re-visit the scenes of its bodily existence. I can keep away any spirit by the force of my mind; they may be outside this building, they may creep and crawl close, close up to the windows to the threshold of the door, but inside, where I am, they can never come. It is not of them I am afraid; I despise them in death as I despised them in life! They were weaker than I when alive, and I am still stronger than they are now that they are dead.'

She had spoken fiercely, bitterly, heated with wine as she was and filled with a sense and feeling of her own power. He gazed at her astonished, seeing her in this new mood; he was getting a glimpse of another side to her character, a stronger, fiercer, more imperious though fascinating personality. She rose from the table with an abrupt movement; they had drunk more than they had eaten. 'Come,' said she, 'I will show you the house, the haunted house, where I live by myself.'

She bade him take up the candelabrum and led the way into a hall behind the great room in which she had met him. Here he had a glimpse of a broad polished stairway to the left, which obviously led up to the third story of the building, a stairway of mahogany with carved ornamentation and well in keeping with the magnificence of this spacious West Indian home. He noticed particularly now the deep embrasures of the windows whose sills of mahogany were comfortable seats; he glanced up at the arched doorway, high and ornamented, which led from the room in which he was into that where he had been received an hour before. 'We'll go upstairs later on,' she said, and led the way outside.

They stood on the flagged piazza; above them a wide balcony extended the whole length of the upper floor, and upon this balcony doors and windows opened. Seen from the rear, the house seemed to be of two stories only; but Robert knew that this was because the ground floor with its many apartments lay under the flagstones he trod. In front of them was a little wooden structure with sharply sloping roof, and in the midst of it an opening into which a flight of brick steps descended. But the lady did not offer to take him down to this region; she turned to her left, indicating a suite of rooms which was attached to the main building by a paved covered way which was the segment of a circle in shape, and curving outwards. This suite stretched straight from the end of the covered way towards a rising in the land to the south. On the opposite hand was another covered path and another suite. A flagstone veranda fronted each suite.

Taking the light from him she led the way. She flung open the first of three doors in this range of rooms; he saw within the room thus revealed a large billiard table, evidently long unused, for there was heavy dust upon it. The second apartment was a concert-room, as its appointments showed; the third was a bedroom, a guest-room clearly, and that too gave signs of not having been for a long time occupied.

'All built regardless of cost,' she said with a little laugh; 'but people were much richer in Jamaica then than we are today. There weren't so many missionaries in those days to preach to them and stir up discontent among their slaves.'

'It is a place well worth having,' he answered for the sake of saying something.

'But almost a prison for a woman who has to live in it alone,' she rejoined.

They crossed over to the other side, through a sort of fruit garden with full-grown trees standing about it. Just as they had nearly reached their objective a puff of wind suddenly coming down from the hills to the south, which rose behind the building, extinguished the candles, and they stood in the soft darkness, with the trees moving and sighing gently, and the dainty, white-robed woman looking, as it seemed to Robert's fancy, very much like a delicate ghost.

'I don't mind the dark, do you?' she asked, coming close to him. 'I can call one of the girls to get a light, but these rooms are not very interesting; they are for the house servants, and that one at the end is the kitchen. You can see them any other time; indeed, there is nothing in them to see. I'll take you upstairs now.'

She took his hand to guide him; he closed his fingers over hers with a gentle pressure; he felt her answering clasp, tender and persuasive.

They regained the rear hall and then went back to the dining-room; she still leading him, for it was dark in the house. She placed the candelabrum on the big banqueting table; then stood still for a space very near to him. He heard her sigh.

'Can I relight the candles for you?' he asked, but this she did herself, not answering. She handed him the lights.

'Hold them high,' she suggested, 'or the breeze may put them out again. We'll go upstairs.'

CHAPTER 6

Annie Proposes

THEY MOVED SLOWLY UP the broad stairway, built in three short flights; arrived at the upper story, Robert walking straight in front him with the candles held high in his hand – for the windows were open – came to the door of a room which faced the steps, and paused. Annie hesitated for a second; then seemed to make up her mind to speak. 'My first husband died in that room,' she said laconically, 'so I keep it closed. The silly slaves are always hearing noises in there, though I have stopped them showing fright when I am near.

'And there,' she went on, indicating the next room, the one farther on, 'is where my second husband died, and this one' – she pointed to another – 'was where my last master passed away – drunk. It's a beastly story, Robert. I tell it to you because others will do so, and they are not likely to tell the truth, or indeed to know it so well as I. You will probably hear that I keep all these rooms closed, and that is so. They are never opened now.'

'Not even by the house slaves?' he asked, gazing curiously at those three rooms where the men who had been successively the lords of this lovely, brave, vivacious little woman by his side had breathed their last. He wondered how she could find the courage to sleep night after night under the same roof, believing as she did, as she had said, that the spirits of the dead could return to earth from hell itself.

'By no one,' she answered, 'such rooms are really graves, or like graves.'

The courage of this admission struck him.

'But if everyone closed for ever a room in which a man or woman died, Annie,' he urged, 'the largest house would soon become an empty ruin.'

'True,' she admitted, 'but I have a wish to keep these rooms so. There is no one to use them, so why should they be opened? This place is far too big for me as it is.'

She took the lights from him, went towards the other side of the landing and threw open another door, stepping inside. 'And this is where your little friend retires at night to her loneliness and friendlessness,' she explained.

He peeped in; he saw a great canopied bed hung with a white mosquito net, a huge mahogany four-poster with the uprights richly carved. Three chairs of expensive wood were in the room, a large dressing-table stood in front of a tall mirror; a mahogany press, and a heavy rug spread upon the floor, completed the furniture. It was a sumptuously furnished apartment, more sumptuous than elegant. She entered it; he stood at the threshold. 'Come in,' she mocked, 'there is not a single soul to see us, and to talk.' She put the candle-holder on the dressing-table and fixed her eyes on him. There was provocation in them; an invitation scarcely to be misunderstood.

He stepped inside, looked round and went up to one of the windows; he was breathing heavily as an unpractised runner might. He saw the lands of the estate rolling away until lost in obscurity, could distinguish the darker shadows as trees towering above the cane, caught a glimpse of lights far below, and knew them to be those from boiling-house and still-house and book-keepers' quarters, and, raising his head, gazed for a while on the innumerable tropical stars which glowed above in the soft silken blackness of the sky. It was all vague and still and lovely out there, and here was he, a few days after his coming to this strange land of slavery and passion, beauty and mystery – for to him it seemed mysterious – in the company of a woman with a strange history, a woman alone, who had passed though more heart-searing experiences than fall to the lot of most women, and who was, to his thinking, the most beautiful of her sex that his eyes had ever seen.

And she loved him, wanted him: he could not be blind to that.

Elsewhere, to some men, she might seem bold and forward, as she herself had suggested she must appear in his eyes. But here it seemed that everything she did or said was natural, inevitable; for her circumstances were not normal and the hardships and distresses of her life were surely a warrant for her splendid independence. She loved him – he could not use a weaker word, though always, in his relations with women he was modest. And he? – he had never fallen seriously in love with a woman before, but for this one he felt that he could do anything, brave any censure, face any desperate risk. She had taken him absolutely into her confidence, told him, at almost their very first meeting, the story of her bitter married life. She had appealed to him for his sympathy and help, and he had promised that they should be hers to the full. She was ready to brave the world's sneers and calumny for his sake: she had more than hinted as much. Could he be prepared to do less for her?

He turned from the window and walked towards her; she was standing by the side of her canopied bed, her back towards it, her hands resting upon it. Again she caught his eyes and held them, with that curious magnetic gaze that had struck him in the cane-fields that forenoon. But while it had then appeared hard and compelling, now it was alluring and soft, for the light of love was in her eyes, and the warm flame of an appealing desire.

'It is a very beautiful view from that window,' he began, banally, for it was not about the outer scene that he wished to speak. The words sounded puerile in his own ears. The wine he had drunk was still heating his brain, still causing his blood to course through his veins in a hot stream; his pulses throbbed under the influence of this bewitching woman's beauty. She nodded her head, agreeing, but looked as though she expected he had something more to say. His arms went suddenly out; he caught her and drew her close to him, tightly, and kissed her hair, her brow, her lips in a frenzy of passion. He felt her answering kisses; they burned upon his lips. She gave herself up to him, a complete surrender. 'So you love me, Robert, love me as I love you!' she panted, and as she spoke a thunderous noise filled the house with weird, nerve-shattering sound. And the lights went out.

'Heavens! What is that?' Robert was startled into an expression of fear. He had started back, but she placed a quick hand upon his shoulder as though to steady and reassure him. 'The wind is stronger now,' she answered, 'a puff of it caused one of the doors downstairs to bang. I have spoken to the women about that before; they should fasten the doors so that they should not bang; I shall have to see that this does not happen again.'

'It sounded as though it were up here, as though someone had struck a terrific blow somewhere near to us, opposite. I thought it was an earthquake: I have heard of them. You are sure it was not up here, Annie?'

'Quite sure. I know it seemed as though it were very close to us; but sounds are peculiar in this house.'

'They would be with those three rooms kept always closed,' he muttered, for a dread of something inexplicable had come upon him, a dread born of the memory of three dead men, one a lunatic, who had, as she had told him, stabbed her and then taken his own life.

'Let us think of ourselves,' she whispered, nestling up to him. 'Let us think of ourselves only in all the world and of our love for one another. There is nothing to fear.'

But now the sound of a horse's hooves came distinctly to their ears, and immediately a murmur of voices below was heard. That someone had arrived unexpectedly was clear. Annie Palmer did not seem inclined to allow that incident to trouble her, but Robert made haste to light once more the candles, then looked at her questioningly. She answered his look with an acquiescent nod; she knew that he would not remain up there with some visitor or messenger waiting for her downstairs. They went down together and found Ashman in the dining-room, standing. He bowed to her as they entered.

'I have just come from Palmyra,' he said at once; 'I found the slaves there in a very bad frame of mind. I surprised some of them at a secret meeting they were having in one of their huts – the ringleaders, I mean. They heard me coming, so I didn't quite catch what they were plotting, but I know it's some rascality. All over the parish there is trouble brewing, Mrs Palmer, as I have told you before, and I think we should do something about it right away.'

'So that's it, is it?' she asked. 'But you could have waited till tomorrow to tell me this. I can't do anything tonight.'

'I thought it was right you should know tonight.'

'You thought you would pay me a visit,' she replied. 'Have you got the ringleaders, as you call them, locked up so that they can't get away?'

'I took jolly good care about that! I told them you were certain to give it to them hot tomorrow and no nonsense about it.'

'There's going to be no nonsense about it! It is their skins or our lives, and I prefer our lives. Very well, Mr Ashman; thank you. You can call for me tomorrow morning, and we'll ride over to Palmyra together. I'll be ready at seven.'

'You're going down, Rutherford?' asked Mr Ashman, now addressing Robert for the first time. 'Our way is the same, and I want to talk to you about some work in the still-house that's got to be done tomorrow.'

'Mr Rutherford is my guest tonight, Mr Ashman,' said Mrs Palmer, not giving Robert a chance to reply. 'He will go when he is ready, and you need not wait for him.' The rich tones of her voice which Robert so much admired, were rather hard now. There was a metallic imperiousness in her voice which neither man could fail to recognize.

'But the estate's work has to be done,' said Ashman stubbornly, 'and it is late already.'

'Late! Are you going to dictate hours to me or to my guests?'

'I am in charge of the estate, An— Mrs Palmer.'

'Under me. I give final orders here. Overseers may come and overseers may go, but I remain; do you understand? Your manner needs mending, Mr Ashman.'

'Thank you for discovering that! Well, you are the owner and so can do what you like. And you are quite right when you say that overseers can go. *I* can go, for instance.'

'*I* am not getting rid of you, at any rate,' she answered, softening her tones a little. For Ashman was angry now and seemed prepared to go to any lengths.

She went up to him. 'Mr Rutherford is out here to learn the planting business; he is not an ordinary book-keeper,' she explained. 'I know about him and his people in England, and that is why I take an interest in him. Don't be silly, John! I know how devoted you are to my interests, but you need not let that cause you to forget your good manners. So you will call for me at seven in the morning? And then we can talk matters over – everything? Where is your horse?'

She had been gently impelling him towards the door as she spoke, and he could do nothing save move in the direction that she wished him to. But he did not bid Robert good night. When he had ridden off she returned.

'Competent overseers are not too easily picked up in Jamaica,' she explained, a little breathlessly, 'and just at this time I don't want to get rid of Ashman; but if he continues to be insolent he will have to go. I suppose that because I just won't put up with everything he says, he will become one of my enemies. Don't pay any attention to what he does or says; just keep away from him.'

'That is not easy, for he is the overseer,' Robert pointed out; 'but I am not likely to seek his company. I disliked the man from the first moment I met him.'

'Keep on disliking him. Where shall we go now?'

'Look at those doors, Annie,' he cried, not answering her question. He had just noticed that the doors were fastened backwards, so that these at least could not possibly have made the reverberating noise that had startled them a while before. 'Those doors did not bang.'

'You forget the drawing-room doors. They are much heavier than these.'

'Let us look at them.'

But those, too, were securely locked.

'Now what made that noise?' asked Robert; 'could it have been an earthquake?'

'I tell you it was one of these doors. The women must have heard the noise and run in and fastened it so that they could not be blamed for neglect. And it is no use asking them anything about it; they would lie for the mere sake of lying. Do you wonder now that I have sometimes to punish them?'

He saw that that must be the right explanation. 'Shall we sit in the drawing-room?' he asked.

'Wherever you please,' she answered softly, 'but I should like to look at the night; it is very beautiful, and I want to look at it with you. Come with me where we can see the sky and the stars and talk about the little things that concern ourselves. Won't you come?'

'Anywhere that you wish!'

She lifted her face towards him; he bent down and kissed her. The doors leading to the courtyard stood wide open, but he forgot that or did not mind it now; her disregard of peering slave eyes affected him also; what did it matter what they saw? She slipped her arms round him and clung to him; he lifted her sheer off her feet and kissed her again and again.

'Carry me upstairs in your arms,' she pleaded, 'I love to feel how strong you are. You can go with daybreak, Robert; not before. My darling, my dearest, how I love you!'

CHAPTER 7

The Brown Girl

THE WEST INDIAN DAWN was breaking when Robert mounted his horse and rode away towards his quarters. He glanced back and upwards when he had reached the lower ground; from the front window of the room above there peeped out a face, and a hand came forth waving farewell to him.

Early as it was the house servants were astir; one of them had even offered him coffee before he should leave, but he had been anxious to get away. He was not yet hardened to the callous frankness of a Jamaican liaison; he now felt ashamed that these menials, slaves though they might be, should see him, know whence he came, and be able to talk about it freely to their companions. The elation of the hours before had vanished; he was secretly startled that he had so quickly succumbed to what he had heard at home were the manners and customs of this country, with a disregard of all concealment, a careless acceptance of any condition and circumstances that might appeal at the moment, however flagrantly might be violated every principle of circumspect conduct. He was suffering now from a reaction. His mood was depressed, his attitude towards himself critical.

But for a moment this mood of censorious introspection vanished before the moving influences of the scene that disclosed itself to his admiring gaze. The sun was surging upwards away to the right; along the edge of a bank of nacre there ran a line of gold. Clouds of soft blushing pink floated lazily against a backdrop of delicate blue; to the left the skies were golden and the green of the earth was alternately dark and light, with deep greys here and there, and splashes of bright scarlet where a giant poinsettia reared its long branches high above the fields of cane.

There had been heavy dew in the long hours of the night. It sparkled now on every leaf and twig; it shone, a million crystal globules, as the sunlight swept down upon the earth; silver and emerald glowed everywhere; it was as though all the land had been bathed in celestial waters. There was a tang in the air from the sea beyond. With the dawning, a light wind had sprung up; it fanned the sweeping expanse of the Caribbean, fretted it here into the frosted azure, transformed it there into glittering jewels. The breeze came laden with the scent of saline waters, cool and exhilarating. And even as Robert stood to gaze, his horse motionless in obedience to his mood, the sun soared swiftly into sight.

It came with a triumphant impetus, as though it knew it were the lord of day, beneficent mainly, but cruel at times when its burning rays would wither the countryside, consume the liquid in rivers and in ponds, cause man and beast to perish, and, day after day, week after week, would flame downwards out of a hard and brazen sky with heat like a blast from hell. But now it was all glorious, and the birds hailed it with song, and the cattle lifted up their voices in a deep, grateful lowing, and men and women rejoiced in its gentle warmth.

Robert drew a deep breath. He knew that in a little while all the moisture at his feet and on the vegetation around would have disappeared, that the softness and sweetness of the early morning would be gone. But for this brief hour the feel of life was perfect, the impulse in one's heart was to shout aloud for the mere joy of being alive. Something of this must have been felt even by those in bondage, for while he stood and looked about him he heard a chorus of merry noises which seemed to come from carefree hearts. Then he gave his horse rein and began to move forward again. And his thoughts returned to Annie and his adventure of the night.

Annie Palmer had not appeared to him to be quite so young in the chilly dawn of the December morning as she had the night before, or when he had seen her on horseback in the fields. There were little lines across her brow, slight it is true, but indisputably there; and just the tiniest of crow's feet about the corners of her eyes. Her full lips which quivered with passion had hinted to him of fervent overwhelming desire; they were the lips of a woman in whom sensuality was temperamental and dominant. She was all fire; there was no restraint about her, but she excused it, defended it, on the ground that she loved him madly; again and again had she told him so, and he believed her absolutely. He believed that she loved him, that he loved her also; yet, he knew, felt, that hers was a volcanic passion, that hers was a tempestuous temperament, wild as the sea fronting Rosehall when it was lashed to fury by the winds that rushed down from the north, fierce as the storms that sometimes ranged over this country, devastating it in an hour or two.

He had pledged himself to her. He had gone to the Great House the night before with no such intention in his mind, although she had fascinated him. He had entered it as a guest; he had left it as a lover pledged, as a lover to whom she belonged and who was hers without reservation; so both of them had passionately asseverated. He was tired now and weary in mind and body. For two nights he had hardly slept, and even his abounding energy was taxed by the exhausting excitements through which he had passed. She had laughed at his protests that he would have to work that day, asking him why he should wish to ride about sun-baked fields or sit sweltering in a boiling-house redolent with the odour of bubbling cane juice and of sweating human bodies; but he had insisted that he must play the game with Burbridge, and she had given in. Nevertheless the task before him was distasteful. This estate life and its exigencies were new to him, and the *malaise* in his mind conflicted with the necessities of a day's laborious and sordid routine.

She was beautiful, strong, passionate, wealthy, self-reliant, and she loved him. He would not live in the Great House with her; on that he had made up his mind; for one thing, he did not wish to leave Burbridge, who so obviously wanted to be friendly with him and who would feel that he had become, in some sort, a master instead of a colleague. There was also his persistent impulse towards personal independence. He had not come to Jamaica to accept anything from a woman; he could not stay in the Great House and not be, in a manner of speaking, a recipient of a hospitality which he could not return.

But how long, in any case, he asked himself, could this life, that had just begun, endure? Annie was a white woman; she had been married; she was still young. Women like her did not, even in Jamaica, contract open, unlegalized connubial relations with men; he knew enough of the colony to be aware of that. Whatever might be done in secret, there was some respect shown by them to such public opinion as existed. Their husbands and sons and brothers cared nothing what might be said about them. Robert had been told in Montego

Bay, by his friend the rector, that these men, even if married, openly maintained other establishments; talked about them, could not imagine why there should be any secrecy or shame in regard to them. But a somewhat different standard for women of the upper orders obtained, and Annie belonged to those orders, was assuredly in the front rank of them. Here was something of a problem; how was it to be solved? By marriage? He had not thought seriously about marriage in his life; he had certainly not considered it a likely, or even possible, consequence of his journey; neither of them had hinted at it last night. But she had been three times married, and if he loved her, and she him, what more logical, more natural, than that this suddenly developed relationship of theirs should end in marriage? But what would his father say?

Robert knew. His father would be startled at hearing any suggestion of an alliance between him and a woman who had already had three husbands and who had herself admitted that she had many enemies in this island who traduced her and kept away from her – who shunned her. His father would be grieved, resentful; there would be an estrangement between them. And he himself; did he really wish for marriage with Annie? Would he willingly, gladly, make her his wife, vow to be everything to her, select her as the companion of a lifetime? He dismissed the question hastily, saying to himself that it was mean and unworthy of him to ask it, feeling indignant that it should have obtruded itself into his mind. Yet the very hastiness and indignation with which he strove to eject it, put it from him, instead of facing it and answering it fairly, caused him an uneasy twinge of conscience; he felt, though he tried not to feel, that he was endeavouring to deceive himself. He said to himself that it was unnecessary, premature, to think of such a thing as marriage now. He meant, and was secretly conscious that he meant, that he did not wish to think of it at all.

He rode very slowly, his horse going at a walk. A delicious coolness was in the air, the sky in front of him was all rosy, with soft white clouds shining in a mellow light, the green of the cane-fields stretching away, a wavering sea of vivid colour on either hand. He could see the wavelets of the Caribbean break gently upon the white margin of beach; the tropical birds had awakened and were calling to one another and singing their morning song, the cattle lowed plaintively as they were driven from their pens to begin the day's work. Now and then a shouted order, sharp, but the words unintelligible, reached his ear.

He suspected that his figure, clearly outlined as it must be from his eminence on a horse's back, was perceptible to every eye that was turned in his direction; perhaps Ashman saw him, Ashman who had arranged to be at the Great House that morning to accompany Annie over to Palmyra. Ashman's conduct last night had been extraordinary; he had acted as though jealous of his presence in the house. Ashman had seemed disposed to make trouble, would probably seek for a reason to do so. Ashman would know by now that he had spent the night at the Great House, and draw his own conclusions. There was some complication to be expected here. Conflict was being ingeminated between him and this aggressive, bullying man.

He hitched his horse to a post standing by his quarters when he arrived at them; he observed that the door of Burbridge's room stood ajar and guessed that Burbridge himself must have already repaired to his duties. But before he could reach his own door that of the middle apartment opened and Millicent appeared. She wore a looser dress than she had worn the day before, and her head was lightly bound up in a coloured handkerchief which she must have tied on just a moment or so ago.

He was surprised to see her; he had not expected her to take up her work as housekeeper so early.

Millicent looked worried, anxious; there was a strained expression on her face.

He would have passed her with a nod, but she stopped him. 'You was all night at the Great House, Squire?' she asked.

'Yes,' he replied shortly, resenting the question. 'You can get some coffee for me.'

'It's boiling already; I soon give it to you. I come here at about eight o'clock last night an' find you gone to the House. I hardly sleep a wink all night.'

'Well, I don't see that that concerns me,' he said irritably; 'is it the custom here for servants or housekeepers to sit up when their employers are away?'

He walked into the room and seated himself on the edge of the bed. There was a close, musty smell about the place; it disgusted him; the contrast between the Great House and these wretched diggings was overwhelming.

Millicent had evidently been preparing for his morning arrival. She went to the back of the house and presently returned with a large mug of steaming coffee and a roasted yam, and a hunch of roasted saltfish flavoured with coconut-oil. She placed these on the table and waited to see him eat.

He drank the coffee, which refreshed him somewhat; the food did not appeal to him, though it was ordinary, good book-keeper's fare.

He felt in a better mood after his coffee; he looked at Millicent good-humouredly. 'So you were up all night, eh? You have taken charge early, but sitting up is not a part of your job.'

'I know that,' she replied calmly, and, to his astonishment, seated herself on the bed beside him. 'But I was anxious about you. You went to a bad place.'

'The devil! My good girl, you may be free, as you have told me more than once; but if you are going to be too free with your tongue you will certainly regret it. How dare you speak of your mistress's house as a bad place?'

'She not my mistress, for I am free – an' educated,' added Millie with emphasis. 'I don't belong to her. An' it *is* a bad place; it is haunted. All sort of noise and cries you hear in dat house at night, an' sometimes in the day too. A lot of people die in there – an' they die funny. You going back, again, Squire?'

'This is impertinence, Millie,' Robert coldly replied. 'You can go now; I don't need you any more.'

Tears gathered in Millie's eyes; she looked hurt. And Robert, who was naturally kind-hearted, and who could not but see that this was a very handsome, well-built girl who had not the slightest intention of offending him, relented. After all, he thought, manners were very free and easy in this country; he had noticed in Montego Bay that even slaves seemed able to take liberties with their masters. And this girl was no slave. 'Now, don't be silly,' he said, 'I didn't mean to hurt your feelings.'

'But you hurt them all the same, an' I only tell you what I tell you because I don't want nothing to happen to you. I couldn't sleep all night because I was fretting for you. Evil spirit is in that Great House, an' God help you if you get in their way!'

'But Mrs Palmer lives there, Millie, and she is not afraid of these evil spirits you speak of.'

'She know why she is not afraid,' returned Millicent significantly, 'though she could be de first to be afraid. You was with her last night?'

'That will do! Just take those things and go!'

'I will go if you send me away; but I told you yesterday that I like you, an' I thought you was going to like me, too, an' that is why I come to keep your house. I am not a poor girl looking for work. Me gran'father – you will soon hear who he is – don't want me to work for any man; he is rich an' strong – as strong as Mrs Palmer.' Millie sprang to her feet. 'And that is why I can talk to you as I talk; I don't afraid of Mrs Palmer and all she can do. She take you up to de Great House last night – oh, I know – like she take up other men; an' you will come to the same end if you don't careful. I pray to God all night last night for you, and I going to ask me gran'father to protect you. But he can't help you if you don't help yourself.'

Robert looked at the girl as though she were insane; and indeed it did seem to him that she might be slightly touched. Of what was she raving?

'I don't think I need even your grandfather's protection,' he laughed; 'but your prayers will no doubt be useful.'

'You laugh at what you don't understand,' she answered sadly. 'Wait till you know more, an' then you might want to cry. I wish you would leave dis place!' she exclaimed fervently. 'Don't stay here; leave as quick as you can – and take me wid you. I will go wid you anywhere. Harm will come to you if you remain, an' then me heart would break.'

'You are excited by your long night's vigil,' he said gently; then, seeing that she did not understand him quite, he added: 'you should not have stayed awake last night. Well, run outside now; I have got to go to work at once. By the way, I am feeling weary; can I get a rum punch or anything like that here? There must be some rum in Mr Burbridge's room. Perhaps Psyche—'

'I can get it out of the room without calling Psyche,' said the girl; 'but rum so early in the morning is bad. Many squires from England die because they drink soon in the morning. You don't want some more coffee instead?'

'No; I need something stronger. Everything that I seem to want you consider bad, Millie, and death is ever in your mind. You are the funniest servant I have ever had.'

'I came as your housekeeper, not as a servant,' she retorted, emphasizing the word housekeeper, giving it the significance of its Jamaican meaning. 'And,' she boldly added, 'I wouldn't care what you did, or whether you live or die, if I didn't love you. So there!'

She went to get the rum, and he mused awhile. This was extraordinary; two women, one white, the other brown, and both indubitably handsome in their respective ways, had told him within a very few hours that they loved him. This was flattering to his vanity, but he perceived that jealousy might be engendered between the two; this brown girl already spoke as one bitterly jealous. She had just said something about Annie taking to the Great House other men who had come to some unpleasant end – other men: what the devil did the little nigger mean? Other men ... Oh! Annie's former husbands of course, and because these had died poor Annie was held as in some way responsible for their death. She had said that some talk went about. But he was not going to have a servant, even if she had independent manners and openly professed love for him, speaking insolently and disrespectfully of Rosehall's mistress!

Millie came back with the liquor and handed it to him with evident reluctance; he took it silently and gulped it down; at once he felt new energy course through his veins. His head swam, for the rum was potent and the quantity plentiful, but it put him in good spirits. He was not disposed to be harsh with Millie now; indeed he suddenly realized that he rather liked this brown spitfire who dared to go great lengths because she was 'free and educated' and her grandfather was a man of wealth and power. He developed an interest in this wonderful grandfather; evidently he was a person of mark. He began to eat his breakfast, and as he ate he talked.

'Is your grandfather a white man, Millie?' he asked.

'One of them was; but he's dead; he was me father's father.'

'Then this other grandfather of yours whom you invoke with such reverence and awe?'

She looked puzzled.

'My language,' he smiled, 'is perhaps not sufficiently "educated". I mean who and of what colour is this other grandfather of yours?'

'He is black, coal black, and he tall and old, very old: he is a Guinea man and wise! He can talk to spirits, like the old witch in de Bible, who call up Samuel. Me gran'father is very great; everybody here 'fraid for him – even Mrs Palmer!'

'I see! An African and what you call out here an obeahman. Is that it?'

'Y-e-e-s; but he's more than an obeahman. More powerful.'

'Originally an African witch-doctor, I suppose, and a hoary old scoundrel. Let him take care that he doesn't get into trouble, Millie.'

'They can't do him anything; him is too strong. He protect me, an' he can protect you, too, if you want. But so long as you stay here you are out of his reach. You better leave, Squire. Trouble coming for you.'

'I will stay and meet it. And look here, Millie, I won't send you away as I threatened to do a while ago. But you are to understand that you must say nothing rude about the lady of this property. Do you hear?'

Millie nodded her head sadly. 'I hear,' she answered, 'and I understand. You love her, an' you don't love me!'

'Perfectly incorrigible,' laughed Robert, now restored to the best of humour by his drink, for that was the effect which drink usually had upon him. 'Perhaps,' he added, 'I will love you too.' Then, to his own amazing surprise, for he had not contemplated any such action, he bent over and kissed Millie on the mouth, and gaily sallied forth. As for the girl, she stood stock still, thrilled to the marrow, exalted to the seventh heaven of delight. A triumphant glare shone in her eyes, the light of victory. Just when she had thought she had lost everything she glimpsed a prospect of ultimate triumph and success.

On the instant her mind was made up, and Millicent had a resolute mind. She was going to fight with Mrs Palmer herself for possession of this man. Other girls like her had fought with as high-placed ladies before in this same parish, and had won. Millie determined to seek Mr Ashman without delay and to enlist him as her ally.

CHAPTER 8

Millicent Acts

FIRST SHE TIDIED Robert's room, though that had not been much disturbed, and she attended to the room in which she had stayed the night before. Then she went to the trash-house, where Psyche was usually to be found piling the dried refuse of the pressed cane, which was used when required as fuel for the mill. She told Psyche that she must look after the lunch of both of the young massas that day, and after their dinner, if necessary; she, Millicent, might not be back before night. She already knew that Mr Ashman was going to Palmyra that day; one of the lads had whispered the news early that morning. He might not be back for a couple of days, and she wished to see him as early as possible. She was of a quick, impulsive character; she hated procrastination; and now especially she was in a fever-heat of impatience. She must act. She prepared at once for her journey to Palmyra.

That estate, which was much larger than Rosehall, was situated behind and to the south of it, and was connected with Rosehall by a bridle-path leading over the intervening hills. It lay in a hollow; it was 'worked' by far more slaves than were to be found on Rosehall; it had its own Great House and overseer's residence, and all the other appurtenances of a great sugar estate. Mr Ashman was in charge of both properties, his energy and capacity rendering him quite capable of handling both. Ashman was an able man in his way; the financial success of Rosehall and of Palmyra in these last two years had been due to his competent management.

Millicent knew that he would ride over to Palmyra, and so be there long before she could come up with him – she did not know that Mrs Palmer was riding with him that morning. But she calculated that she could get to the next property soon enough to catch him at the overseer's house; if he were out riding round the estate, however, she would have to await her opportunity of speaking to him. What she was going to say she had not yet thought out; she must feel her way when she met him. But she knew that everybody said he had been Mrs Palmer's lover, that everybody said he was still enamoured of her, and that lately there had been a coldness between them that had preyed upon his mind and worsened an already nasty temper. That he was a strong and determined man Millicent was well aware; that he would fight to regain his old ascendancy over the mistress of Rosehall she guessed. She wanted him to do that, without harming Robert, of course, whom Millicent regarded as merely a victim of Annie Palmer's. Millicent, young and, on the whole, unsophisticated though she was, shared to the full the ordinary feminine distrust of her own sex and was ready to attribute what a man did that was not right in her sight to the wiles and machinations of some other woman. Robert, having come to Rosehall but two days ago, she told herself, could not be blamed for anything he did in connection with Mrs Palmer. It was the lady who was responsible; it was from the lady – a very terrible character – that the young squire must be rescued by any means; and if those means were not fair Millicent would have not the smallest objection to them or experience the slightest sting of self-reproach in employing them.

She walked with a rapid stride, swinging her upright body smartly and easily as she marched, communing with herself, filled wholly with her purpose. The young 'massa' – she called him so in her mind, yielding to custom, in spite of her freedom and education – had kissed her, and, in spite of all that she had said about Mrs Palmer, had decided to let her stay on in his service. He had confessed that he might come to like her. But he had been with the white lady all the night before, as other men had been, and she had heard a great deal about the fascination which that woman exercised over those who loved her until she wearied of them. If she could break that enthralment at once, the young, handsome squire would be saved and would leave Rosehall, taking her with him, as she was absolutely determined that he should do. He was not the first young white man that had liked her; others had suggested an establishment to her, and they were not mere overseers either, but owners of their own properties. If she had remained 'single' up to now, it was of her choosing; none of her suitors had touched her heart, or, as she put it, 'filled her eye'. But Robert Rutherford did; he stood forth in her imagination like a god. She had seen and loved him, just as Annie Palmer had done. She was as resolved to fight for possession of him as Annie Palmer was.

It was pleasant walking; the path led through leafy woods and the sun was not yet strong enough to cause discomfort. Besides, Millie was well accustomed to lengthy peregrinations; walking was second nature to her. But she was some time behind Mr Ashman when she came to Palmyra, and as she neared the overseer's house she saw at once something unusual was forward.

A sort of court was being held. Half a dozen men were being tried for plotting something; just what, no one was certain of, for the men were obstinately reticent and asserted that they had met the night before, in the hut in which they had been caught by Mr Ashman, for purely social purposes. Ashman again and again pointed out to them that, if that had been so, they would not have ceased suddenly to talk when they, much to his annoyance, heard his footsteps, and would not have attempted to bolt, an effort which he had frustrated by flinging himself into the doorway and barring their egress with his body. That they had been planning some mischief, he averred, was beyond all doubt, and Mrs Palmer, who stood listening to him and to them, nodded her head in agreement.

She was looking very grim and serious this morning. There was resentment in her heart against Ashman, who had spoken plainly to her about Robert Rutherford as they rode over to Palmyra; she had repressed her feelings (a matter of difficulty with her), and the repression was clamouring for explosive relief. There was relief to hand. These slaves were unruly, secretive, dangerous; at the very least they had no sort of right to be where they had been found by the overseer last night. To punish them severely might be to lose their services in field and sugar works for some time, but to order their condign chastisement, and to look on while the lashes were inflicted, was a joy and satisfaction which she could not at that moment forgo.

Annie ruled her people with terror, white and black alike. She had witnessed whippings for years and years, and her appetite had grown with what it fed on. The first flogging she had seen had made her ill, yet she had found a terrible fascination in it. She had gone to see another, and yet another; that first tasting of blood as it were, had awakened a certain lust in her which had grown and strengthened until it had become a powerful and abiding obsession. Had she lived fifty years before, when slaves could still be procured from the coasts of Africa, and when the law gave the slave-owner far more power over the life of a slave than it did in these days, she would sometimes have had an erring bondsman or woman whipped to death in her presence. At this moment her full lips were set hard, and the little lines running from the nostrils to the corners of her mouth were grimly perceptible. When she spoke it was in tones of cruel finality.

'Give them twenty-one lashes each: it ought to be more, but we want their labour today. Lay on the lashes well, though; make them feel! That will teach them to plot mischief again!'

There were two executors on this occasion, for one would be too tired to apply the blows with sufficient vigour on all the culprits condemned. Millicent had seen something of this sort before; she was sick with disgust and anger, but she did not forget her purpose. She worked her way as close to Ashman as she could, and then fixed her gaze upon his face with the idea of communicating to him by movements of her eyes that she wished to speak to him.

When the flogging was finished and the men ordered to resume their work immediately, Mrs Palmer, casting a glance over those who had been summoned to witness this vindication of authority, observed Millicent staring at Ashman and, not remembering her, noticing too the girl's good looks and superior attire, asked sharply: 'Who is that young woman? Not one of my people, is she?'

Ashman turned and saw Millie for the first time. 'No,' he said, 'she's old Takoo's granddaughter.'

'Oh!' A note of interest crept into Mrs Palmer's voice. 'I have heard of her; I must have seen her before, too.' She looked piercingly at Ashman.

'She evidently has come to you; she is staring at you. She is very pretty, John.'

'Yes,' dryly.

'Treat her nicely; she looks as if she was worth it. You like pretty things. I shall see you at the Great House when you come up.'

Mrs Palmer rode off with a knowing smile, a smile of great satisfaction. She had at once concluded that this girl wished to see Ashman for intimate reasons, upon which but one construction could be placed, and she was glad that Millicent was so well favoured. Ashman's talk that morning had aroused in Mrs Palmer's heart a dangerous feeling towards him, but she wished to avoid trouble with him if it were at all possible. He was too useful to be dispensed with lightly.

'You want me?' briefly demanded Ashman. He was in something of a hurry and did not wish to devote too much of his time to a girl on whom he had smiled in the past, but who had shown only too clearly that for him she had not the slightest use, and was never likely to have.

'Yes, sir' – Millie strove to speak her best; 'I want to speak to you – private.'

'Well, I haven't much time. Come this way and tell me what it is.'

He took her out of the hearing of the people around, but he did not get off his horse to listen. 'What is it?' he demanded impatiently, seeing that she hesitated.

She took her courage in both hands; she plunged into her tale without circumlocutory preliminary, though it had been in her mind to lead gradually up to the heart of it.

'You know that the new book-keeper sleep at the Great House last night? You know he was there wid Mrs Palmer?'

'And what the hell has that got to do with you?' he burst out, scandalized at her telling him this, regarding it as a gross offence, partly because the very fact that she stated was rankling in his heart.

'Don't hell me, Mr Ashman!' returned Millicent with spirit. 'Don't hell me! I am not one of you' slave that you can flog like dog; and me gran'father know how to deal wid anybody who ill-treat me.'

'Your grandfather can go to hell as well as you; some day he will swing from a gallows. And don't be too sure that I can't flog you and make you pay a fine for it, if you are impertinent. Mrs Palmer would have you flogged now, on the spot, if only I told her what you have just told to me!'

Millicent realized, with a sickening spasm of fear, that what he said was only too true; Mrs Palmer might, in a paroxysm of fury, order her to be whipped until she bled, no matter what the after-consequences might be. She had done some daring things in the open light of day, and some still more terrible, horrifying things, by the dim light of candles within the heavy walls of Rosehall, if what was whispered about her was true. Millicent trembled.

But she held her ground and she spoke out with courage.

'Try it if you dare,' she volleyed back. 'Try it, an' as sure as there is a God in Heaven me gran'father will poison both you and she before the week is over.'

Ashman realized in his turn that that also was very probable. Takoo would undoubtedly take vengeance for any injury inflicted on his granddaughter: no one who knew him could doubt that. And he was considered in these parts a master in the art of poisoning. There was a white planter who had died in agony, and Takoo had been suspected – though nothing could be proved against him. Ashman temporized.

'If that is all you have come here to say, you had better clear out,' he ordered.

'I come here to tell you that – that you should try an' stop this thing between Mrs Palmer an' the new book-keeper. If you don't do it now it might be too late next week, and *you* won't like that.'

'Oh,' he said grimly. 'But you don't care a curse about me; so it's not in my interest you are speaking. What is your object?'

'Say what?'

'What do you want? What are you telling me this for?'

Millicent dropped her eyes.

'I know you been friendly with Mrs Palmer.'

'That is none of your business. I will thank you not to mention it again.'

'An' if she love this new massa she not going to love you any more, an' she may turn you away or—'

'Yes?' ominously.

'Well, you know what happen sometimes when she done finish with anyone she used to love.' Millicent spoke in a whisper, as one very much afraid.

'Yes?' There was now a fierce harshness in Ashman's voice. Again had Millicent echoed his own unpleasant thoughts.

'And' – desperately – 'I like the young massa, an' I am his housekeeper.'

'So, that is it at last! Now we have the motive.' He thought a moment, then suddenly looked at Millicent with a new light in his eyes. His voice became friendly on the instant. 'What can I do, Millie? I don't see that I can do anything.'

'Can't you turn him away as soon as you go back to Rosehall?'

'I? But she would take him back if she wanted to. I would only be making a fool of myself if I did that.'

'Then why don't you tell him all about her, massa? You know everything. Tell him!'

'He wouldn't believe me if I did; and he would repeat to her everything I said. It would be no use. But you – *you* could tell him. Does he like you?'

'I think so,' diffidently.

Ashman was ready with advice; he had made up his mind.

'That is good! Make him like you more. Don't leave him if you can possibly help it. Stick to him all the time; show that you love him. You are a very pretty girl; I am sure he will like you. And tell him all that you know, Millie; tell a little now and a little more later on; but rub it in as much as you can. And look here, don't for God's sake, let Mrs Palmer know that you are his housekeeper, for she would give orders that you were not to put your foot into Rosehall or Palmyra again. You understand that, don't you?'

'I know.'

He thought a moment. 'I tell you what,' he said. 'You'd better come up to my place sometimes as if you came to see me. That may make her think that you are coming to me.'

'But suppose Mr Rutherford think so, too? He's a stranger. What will him think of me?'

'He isn't likely to have any thought like that; and you can always find reason to give him. But if Mrs Palmer imagines there is anything between you both – God help you! You ought to know that.'

'I know that,' said Millicent miserably. 'She is hell. She is de devil himself. She is the worse woman in Jamaica!'

John Ashman looked at the girl with a lowering face, thinking that she was saying things distasteful to hear, almost unbearable. It was impertinence in her, stark impertinence which, in other circumstances, he would have regarded as intolerable, but did not the whole parish say the same? And did he not know it himself? Besides, he and Millicent must be allies now; they both had much at stake. 'Do what I tell you,' he urged, 'and now go back to Rosehall.'

She nodded understanding, turned and retraced her steps.

CHAPTER 9

The Overseer

MR ASHMAN was sitting on his veranda, moodily looking towards the slave village where dwelt the workers on this estate; the scene was so familiar to him that, while seeing, he might be said to see it not. The huts of the slaves stood in their own little gardens in which grew the fruit-bearing trees and vegetables that these people cultivated for their own use. Breadfruit and banana spread luxuriant leaves above and around the houses, creating a welcome shade during the warmer hours of the day; yam-vines clung to sticks stuck almost upright in the soil; the purple of the potato plant showed itself on tiny hillocks in which the tubers ripened. It was a settlement, this, and those who inhabited it were mostly at home at this hour; work had ceased in the fields, and from numerous fires trailed upwards into the air blue smoke of burning wood with which bondswomen cooked their families' evening meal. The fires themselves could be seen shining in the dusk, lending a touch of bright picturesqueness to the village. Stars were peeping forth, and the breeze of the December evening was delightful after the heat and turmoil of a strenuous day. Mr Ashman looked upon it all, but gave it no thought, for his mind was on far weightier and more intimate subjects. He was deeply troubled, and anger smouldered in him. His concern was to find a way by which to solve his difficulties, and no way that promised success could he discern at the moment, think he never so deeply.

As the man in charge of Rosehall and Palmyra he was somewhat anxious about the dangerous situation which he knew was developing in this part of the country, and perhaps in every other parish, though just what and when the climax would be he could not guess. There was trouble abroad. Word had got about that a decree which freed the slaves had arrived from England and was being kept back by the masters, and the slaves were in a state of dangerous excitement. The work on estates went on as usual, force of habit and fear of the whip were still potent with these people. But there were grumblings, plottings, and the belief was spreading that, at some date not distant, and at a given signal the slaves would rise, give the properties over to the flames, loot, murder their masters, and thus would take by savage means what they believed was being withheld from them. That some outbreak would occur Mr Ashman did not doubt; but in the meantime he knew he could do nothing. Even the whipping those six men had been given at Palmyra had not wrung a single word of confession from them. One could only wait and be vigilant. And, anyhow, the threatening danger, though it might be serious, was general; of more importance to him was the danger that menaced him personally and alone, and from an altogether different quarter.

For three years he had been practically master of Rosehall and Palmyra, their affairs having been entrusted to his management. He had been more than that, too; he had been Annie Palmer's lover. He recalled their first meeting, Annie's husband had been dead a month, and had, as was the custom, been buried on the estate, and some ugly rumours had floated about as to the cause of his death. The slaves of Rosehall had whispered, the white mechanics and book-keepers had also talked below their breath; but no one had come forward to make any positive assertion, and he would be a bold officer of the law who should charge the owner of great estates, and a woman at that, with murder, unless he possessed the amplest, most convincing proof. Yet Montego Bay wondered and hinted, and he had heard this talk. He had gone to the Bay on business at about this time, he having terminated his connection with a property in Westmoreland and being engaged in looking for another position that should suit him. He had an excellent reputation as a capable overseer; he was not doubtful about his future. Certainly he had never thought of making application to the owner of Rosehall, would have laughed at a suggestion that he should do so. But while he stayed at Montego Bay Annie Palmer had ridden into town one morning. Chance brought her to the lodging-house at which he stopped, and in the corridor leading to the dining-room they met that day.

John Ashman was muscular, well set up, arrogant in mien, rough in manner, but of a certain handsomeness of which he was very well aware. Annie was dainty, bright, alluring, with an eye for a fine-looking man and a rage for the possession of anyone she fancied. Her impulses were lightning, her will imperious; she overrode obstacles in her path with a fine scorn and disregard of consequences. She did not know who this man was, but she saw at once that he was well-favoured and that he gazed at her intently and with admiration flaming in his eyes. He knew who she was; word had gone about the house that Mrs Palmer of Rosehall was in it, and at first sight of her he was aware that this could be no other than the woman about whom all the town had been talking, the woman whom most people had begun to whisper of as of dreadful character even in a land where there was not much delicacy and where the uncertainties of the immediate future (due to the rumoured abolition of slavery and the equalizing of master and slave) had soured tempers and turned many men into disgruntled brutes. She seemed to Ashman more lovely than common report had painted her, more fascinating than he could possibly have dreamed. Her character? What did he care about that? Or rather, it rendered her more enticing to him, for now he was filled with admiration of her force and daring. It came to him swiftly that only a bold and ambitious man deserved to win and hold such a woman, and if any man failed to hold her and perished, there was little reason to waste tears over such a weakling.

But Ashman, even as he thought, while, with unconscious rudeness, he stared at Annie, did not dare to put himself forward, in his own mind, as the young widow's suitor. Her husbands had been gentlemen, men in independent positions and of the class that ruled the country; he was but an overseer. A domineering, imperious man who had won upwards from the ranks of the book-keepers; but an overseer only; and such did not aspire to the hands of great ladies unless those ladies showed for them a marked preference. And even then it was not marriage that was usually suggested. Barriers of class were upheld where sometimes every other barrier went down.

Annie Palmer knew much about the nature and the impulses of men, and something of what was passing in Ashman's mind she understood. She saw that his stare was not that of curiosity only. It was that of a man who was taken by a sudden admiration, one who required but little encouragement to be brought to a lovely woman's feet. She seized the opportunity; a trifling question – 'Where is the dining-room, please?' –

opened an acquaintanceship between them. She told him that she wanted someone to manage her estates, now that her last husband was dead. She learnt from him that he was free; when they parted that day he had been appointed overseer of Palmyra and Rosehall, with more than an overseer's general authority. Within the next few days he was Annie's accepted lover. This relationship had endured for nearly three years; then he had noticed recently that she had grown cold, more difficult to deal with, less satisfied with him. Then happened the advent of Robert Rutherford, and Ashman had realized that he must fight for his ascendancy or lose everything, must break the intimacy between Annie and this upstart or be speedily broken himself.

He had never lived at the Great House; Mrs Palmer had never suggested that he should do so. But then his quarters were comfortable, and an overseer must keep constant watch over his charge. He had been often and often at the Great House, and had learnt, indirectly, all that there was to hear about Rosehall and its previous owners. He did not doubt now that they had come to their end by violent means; Annie Palmer was capable of anything that her passions or her interests might suggest. When once she was on her estates she made little effort to disguise her disposition; it was irksome, painful to her to be anything but herself; she had for too long given free vent to her feelings, yielding swiftly to the inclinations she experienced, to care to pretend before him. She might make him her lover but she did not forget that he was her inferior, and she was not accustomed to caring about what her inferiors might think of her. They were there to obey, to administer to her convenience or her pleasure; if she chose to be gracious to them, that was kindness on her part, but with them she would be herself always. Queen of Rosehall by unquestioned, imprescriptible right, her subjects must submit to her will and be delighted when she showed them the smallest degree of favour.

But if that favour were withdrawn! That was the thought which rankled in John Ashman's brain just now. A week had passed since Robert's coming to Rosehall, and already some ominous things had happened. Last night Robert had been to the Great House again; Ashman himself had seen him ride away from it this morning. Yesterday Annie had sent for her overseer and instructed him to employ another book-keeper, a man who might do for a temporary job on the estate. 'Another man is needed, John,' Mrs Palmer had said; 'Mr Rutherford is not accustomed to this work, and it would be folly to depend too much upon him.'

'Then why not get rid of him?' Ashman had not unreasonably asked. 'Why keep a useless person on the estate?'

'He is here to learn planting,' she replied; 'I have explained that to you before. And he is a friend of mine. That is another very good reason.'

'Let us understand one another plainly, Annie,' Ashman said. 'This book-keeper was with you on the very first night he came to Rosehall. What does this mean? That you have taken him as your c—?' He paused upon an ugly word. He did not wish to press the quarrel too far.

'Say what is in your mind,' she smiled, looking him straight in the eyes. 'Don't think about my feelings, I beg of you. Don't let me trouble you in the slightest. Go on! I am taking him as my what?'

'You are throwing me over for him?'

'You haven't been so much of a devoted lover of late, have you?' she asked him, with a little sneer.

'Are you trying to make out that I am to blame for your treatment of me?'

'Well, there are your twins over at Palmyra, you know, John, and they are not yet three months old. And there is – but this is all unnecessary. You are a good man on the estate, and you know you are welcome to remain as overseer. But please remember that we are not husband and wife.'

'Perhaps I am lucky in that,' he answered grimly, stung to a significant remark.

She started. Annie Palmer hated any allusion, however indirect, to the death of her husbands; she would occasionally speak of it herself, but grew white with anger (with which was blended dread) whenever she thought that someone else was hinting at it. Ashman had been wise hitherto to keep off that forbidden ground. Jealousy and temper had now betrayed him on to it.

Annie's gaze narrowed, and for one long minute she sat silent, her fingers beating a tattoo upon the table at which both of them were sitting. She would have ordered this man peremptorily out of her sight and off the premises at once but that the crop must be taken off day by day now, and that there were disquieting rumours about the disposition and plottings of the slaves. But, if not now, a little later certainly Ashman must go. But if he knew too much – and he could have found out much in these last three years – was it safe that he should be allowed to go, with a thirst for revenge in his heart? That was a question to be answered later on.

Ashman saw the look in Annie's face, had a startled realization of the trend of her musing, and when he had left her yesterday it was with less self-assurance than he had ever felt. He had wounded Annie, who had evidently ceased to care for him; who indeed had never deeply cared for him. He must be wary in his movements now; she would plan to keep him silent if she could not keep him tame. But if Rutherford could be got rid of? In that case present disagreements might be forgotten, old relationships resumed: he wished that, for in his own fashion he loved this extraordinary woman. But how to get rid of Rutherford? Annie had killed one of her husbands, it was said, with the aid of the old devil, Takoo, and by herself the others; but Takoo was the girl Millicent's grandfather, and Takoo would protect the boy. Besides, murder was terrible; if he struck at Rutherford he could never escape suspicion. His only hope was that Millicent would be able to convince Robert that he ran an awful risk by continuing to be Annie Palmer's lover, that she would be able to assure the new book-keeper that Annie had been thrice a murderess, and that, shocked and rendered afraid, young Rutherford would flee from the estate.

As to his remaining as a book-keeper, that was but a mere farce now. Even now he, Ashman, was waiting for the man for whom he had dispatched a messenger that same day, after receiving Mrs Palmer's orders that Robert was to be relieved of much of the harder work which a book-keeper was expected to perform. Robert clung to his book-keeper's room, shame, pride, a feeling of loyalty to Burbridge, all operating in his mind to keep him to that decision; but Ashman wondered how long it would be before he broke down under the pressure of Annie's wish and solicitations – for Annie had said plainly to John Ashman that Robert might come shortly to take over one of the vacant rooms in the Great House. Annie cared less than ever she had done for such public opinion as existed; her strong will would undoubtedly influence the young man. Ashman had seen many a man arrive from England with the noblest resolves and the highest ideals, and sometimes in a week these all seemed to disappear as completely as if they had never existed. Why should Rutherford be different? He was not acting differently, anyhow, thought Ashman with a bitter smile.

He saw, for there was a young moon in the sky, the figure of a man approaching him, a white man quite evidently. He knew who it was.

The stranger approached the veranda confidently, but waited at the foot of the steps leading up to it before venturing to ascend. 'Come up!' Ashman ordered, and the man obeyed.

Even in the obscurity of the veranda it could be seen that this person was in shabby attire, and in the light his shoes would have been perceived to have gone some way towards dissolution. That he had walked it from where he had come, too, stamped him at once as a poor white, 'a walk-foot backra', a man who was down in the world pretty badly, since to walk in a land where all white men rode or drove was a flaunting advertisement of poverty and degeneration.

'You applied to me for a job some months ago, Rider,' Ashman began without any preliminaries. 'Do you still want a job?'

'I do, sir.'

'And you think you can keep sufficiently off the rum during this crop to be worth your keep?'

'I should hope so. 'Tis not in mortals to command success, but—'

'You are not in the pulpit now; you haven't been there for many years, Mr Rider, so you needn't preach to me,' interrupted John Ashman roughly. Yet, curiously enough, he had a sort of respect for this peculiar, shabby individual standing quietly before him, for he knew that Rider was considered a highly educated man. Richard Rider, M.A., had been a curate in the Kingston parish church ten years ago, and would probably have been its rector in another five years but for his predilection for drink. He had drunk himself out of a church that had been quite ready to overlook occasional lapses and even a constant state of intoxication which did not include exhibitions of street staggering and lying down in the gutter; but when Mr Rider had been often drunk both in and out of church, his bishop was compelled to take some notice of his actions. Accordingly, Rider had been demoted to a country church, but there, free from all restraint, and finding nothing in the manners and morals of his congregation to inspire him with the belief that they cared sixpence about religion, he had become more frankly an adherent of the bottle than even when in Kingston. So he had been permitted to retire from his office as practising priest and had found situations as a book-keeper in those times when he kept sober; for there were occasions when he was comparatively sober for weeks and months. Ashman, who knew a good deal about him, hoped for the sake of the work to be done that the present was one of the sober interludes of Mr Rider. 'You can live in that room,' he said to him, pointing to a little annexe to his own house. 'The other two book-keepers live together and there is no space there for you. How long you remain here will depend upon yourself. Where's your luggage?'

'It is not considerable, a nigger could bring it on his head.'

'I should think so. We'll send for it tomorrow. If you go outside now they will give you some grub.'

Rider went off, but Ashman continued to sit and stare at nothing and think his own sombre thoughts. It was about nine o'clock now; the fires in the negro village had long since died down, the slaves had all retired, weary from their long day's labour. A sound as of footsteps again broke the silence; Ashman observed a figure which resolved itself into that of a woman as it drew nearer. She came right up to the house, saw him, and ran up the veranda steps. She seemed to know the place very well.

'Millie? I have been expecting you! Sit down.'

This invitation was a token of friendship; Millicent looked about her, noticed a chair in the corner and plumped herself into it.

'Well, how goes everything?' questioned the overseer keenly.

'He went up last night to the Great House again, an' stay there all night, Busha.'

'I know that.'

'It don't do him no good, for when he come back home he wanted to drink. He drink more all day today than I ever notice him do before, though,' she added truthfully, 'he went to work all the same.'

'I know that too,' said Ashman moodily; 'and have you said anything to him?'

'I tell him about Mrs Palmer; what she is and what they say she do to all her husband, but it don't make no difference. Sometimes he insult me by shutting me up, sometimes he only laugh and say I forget myself an' that I better be careful. But he don't seem to care.'

'Did he say he would tell her?' anxiously asked Mr Ashman.

'No; I ask him straight if he was goin' to, an' he say no, but that I am running a big risk. But it's not doing him any good, for though he been here only a few days he is different already. He's more careless-like, don't seem to mind nothing at all now. She is doing him bad. I hate her!'

'So it doesn't seem as if he loves you, does it?' inquired Mr Ashman mockingly.

'I don't know.' Millie hesitated. 'He talk to me now more than before; and ask me a lot about meself. I think he getting to care for me, an' that is natural, Squire, for I care for him an' I am pretty.'

'Millie,' said Mr Ashman slowly, following an idea that had come into his mind, 'don't you think your grandfather might help you? He is fond of you, isn't he?'

'He love me to death,' said the girl proudly. 'But what is he to do? He is strong, but' (dismally) 'Mrs Palmer strong too. She is so strong that she can live in a haunted house, where they hear all sort of noise day an' night, and yet she get no harm.'

'The haunting is probably done by some of the damned house people,' remarked Mr Ashman scornfully. 'That banging of doors and murmuring is all the work of one or two venturesome brutes who want to keep up the story of duppies in the place for their own reasons. If it was worth while I would investigate it. Perhaps your very grandfather put up one of the house servants to bang those doors! I have long suspected it. Mrs Palmer is not as strong as your grandfather, Millie.'

She shook her head doubtfully.

'Your grandfather must know that you are living on this estate now?' he asked.

'Yes, he know, and he don't quite like it. Only yesterday he say to me that trouble going to come on me because I live here as Marse Robert's housekeeper, an' I tell him I am not a real, regular housekeeper, but he say that I will be – and that make me glad. But me gran'father very sorrowful; he warn me against Mrs Palmer.'

To this, for a while, Ashman said nothing. He was buried in thought. At last:

'So old Takoo thinks you are in for trouble, eh?'

'So he tell me, but perhaps he is wrong.'

'Perhaps; but suppose he thought that Mr Rutherford had anything to do with your trouble; would he be angry with him?'

'Lord! He would kill him!' exclaimed Millicent, raising her voice in sheer terror. 'Me gran'father is awful when he get out o' temper; and if you or anybody else do me anything he would never rest till he revenge me.'

Ashman knew that Takoo would not consider as an ill deed the taking of this girl as a mistress, or 'housekeeper', by any white man for whom she cared; that kind of action Takoo would look upon as normal and even as highly meritorious. But should Robert lead to any harm being done to Millicent, whether by Annie or someone else, the old man might hold him responsible; and, of course, it would be easier for Takoo to wreak his vengeance on a mere book-keeper and a stranger than on Mrs Palmer or even on the overseer. Ashman wished no particular harm to Millicent, though he saw no reason why he should particularly wish her well. She was a mere pawn in the game he was playing. He had always been hard and selfish; his life, his circumstances, had further helped to make him so. He was known as a stern taskmaster; his object in life had been the material advancement of John Ashman; his great ambition had always been to rise from overseer to attorney, to the position of a man in charge of many estates, with overseers under him. From that to ownership was often but a short step, as he well knew. He would have worked with Millicent to get rid of Robert Rutherford; if that end could not be achieved with the girl's aid, why should not her grandfather be the instrument of Rutherford's disappearance from the scene? She might suffer, but she would have to take her chance of that. Robert Rutherford must go; must go absolutely; there must be a complete severing of the ties that now existed between him and Annie Palmer. And Millicent had just given a hint as to how Robert's elimination might be brought about.

'It's getting late, Millie,' said Ashman, rising. 'Come and see me soon again, and tell me everything that happens. By the way, are you going to Marse Robert tonight?'

'Yes,' she answered simply.

'Well, good night.'

CHAPTER 10

The Explosion

WITH RAPID STRIDE and sinuous swinging of the hips, Millicent took her way towards the book-keepers' quarters. She knew she would find Robert in his room tonight, for Burbridge would sit up in the still-house. Tomorrow night would be Robert's turn, if he wished to undertake the work. For it was no longer compulsory for him, and she had heard that another book-keeper would be about on the following day. Mr Rutherford was being allowed to do much as he pleased.

When she reached the little house she perceived a light shining through the crevices. She was going to the room which she had, without invitation or specific permission, made her own, when she changed her mind. She knocked at Robert's door.

'Come in,' his voice bade her, and she entered to find him sitting by his table, a glass of rum and water by his hand. He had thrown off his jacket and was taking a 'night-cap' prior to going to bed.

'Well, Millicent, what's all the news?' he asked her cordially; 'what brings you here at this time of night?'

'You know I live here, in de next room,' said Millicent, looking down at him, 'an' I thought as I would ask how you are, an' tell you good night.'

'I am very well, thank you, Millie, though I have had a pretty strenuous week of it.'

She did not know what 'strenuous' meant, but guessed its meaning.

'You was up last night?' The inquiry was really an affirmation.

'Yes, mentor; I was up some part of the night.'

'You didn't come in till morning, an' you work all day today. That don't good for you, Marse Robert; don't you know you may get sick an' die?'

'It is possible. But I say, Millie, I never imagined when I left England that I should find here a brown lady to take such an interest in my welfare, and lecture me on the error of my ways. Is that customary with housekeepers?'

'Yes; if they like you. Tell me something, Marse Robert.'

'What is it?'

'You ever say anything to Mrs Palmer about me? You ever tell her I am looking after you?'

'I haven't mentioned you, no,' said Robert, conscious now that he had deliberately refrained from saying anything about Millicent to Annie. She of course had asked him who was attending to his creature comforts in his quarters, and he had assured her that Burbridge had made ample arrangements for him. Mrs Palmer had come to the conclusion that Burbridge's servant was attending upon Robert also.

'Don't tell her.'

'Why?'

'Because she might want to stop me. She can prevent me coming here, you know.'

'Of course. But frankly, Millie, why shouldn't she if she wants to?'

'You want her to?' asked the girl plaintively.

Robert looked at her. She was undeniably pretty, and though he guessed she could hold her own and did not lack for strength of character, she was very gentle in dealing with him. He felt he should be very sorry if Millicent were to leave his service. 'Well, no, I don't want her to,' he admitted.

The girl's face lightened in a flash. A happy smile showed her white, gleaming, even teeth and shone in her eyes. 'Then you like me, Marse Robert!' she cried confidently. 'You like me, or you wouldn't mind whether I go or stay. Don't I right?'

'I think I have told you before that I do like you, Millie,' he laughed, sipping his rum and water, 'though you have been awfully cheeky.'

'Because I tell you about Mrs Palmer?'

'Yes. Had you been a man, Millie, you would have been out of this place long ago. But I am afraid I am weak where a woman is concerned, especially a pretty woman.'

She came nearer to him. 'You think I am pretty?'

'You know you are.'

'Yes, I know I are; but I want to know if you think so too. You think so?'

'I am sure you are, Millie.'

'Yet you like the mistress better than me. Because she is white an' you are white? But she don't love you better than I do, and she is wicked, I tell you, wicked—'

'Millicent!'

'I don't care! It is true. An' I tell you so because I love you an' I am afraid about what might happen to you. You don't know everything. You running a big risk; it may kill you.'

Robert thought that it was treason to Annie for him to allow this coloured damsel to run on in the way she was doing, to permit her to traduce the woman to whom he had sworn eternal devotion; and yet, he asked himself, how could he prevent it? She was retailing lies, of course, but she believed them; and if she repeated them it was because of her sincere affection for him. He could not be a brute and order her away! He loved Annie – (an uneasy questioning in his mind made him wonder whether he loved Annie as much as he said he did and as he clearly ought, but again, as on previous occasions, he tried to dismiss this question from his mind). But he liked this girl also; with something like comic dismay he had discovered that, in spite of all he had believed to the contrary, a man could care for more than one woman at the same time, even if not with the same degree of intensity. He did not realize that Annie Palmer fascinated him but that he did not love her with such devotion that no other woman mattered to him; he was not sophisticated. He had faced for a few moments the question of marrying Annie. He had hurriedly dismissed it. He had accepted the existing situation, had noticed too that Annie herself never once mentioned marriage, but seemed content with their present irregular relations. His father would not approve of them? No; but his father was thousands of miles away, in a different land, in a different world. Why should he bother to think of what was so distant? This was Jamaica, and why would he not do in Jamaica as others did? To be a model of virtue here would be merely to make oneself ridiculous. In the meantime, here was Millicent, and her society was not unpleasant.

'I am not afraid of being killed,' he said with a laugh. He finished his drink of rum and water, and mixed himself another. He rather liked the flavour of Jamaica rum.

'You don't believe what I tell you?'

'Of course not! I am not going to believe every lie that you have heard, Millie.'

'Some day she will know that I looking after you, an' she

will order me not to come back to dis place. What you will say then?'

'Sufficient to the day is the evil thereof, Millie. Meantime you are still here, and, as you want to be here, that should content you.'

'Very well, Marse Robert.' She looked at him in silence for a few moments, then added, in a low voice, 'good night.'

'So soon?' he asked and drained his glass. 'Why don't you stay a little longer?'

'You mean it? You want me to stay?' Millicent asked eagerly.

'Of course I do. Take a chair. Better still—' He drew her down to him and sat her on his knee, laughing the while. Then he kissed her. She threw her arms wildly about his neck and kissed him in passionate return.

Millicent's eyes were shining now. Her grandfather had told her, only the day before, that she would become the young book-keeper's 'real' housekeeper, and it seemed as though this prediction were in the way of being fulfilled.

Robert stroked her cheek gently. Then he slipped his left arm round the girl's waist. 'You want to know if I think you pretty, eh?' he asked. 'I think you very sweet and lovable, Millie, and I am glad that you care for me. Do you like to hear that?'

For answer she kissed him; then:

'You will leave here, Marse Robert?'

'Leave here; but why?'

'If you love me more than you love she, you will. But I wouldn't mind so much if she was different. The two of us could have you. It is because I am afraid that I want you to leave. Don't you understand? She may kill you an' me together – she will hate me, and if she think you don't love her as you should—'

'Don't talk about Mrs Palmer, Millie!'

'All right' (with a sigh). 'But you like me all the same?'

'Yes; I do, and I am going to keep you with me always, do you hear? You are going to stay with me and I am going to care for you.' ('Why not?' he muttered to himself. 'Other men do the same. Why should I be a prude?')

'You don't want me to – to go into my own room tonight?'

'No; you are going to stay with me. You don't mind?'

'I want to,' she said simply, and her arm stole round his neck once more.

Not more than ten minutes had passed before they heard the sound of a galloping horse. It approached and halted before the book-keepers' quarters. Someone alighted, came up the steps; then there was a sharp rap on the door.

'Who is that?' Robert called out sharply.

'I. Can I see you for a few minutes?'

'Mrs Palmer!' whispered Robert, startled and guiltily ill at ease. 'Slip into the next room, Millie, and be quick, for God's sake.'

'In a moment!' he said aloud.

In a couple of minutes he opened the door and stepped outside; but Annie Palmer did not choose to talk with him on the veranda. She passed into the room, he following. She glanced keenly around, noticed the door that led into the adjoining apartment and pointed to it. 'Who lives in there?' she asked directly.

Robert, glancing at her face, saw it dark with anger and suspicion. Another thing about her surprised him. She was dressed in man's clothing, in a black suit which had evidently been made for her. Millicent had told him that she was in the habit of riding about the estates at night, habited like a man, but he had thought that this was but one of the inventions of the slaves, who felt that their mistress's eyes were always upon them. Now he knew that it was but the sober truth. Annie, looking more diminutive than ever in her man's clothes, stood before him, a heavy riding whip in her hand. And her manner was imperative and stormy.

He was about to answer her question, saying that the apartment was occupied by the girl who looked after his meals and room, when she suddenly walked over to the door and gave it a push. It yielded, after a slight resistance; for Millicent realized that nothing was to be gained by her struggling against Mrs Palmer's determined resolve to enter.

Millicent was standing and breathing heavily. Annie Palmer looked her up and down with a wide-eyed contemptuous stare. 'So you have Ashman's woman as your servant and "housekeeper"?' was the question she flung at Robert.

'I am not Mr Ashman's woman,' volleyed back Millicent, stung to a spirited protest by Mrs Palmer's assertion. She looked sharply at Robert to see how he took this remark.

'Speak when you are spoken to!' ordered Mrs Palmer. She turned to Robert. 'I could not sleep; I thought I would go for a ride about the estate; I have to do that sometimes, to see that everything is in order. I fancied that perhaps you might like to come with me. You didn't tell me it was this woman who was looking after your room, Robert, or I would have told you she is the last person that I care to have on Rosehall. She is a well-known character about here. I suppose she is trying to get you to make her your "housekeeper", isn't she? And has perhaps already succeeded?' Annie spoke with an effort at composure, thinking no more about what Millicent might feel than she would have done had she been speaking about a dog. 'If you want one of this type,' she went on, 'you might select a better specimen. This one is rather notorious. Anyhow, if I had known she was here I should have seen to it that she did not remain. I only hope she hasn't yet stolen anything from you. They all steal.'

'I am not a thief, Mrs Palmer!' cried Millicent, furious now beyond the restraint of fear. 'I am neither a thief or a murderer, an' that is more than everybody can say!'

'Indeed!'

'Yes; an' the reason why you don't want the Squire to have me for his housekeeper is because you want him for you'self an' you are jealous!'

'Jealous of you, a creature like you – *you*? Girl, are you mad? Do you want to be whipped within an inch of your life? Do you remember who you are talking to? Dirt that you are, how dare you! Leave Rosehall this minute, or—'

'I won't!'

'You won't?' shrilled Mrs Palmer, and that shrilling voice was new to Robert and shocked him. 'You won't! Surely you must be mad!'

'I am not one of your slaves. Dis place is yours, but the Squire is a free man, an' a white man, an' if he say I am to stay here tonight I can stay. And you can't flog me. You can't!'

'We'll test that now,' said Annie softly, narrowing her eyes. She lifted her riding whip and brought it down sharply on the girl's shoulders. Swiftly she raised it again for another blow.

Robert darted between them.

'Annie, Annie,' he implored, 'remember your position.'

'I am a mistress of slaves, that is my position,' she retorted; 'and this woman is little better than a slave. Leave me to deal with her, Robert; I know her kind.'

'If you touch me again I will dash your brain out,' shrieked Millicent, seizing a chair. 'I am free like you are, and, so help me God, I rather die than let you beat me!'

'We shall see,' replied Annie, shaking off Robert's arm. Her face was set; there was a light in her eye which indicated an irrevocable determination to chastise and humiliate this girl in the young man's presence. Robert realized her resolve, and nerved himself to frustrate it. He felt sick, ashamed, loathing himself and the scene in which he played a part. Yet Annie seemed to have no reproaches for him. It was the girl alone upon whom she was bent upon exhausting all her fury.

'You cannot help her, Robert,' she said with icy finality. 'She has to be flogged for her impertinence, and if not by me it will be by one of my drivers.'

'Annie be reasonable: she will do you hurt!'

'She wouldn't dare. Stand aside. She won't lift a finger to me.'

The whip was raised again. It was about to descend when it was suddenly seized.

She swung round, furious and astonished. A tall, gaunt, savage-looking black man, with grizzled hair and heavy features, held the whip. Deep-set eyes glowed as they answered the glare from Mrs Palmer's eyes; a long, deeply-lined upper lip closed firmly over the projecting lower lip; old though he was there was nothing feeble about his appearance.

'Takoo!' The name came in a gasp from Mrs Palmer.

'Grandpa!' cried Millicent, frantically joyous.

Robert gazed at the man bewildered. To him it was a thing astonishing that a negro should thus have dared to stay the hand of Annie Palmer.

'Patience, missis,' said the old man calmly. 'Remember Millie is my gran'child; I am begging you, for my sake to spare her.'

He spoke very good English, but though his words were humble his demeanour was not particularly so. He still held the whip.

'What are you doing here, Takoo?' demanded Mrs Palmer.

'I was about you' estate tonight, as you sometimes allow me to come, missis. I knew Millie was this new massa's house-keeper, an' I wanted to see how she was getting on. I was out there for some time; I see you ride up. We didn't know you would have any objection to Millie; but as you object I will take her away.'

But Millicent, who was never a coward, would not stand silently by and hear her fate decided by others. 'Grandpa,' she sobbed, 'Mrs Palmer say all sort of bad things about me. I never had anything to do wid Mr Ashman. I love the young Squire, an' the Squire love me—'

'You fool!' Mrs Palmer burst out. 'How could a gentleman love you? Do you still forget yourself?'

'Patience, missis, I beg you to have a little patience. She is my gran'daughter,' said Takoo. 'Get your clothes an' come, Millie.'

Millicent glanced at Robert, but knew in her heart that from the doom pronounced there could be no appeal. He could not help her. She was to go, and that immediately. Just when she had triumphed her cup of joy was dashed from her lips.

She went into her own room to gather her few articles of apparel, while the others waited silent. She returned within a couple of minutes, and looked with open-eyed malignancy at Annie Palmer. She passed out of the room followed by her grandfather, but at the steps of the veranda she turned round and flung out her hand with a fierce gesture.

'You will try to murder Marse Robert as you murder you' husbands,' she hurled at the stern woman who stood tapping the table with her whip. 'I done tell him all about you, you bloody witch! Some day I will live to see them hang you in Montego Bay!'

Old Takoo uttered a cry of warning and anger, and literally pushed his granddaughter down the steps; Annie made no reply, but a rush of blood to her head showed itself in the sudden crimsoning of her complexion. The accusation, openly and defiantly thrown at her, was terrible: that it should have come from a native woman constituted the quintessence of an unbearable insult. This girl regarded her as a rival, had dared to struggle with her for the affection of her own book-keeper. She trembled with passion, held now in restraint by an almost superhuman effort of will. But she said never a word.

'Fool,' hissed Takoo to his niece, 'you want to dead? She will never forgive you!'

'I don't care!' exclaimed Millicent. 'If there is a God in heaven He will see that she is a beast. An' sooner or later she will kill him, Tata.'

'She may kill you first,' muttered the old man, as they hurried away. 'You must go far from here, Millie, an' you must go tonight. It is hell you have to face now.'

'I don't care.'

'So you say now, but wait.'

'She is a she-devil. She is a witch!'

'Yes; an' what that mean for you?'

'I have you, gran'pa; you can protect me, and bring the young Squire back to me.'

Takoo answered nothing; he was thinking of the blow with the whip which Annie Palmer had dealt to the one being on earth whom he cared for. He was thinking also of Annie's certain future vengeance for the words so daringly spoken by

Millicent. He knew the mistress of Rosehall; she would strike at Millicent; such an affront could never be forgiven.

He had been Mrs Palmer's tool more than once; they had been secret allies. Now he saw her as an enemy and an antagonist. And he feared her.

CHAPTER 11

The Apparition

ON THE CHAIR upon which Robert had been sitting Annie seated herself. She was thinking moodily, her fingers tapping the wood, her eyes bent upon the floor. She had seen Robert's face when Millicent had openly flung at her the charge of murder. Its expression had not been wholly reassuring.

She mastered her voice; she wished to speak calmly.

'You see,' she said, 'it would have been better if you had decided to live up at the Great House. You would have escaped all this. These girls hang about the white men on the estates for what they can get out of them, and often they have their own nigger lovers at the same time. This one seems to have deceived you badly, Robert. She was Ashman's mistress; he told me so himself.'

'He is quite capable of lying.'

'You are defending her, then?'

'There is nothing to defend. She is gone; you saw to that. But don't you understand, Annie, how revolting all this is? You are a white woman, a lady, the mistress of Rosehall, and you come here and engage in a row with a coloured girl, a row that might have been a fight if her grandfather had not happened to come in when he did. You say that she is a common woman, and she says that—'

'I killed my husbands. Oh, yes, I heard her very distinctly. Well, and what do you say to her story?'

'It is all rubbish, of course; yet she will repeat it. She or her grandfather will probably tell other people, white people, about what happened tonight. There doesn't seem to be much reticence in this country. Your name—'

'Is gone already,' interrupted Annie brutally. 'Any number of people here know that you have stayed all night at the Great House with me; there is no secret about that. Why should you care? Why are you always dwelling on what other people may think or say?'

He gave no answer.

'You will soon get over your prudishness,' she smiled bitterly. 'Indeed, considering the company you had tonight, and after having been with me last night, too, I should say that you were already the complete West Indian gentleman!' She sprang up, placed both her hands on his shoulders and looked searchingly into his face. 'Robert, don't let us quarrel over a woman – especially a woman like that. You know I love you; I am yours entirely; you believe that, don't you? This is my own little kingdom; we have no need to bother ourselves about outsiders. Come to the Great House with me, stay there; if you want me to marry you, I will, and as soon as you like. If you don't want to get married, it doesn't matter, so long as you are mine and I am yours. You can be master here if you like. You will stick to me, won't you, darling?'

'Yes,' he said, but without any great heartiness, 'but I won't live in the Great House, Annie.'

'And that girl will not come back to Rosehall,' she rapped out, her naturally high temper getting the better of the prudence with which she was endeavouring to regulate her words and conduct just then.

'She would be wise not to,' he answered dryly, and she winced. He was alluding, quite obviously, to Annie's thirst for inflicting corporal punishment on others.

She changed the subject.

'We have a new book-keeper, Robert; I told you we were going to get one. You will see him tomorrow.'

'Yes.'

'And I want you to come up to the Great House tomorrow for lunch, and we'll talk over matters. You must not be hard in your judgement of me; remember, if I lost my temper tonight it was because of you. I could not bear to see that girl making some sort of claim on you. You don't blame me for that, do you? It wouldn't have mattered to me if I did not love you.'

He could not but be mollified by this; she was pleading now, not fighting, and there were actually tears in her eyes as she gazed at him.

'It is all right, Annie, don't dwell upon it. Yes, I will come to the house tomorrow.'

'Good,' she cried. 'Good night, Robert!'

She kissed him warmly; he took her to where her horse was standing; she leapt into the saddle easily and rode away. He returned to his room to think.

As his room-door closed behind him a man, who had been hidden in the shadows on the southern side of the building, came forth cautiously and made his way on foot towards the overseer's quarters. Ashman had heard enough to know that his plan had failed. He had not calculated upon all the possibilities of failure; indeed, how could he have foreseen everything? After Millicent had left him that night he had hurried up to Mrs Palmer and told her bluntly that the girl and Robert Rutherford were lovers. He had pretended jealous anger; he knew that that alone could be his excuse for going to her with the story. He had told her bluntly that Robert was her special protégé and therefore could protect Millicent on the estate, but that, for his part, he wished to forbid Millicent to come near the estate again, and would like to chastise her for deceiving him. He had suggested deep resentment that Robert should have taken both herself and Millicent from him. Then he had left, still in simulated anger, had ridden to within a furlong of Robert's quarters, dismounted, and given his horse a slap on the buttock which had sent that animal cantering to its stables. On foot he had crept down quietly to the book-keepers' house, intent on learning all that should subsequently happen. For he knew Annie Palmer. He expected that, on that same night, without delay, she would bring matters to a crisis.

What he hoped was that she would surprise Robert with Millicent (as indeed she had done) and that Robert, not daring to oppose her, would allow the girl to be badly treated. Ashman, living mainly for his own advancement, of a naturally coarse disposition, and feeling confident that the opportunity of being Annie Palmer's lover (and so virtually master of Rosehall) would outweigh any tender feeling that Robert might have for Millicent, had not imagined that the young man would try to aid the girl. Millicent would therefore feel the full effects of Mrs Palmer's wrath and vengeance, and would be sent ignominiously and in bitter pain and humiliation from Robert's presence. Her grandfather would hear of it: Mr Ashman had made up his mind that Takoo should, and Takoo would hold the young man at least partly responsible. He would hesitate to strike directly at Mrs Palmer; everybody feared that lady, who in her turn despised others. But of Robert, Takoo would have no dread at all, and would injure him, thus avenging his granddaughter and at the same time hurting Mrs Palmer. Ashman hoped that the old wizard and murderer – for no one doubted that Takoo was both – would poison Robert Rutherford before a week had elapsed. Thus a dangerous rival would be disposed of, and white men of the better sort, already suspicious of Rosehall and its mistress, would in the future come no nearer that property than its gate.

But Takoo, it now was clear, was watching over his grand-child; by a cursed mischance the old African had been on the spot during the stormy scene in Robert's room. He had taken Millicent safely away; he must have noticed that Robert had endeavoured to help and befriend the girl. Takoo would not now move against the new book-keeper, whom he knew was guiltless of any wrong – or what Takoo would consider to be wrong – against Millicent. The plot had failed.

When Ashman got back to his house it was to find Mrs Palmer awaiting him. He was surprised at this, but had a tale ready to account for his absence from home. To her query where he had been, since she had expected to find him at home, he replied that he had gone for a walk, as usual, to see that everything was fixed for the night. It was what he sometimes did, and Annie never suspected that there was any reason to doubt him.

'And why are you here?' he asked. 'Anything important?'

'Yes.' She came to the point at once; she knew that in another few hours Ashman must hear of the encounter in the book-keeper's room. Annie was too well acquainted with the customs of her estate and its people to doubt that there had been ears to hear and eyes to see what had passed; Burbridge's housekeeper, she realized, must have been awakened by the sound of voices, if indeed she had been asleep. And there may have been others in the neighbourhood; you never could tell. Ashman would know. Just as well that he should hear about it all from her lips.

She told him briefly. 'And your girl went off with her grandfather after speaking to me as no one ever did before. She doesn't care a straw about me, John.'

'I can see that.'

'She ought to be punished for her impertinence, and worse, to me.'

'But how?' He was interested in her remark. He was not very quick-witted, but it struck him suddenly that, if Robert truly liked Millicent, as it seemed he did, anything done against her by Annie might drive the young man in anger and disgust away from Rosehall, a possibility which Annie in her offended pride and jealousy had not perceived. Ashman himself had learnt a lot about Robert's character in the last hour or so.

'I don't know how – yet. Perhaps you could say. But first of all we must find out where she is. She has left the estate, of course; she is out of it already. Can you find out where she is gone to?'

He did not wish to appear too eager. 'If she has gone,' he said, 'why do you want to follow her? Isn't that a good riddance of bad rubbish?'

'And am I to rest content while that wretch spreads lies about me, and while everybody knows that she abused me to my face and was not punished? Besides – well, I have given you my reasons.'

But he finished her sentence in his mind: 'Besides, my lover may seek her out and she may share him with me, and that I will not have at any cost.'

'I will try to find out where she is,' he said aloud; 'but you have to be careful, Annie. You can do much as you like on Rosehall and on Palmyra, though even here, in these days, you have to be careful. Outside of the estates you run a great risk if you go beyond the law. The missionaries are very active now, and they force the magistrates to take action.'

'Are you, also, suggesting that I murder people?' she demanded harshly.

'I suggest nothing. I am only thinking of your safety. After all, you know that I love you, Annie.'

'And love yourself more,' she sneered, 'not to mention the estate wenches. But don't be afraid. There are more ways of hanging a dog besides putting a rope round its neck. I will show you something, John; I will show you that I have other means of dealing with these people than the whip and even death – it is death to them in another form, and I cannot be hurt by the law.' She was wrought up to the highest possible tension; her eyes were blazing; there was an evil look in them. 'Call up some of your people,' she commanded, 'on any pretext; send them outside, not too far. You'll see.'

'What is it? What do you intend to do?' he demanded startled.

'Do what I say! Don't argue!' she cried peremptorily; and he went outside and shouted for some people to come out. He thought, he said, that a cow had escaped from her pen and was roaming about the field near the house; that was the first excuse that came to his mind, and all the more readily, as cows were always breaking out.

Three or four men came tumbling out at the sound of his voice, and with them the Rev. Mr Rider, the new book-keeper. They ran towards the field indicated, though no sound came from it. Annie Palmer stood on Ashman's veranda staring towards the field. Suddenly Ashman gave a gasp of astonishment and horror.

At the same moment a terrified shriek burst from the men who had gone to search the field for the errant cow, and they came flying back, all except Mr Rider. They rushed up to the veranda, their teeth chattering, their eyeballs gleaming white in the faint light of the moon. 'The Horse,' they gasped, 'the Three-footed Horse from Hell!'

And out yonder, glowing phosphorescently, loomed the figure of a gigantic horse, which seemed to have one leg in front and which loped slowly on, as though coming towards them, a horse like to the pale spectre described in the Apocalypse and ridden by Death, frightful to look upon, awe-inspiring, terrifying.

It stood out distinct, but made no sound. The frightened negroes shuddered abjectly and moaned. Even Ashman, who had turned pale, muttered blasphemies, as if that could protect him from whatever danger might threaten.

Then, in a flash, the apparition was gone.

Mrs Palmer laughed softly. Leaning over the balustrade of the veranda she called out to the terrified slaves, 'You see what you have to fear if you dare to forget yourselves? You have seen with your own eyes!'

'Send them back to their beds, John,' she continued, 'they haven't had a lesson like this since you have been here; but it was about time that they had one. They will tell others. Who is this man?'

She alluded to Rider, who was slowly coming towards them.

'Rider, the man we employed tonight.'

'The book-keeper? He seems very nonchalant.'

'He is probably drunk, or a fool. What was that thing out yonder, Annie?'

'You heard what the niggers said – the Three-footed Horse.'

'But I always believed that that was a foolish superstition,' protested Ashman, trembling slightly, in spite of his efforts at self-control. 'I never believed that mad story.'

'You saw for yourself, didn't you?'

'And you – you summoned it? You knew it would be there?'

'Yes; and now you know how I can deal with that wretched girl if only I find out where she is, if only I can bring her within my power; and, by God, I will do it!'

'Annie,' said John Ashman, and there was fear and revulsion in his voice, 'they have said about here that you are a witch. I have never listened to that talk. But this, this – what does it mean? That thing that I saw out there came from hell, and you brought it!'

'I brought it,' she admitted, and there was mocking triumph in her tone; 'and now you know more of me than even you did before. So be careful, John, and find that girl for me.'

'If Rutherford still sticks to her—' he began.

'So much the worse for him also!' she flung out savagely. 'I am stronger than he or you or anyone else here. Begin your inquiries tomorrow.'

He took her down to her horse, and she rode away, right through the spot where the strange animal had shone and then disappeared. Ashman shuddered. He would not have gone alone into that field that night for any recompense; he was too shaken in nerve. It came into his mind that Rider alone had not seemed much perturbed. And he did not really think Rider was drunk or a fool. 'Perhaps,' he thought, 'it is because he is a man of God' – for again his queer respect for this dissolute priest asserted itself. He went to his sideboard and mixed himself a strong draught of rum and water.

Meantime Annie Palmer galloped home and in a very little while came to the Great House. Her servants knew her moods from the tones of her voice; hearing her call now they hastened out precipitately, nervous and apprehensive. She flung into the house and up the great stairs; arrived in her room, she threw open a front window from which she could survey the property down to the gate, and see in the distance the low small building in which Robert Rutherford lived. She half-leaned out, staring fixedly in that direction; her teeth bit into her lower lip, sobs of wild anger half choked her. She loved him. She cried aloud that she loved him, that he was the only man she had ever loved, and that he cared but little for her after all; was only taken with her as a child might be with a new toy, but was ready to desert her – she felt that in her heart. 'But I won't let him,' she gasped, 'I won't let him! He is mine, and that wretch shall not take him from me, nor Ashman prevent me from doing what I please. Ashman! I don't trust him; he is working for himself. Let him be careful! That woman will die in a week, and no one will ever dare to say that I had a hand in it.'

She felt deathly weak. Her vitality was enormous, but she had taxed it greatly that night. She had admitted to Ashman that it was she who had evoked that pale, vast spectre, a giant horse with but one leg in front, the Three-footed Horse of a profoundly held Jamaican belief, which had been seen on Rosehall before, and which, some said, had only been seen when one of her husbands was about to die. It had been associated with her; it was always the herald of some terrible happening; its appearance had inevitably served to strengthen her hold on her sullen, bitterly-discontented slaves. It was not only by bodily fear that she held them, by dread of the whip and the iron chain, but by far more potent spiritual terrors, by the report, the conviction, that she could summon fiends from the Pit to work her will if she were minded to do so. And tonight she had done so; but the effort, and the emotional stress through which she had previously passed, had exhausted her. Slowly she sank by the window, in a dead faint, and when she came to herself it was dawn.

She had been through a desperate crisis, and her waking brought her no surcease of agony and apprehension. She had never had to fear a rival before; it was she who in the past had sickened of the men she loved, or thought she loved; and when weariness and distaste supervened, when an uncontrollable aversion asserted itself, she had succeeded in ridding herself of them. Ashman had no claims as a husband, his existence could not trammel her actions: he could not venture to exercise authority: that perhaps was why he was still alive; besides, he was very useful to her in practical affairs, far more so than her husbands had been. He had to cease being her lover when she willed it so; he understood that clearly. But she wanted love, what she considered love, and this boy, some six years her junior, fresh from England, tall, manly, handsome – her senses had thrilled at the sight of him, her blood had grown hot with desire for him; she felt that she would gladly, willingly, make any sacrifice for him – and he did not love her! Attracted, yes; fascinated, undoubtedly; but nothing more. She had seen this in his attitude of a few hours before; she would be much exercised to hold him for much longer now. The girl with the brown complexion and the defiant look, that granddaughter of the negro most feared in all the parish of St James, had deliberately challenged her, Annie Palmer, and might yet draw her lover from her. So again must she strike, and this time with weapons that might not succeed with a white man and by means that must not easily be detected. Through fear and horror she must rid herself of this rival. But what if those instruments failed, as they might fail? As Annie threw herself upon her bed, in the dawning, for a few hours of rest, she vowed that if the means she proposed to use should not succeed, other and more material ways should be found to achieve her object, however great the risk might be.

Chapter 12

Who is Annie Palmer?

THE THREE BOOK-KEEPERS were sitting at dinner; it was about eight o'clock. A half-moon glowed in the east with the greenish tinge of the tropics. An hour or so later Mr Rider would take up his station in the still-house; now he was making the acquaintance of young Rutherford; Burbridge he knew already.

Robert was in a silent, surly mood. He had lunched that day with Annie, as arranged, but the lunch had been a depressing function. Each party had something to say to the other, but had refrained from saying it; each felt that a barrier had sprung up between them since the night before; each was conscious of it, but wished to disguise the fact from the other.

Annie had, casually as it seemed, asked him if he were coming to the Great House that night; he had answered, no, he did not think so, and she had not pressed him to come. Indeed, she had seemed relieved at learning that that was not his intention. She had made no reference to the scene of the night before, although it would have been very natural for her to have done so. He himself did not, although he would have liked to ask one or two questions. But she was hardly the person whom he could question as to the whereabouts of Millicent.

He had gone about his work that day with a dogged determination, though he had no inclination for it. Psyche was looking after his room and his food now; he had asked her that morning to undertake that duty. Rider was to live in the small building attached to the overseer's residence, but would take his meals with the other book-keepers. At this moment he was trying to appraise Robert; already he had heard a good deal about him from Burbridge.

The talk on the estate that day had been of the appearance of the strange apparition so distinctly seen by many persons on the previous night. The news had spread with a rapidity of a cane-piece conflagration; there was not a slave, not a white man, on Rosehall who had not heard of it by this; on Palmyra also it was being discussed. The people could think and speak of nothing else. The slaves were frightened. The Horse with three feet, luminous, ominous, of which they had heard all their lives, and which they believed to be an infernal spirit, dominated their imaginations now that it had been seen by so many living witnesses.

'And you yourself saw it?' said Burbridge to Rider, not for the first time.

'As I have said more than once before, yes. It was very distinct, very horrible; it had only three legs, and the foreleg seemed to grow out of the creature's chest; it was just as negro tradition and superstition have described the Three-footed Horse as being.'

'Then there *is* such a fiend,' muttered Burbridge, troubled; 'and it is seen on this estate of all others!'

'Is there such a fiend?' inquired Rider, with a slight smile.

'You just said that you yourself saw it,' Robert reminded him gloomily. 'You should be far more convinced than we.'

'I am merely wondering if it was a fiend,' Rider explained. 'That I did see something, I admit. Exactly what was its nature,

I am not prepared to say. It may have been a fiend or a ghost, that is possible. But, again, it may not have been.'

'Then what was it?' demanded Burbridge irritably.

'I do not profess to know; I think I have made that quite clear. But I heard today that these strange visions appear only when something dreadful is about to happen on this property. You have heard that too, haven't you, Burbridge?'

'Often.'

'Then I suppose, we had better be looking forward to trouble, to dreadful occurrences?'

Burbridge glanced doubtfully at Robert. He did not want anything he said to be repeated to Mrs Palmer.

The glance was intercepted; Robert spoke out.

'From what I have heard,' he said bitterly, 'dreadful things seem a specialty in this place. No doubt all these tales are lies; they get on one's nerves nevertheless. I am beginning to regret that I ever came to Rosehall.'

'So soon?' interjected Rider lightly. 'Well, being sober and in my right mind – a dreadful state that will not last for long – I am inclined to agree that you are right. I can speak out plainly, you see, Rutherford, for my tenure of office here is not likely to be lengthy. I am very fond of resigning.'

'You would not be here if I were doing my work properly,' said Robert, with a touch of self-contempt.

'Please continue in your bad course for a little while yet,' urged Rider. 'I need to recuperate before I become a gentleman of insobriety and leisure again. Pardon the impertinence, Rutherford, but you have people in England, haven't you – people in good circumstances?'

'Yes; why do you ask?'

'No offence intended, old man; but of course I know you are from a 'varsity, like myself, and your sort don't become book-keepers – if our friend Burbridge will excuse a remark which is not intended to be rude. I am a book-keeper now, but that is because of circumstances. "How art thou fallen, O Lucifer, son of the morning!" And I have no people in England to whom I could turn; a nephew and a couple of cousins only, and their interest in me is very properly nil. They do not specialize in the appreciation of black sheep. You are different. And since you have begun to regret coming to Rosehall you will certainly go on regretting that you ever came to Jamaica. The logical sequence is that you should leave Jamaica as soon as you can. But men, alas, are not guided by logic!'

Robert smiled, in spite of his depression; he rather liked this quaint parson who was so obviously down and out, and yet who spoke so well and seemed so intelligent.

'You take a great interest in me, a stranger,' he replied.

'I do. Both sober and drunk I am one of the most curious of men. I don't want to appear a Nosey Parker and that sort of thing, but I have heard all about last night's little business in these rooms; it is all over the estate. And that, coming just before the appearance of that peculiar-looking ghostly animal, suggests trouble. I am not courageous! I would always avoid trouble precipitately; hence my warning to you. I don't think you are quite ensnared by the tropics yet?'

'What do you mean?'

'Well, there are men like me who, having once got all this sunlight into their bodies, and a good deal of the fermented cane-juice into their veins, can never get rid of the fascination of the tropics. Add to those influences a pretty native girl or two, and they are completely lost. They are bound to these lands for ever. I have escaped the wiles of the feminine sex; the bottle has been too powerful a rival to them. But I am doomed to remain here; and so is Burbridge; with him it is financial disabilities mainly. You – you don't seem to suffer from all these hindrances and drawbacks; therefore I don't see why the devil you are here.'

'But I am.'

'Quite so. And last night – all right Burbridge; our friend Rutherford is not the sort that blabs; you need not signal caution – last night showed that you are in a somewhat dangerous position. But you can escape from it if you wish.'

Robert did not appreciate this direct interference with his affairs. He wondered if Rider could have any ulterior motives for speaking as he did? Had Ashman set him to it? He threw an angry, suspicious look at the ex-clergyman, who understood it in part, but smiled easily.

Rider sat facing the door. He rose quickly just then, staring towards the dusty path that led from the gate up to the Great House.

'Our mistress seems to be going for a ride,' he observed, indicating a figure on horseback which, followed by another, was riding towards the gates.

That it was Annie was quite evident. Another rider attending her was probably her boy.

'This is the first time since I have been here that she has left Rosehall at night,' said Burbridge, surprised, after the two figures on horseback had passed through the gates.

'An unusual occurrence, eh? Then the object of her ride must be unusual also. That is a very singular and striking woman,' said Rider.

The lady and her attendant had now turned their horses' heads in the direction of Montego Bay. They rode at an easy pace; later on, the road being bad, they would have to go at a walk; they would not reach Montego Bay before eleven o'clock, if that place were their destination.

'It will be late when they get to town,' continued Rider; 'and that virtuous and somnolent place retires early. Now, what sort of business can be taking Mrs Palmer to Montego Bay tonight?'

'You are very curious,' observed Robert with a short laugh, but he too was conscious of a great curiosity.

'I am curious,' confessed Mr Rider. 'I have already said so. Mrs Palmer's doings have exercised a good deal of fascination over me ever since I came to this part of the island. Who is she? What is she? She has had three husbands and – well, it is a fact that she has had three husbands and that all three of them have died. She is a determined woman; she can bend people to her will; she is feared; she can call spirits from the vasty deep – or things that look like spirits. And last night she threatened a young coloured woman with condign punishment, and nearly inflicted that punishment herself. Now she goes riding out at night, with but one boy attending her, and that is hardly what any other white woman in Jamaica would do. She is a mystery. I can't say that I like mysteries unless I can solve them.'

'She can be very friendly when she wants,' broke in Burbridge haltingly. 'And she is our employer, after all.'

'I am here for just so long as it will take Ashman to get someone else to fill my place,' said Rider derisively. 'I am merely a convenience and therefore not affected by that strong spirit of loyalty (which seems to me indistinguishable from self-interest) that the ordinary book-keeper may be expected to display. I am here today and gone tomorrow, friend Burbridge, and the benefit of such a situation is that I can speak my mind plainly now and then, knowing that once I depart from any estate, I am not likely to be employed on it again. Anyhow, after what happened on Rosehall last night, I don't wish to remain here long. A few weeks will be sufficient for me; it would be a few days only were not my exchequer in a deplorable condition. I am now going to keep watch and ward over the still-house, which is a den of thieves. I shall endeavour, myself, to keep my hands off the rum.'

He laughed but made no movement to leave. Instead of that he lapsed into thought as though something were on his mind.

'We know what she is, more or less,' said Robert, as if to himself, 'but down in the Bay, I remember now, even the rector was puzzled as to who she was and where she originally came from. He said something of the sort to me when he learnt I was coming here to work. The matter seems to have been much discussed, but no one is any the wiser.'

'The matter has been much discussed,' said Rider, waking out of his reverie; 'all personal matters are canvassed in this country with a good deal of energy and even more impertinence. Witness our conversation now. But Mrs Palmer has not been communicative. Still—'

'You know something?' quickly inquired Burbridge.

'Merely rumours, but I fancy they are true. You see, she lived in Kingston before she appeared as a bride in St James, and Kingston is a town where news spreads far more rapidly than it can down here. I was in Kingston when it was said she was going to marry John Palmer, and as he was known as one of the biggest of the planters, and the owner of the finest residence in rural Jamaica, naturally there was some talk about the woman he had selected as his wife. Some of this talk came my way; I was then curate in the parish church, and the proper thing is that all the gossip should be related to the clergy; apparently it assists them in their spiritual work.'

He paused for a moment, and the other men waited expectantly, not wishing to press him to detail the early history of a woman, but eager to hear it nevertheless.

'I forget now what her maiden name was,' resumed Rider, 'but that doesn't matter. The story was that she came to Jamaica from Haiti.'

'Haiti?' cried Robert; 'then she is French?'

'Probably both French and negro,' suggested Burbridge; 'I hear there is a lot of mixture of blood in Haiti; she may have some. That might account for her witcheries!'

'There is hardly any need to find the blood of the negro in every villain, male or female,' chuckled Rider, 'though that seems to be the fashion in the West Indies. The world is not divided into black devils and white angels; anyway, we three could hardly claim to belong to the angelic confraternity, could we? Besides, there were plenty of white people in Haiti once.'

'Yes, but after the French Revolution the negro leader Dessalines had them all driven out or massacred,' Robert reminded him. 'Those who seemed to be white and were allowed to remain really could prove that they had some negro blood in their veins. I was told that in France. Annie may be one of those.'

'You forget, my friend, that Henry Christophe succeeded Dessalines as ruler of the northern part of Haiti, and he was a white man. And in the south, Petion, the President, encouraged white people to remain. No; you are quite wrong about Annie Palmer's origin. Her mother and father were said to be Irish; she herself was born in England or Ireland – both countries have been mentioned – but they took her over while she was yet a little girl. She speaks English perfectly; she would have learnt it from them. She probably speaks French fluently, though no one here has heard her speak in that language.

She must have heard and seen some strange things in Haiti; it was there, if anywhere, that she discovered she had powers out of the ordinary. As a growing girl she must have been even more beautiful than she is now, and if her parents were in favour with either Christophe or Petion she would have been regarded as a sort of goddess by the common people. White, lovely, imperious, strong, fearless: don't you see she was just the sort of girl that a superstitious people would have worshipped?'

'I can understand that,' said Robert; 'but what follows from that?'

'This – it is merely a deduction of mine, but I don't see why it shouldn't be true – the voodoo priests there, who are versed in all the old African sorcery, and who do understand how to influence the minds of their dupes in all sorts of extraordinary ways, may have seen in this wonderful young girl great occult possibilities, and have taken pleasure in teaching her how to develop those possibilities. She knows how to terrorize the people on her own estates; she has always known it. She can beat down the resistance of white men weaker than herself. I have spoken about the Haitian priests. As a matter of fact, the priestesses of Haiti are quite as powerful, in every way as influential, as their male colleagues. Given a woman of that description thrown in contact with Annie Palmer when she was growing into womanhood, when her mind was maturing, when her curiosity was at its keenest, and anything might happen. She may have had a voodoo priestess for nurse when her parents took her to Haiti; it is quite likely. And Haiti, we all know, is the very stronghold of devil-craft in this part of the world. There the people see visions and the dead are brought out of their graves, or seem to be.'

'It is all guess and hearsay,' murmured Burbridge.

'It is most of it conjecture,' admitted Rider. 'I said as much at the beginning; and that is why I have never mentioned the matter before. Still, she did come from Haiti to Jamaica, and she was of English or Irish parentage; so much was believed in Kingston, and that belief would not have got about if it had not its foundations in fact. The rest may not be true, but I think it is. The circumstances suggest that it is.

'But I have been talking too much,' he added abruptly; 'I must go on to the still-house now.'

He rose quickly, nodded to the others, then went his way. Robert turned to Burbridge.

'That fellow has been saying some peculiar things,' he remarked. 'Tell me, do you believe these stories about Mrs Palmer's murdered husbands?'

'Good God, Rutherford!' exclaimed Burbridge, 'do you want to get me in trouble?'

'That question alone is an admission,' said Robert grimly. 'Rider clearly believes that there is some sinister history connected with this place, and so do you. And I am coming to believe it myself. That is the worst of it. My mind is plagued with doubts and suspicions.'

'But you' – Burbridge hesitated a moment, and then pursued the topic resolutely; he felt he could trust Robert. 'You are not like us, as Rider just said; if you don't like staying here you can leave when you please, unless—'

'Unless what?'

'Unless – you won't mind me saying so? – you are in love with Mrs Palmer. I can understand that you should be. She is a wonderful woman.'

'I will be frank with you, Burbridge; I am and I am not. She is wonderful, as you say, and she has been extraordinarily kind to me. But since you know what happened here last night –

of course Psyche told you – I don't mind admitting that I am startled and disgusted and afraid. I am not afraid for myself, but for Millicent. I don't know what is going to happen, but I feel that something is. I feel mean when I speak like this; I feel as if I were a traitor. Yet' – he broke off abruptly. 'Have you any idea where Millicent may be?' he asked, as if changing the subject.

'There is no particular secret about that. She has an aunt who lives just outside of Montego Bay, on the road to Hanover. I suspect old Takoo took her there last night, but I don't suppose he will keep her there for long. He will remove her as soon as he can, if he wants her whereabouts to be unknown. Meantime, as she is over twelve miles from here, she should be safe for the present.'

'Safe from whom?'

Burbridge did not answer.

Robert, who had suddenly decided that he was interested in Millicent's welfare, was frankly and sincerely worried; Burbridge, though personally indifferent, felt that perhaps there might be much to be worried about.

'You, or Rider, said a little while ago that Mrs Palmer was going in the direction of Montego Bay,' insisted Robert. 'Do you think—?'

'I would not dare to think anything,' replied Burbridge, lowering his voice. 'I don't want to get mixed up with this business, Rutherford; I have enough of my own difficulties to contend with.'

'But surely she wouldn't dare!'

'I don't know what you mean,' said Burbridge guardedly, 'but I believe Millicent is perfectly safe where she is, for the present at any rate. She is probably in bed by now, and even in Jamaica a man or woman is secure in bed. There is nothing to worry about.'

'Will you find out for me, tomorrow, without fail, just where she is?' asked Robert. 'Can you get the information? I will pay any expenses that may be incurred. Will you?'

'I will try,' promised Burbridge. 'I can send a boy I can trust down to the Bay on an errand, and he will go to the place I told you about. If Millicent is there he will find out.'

'Send early,' urged Robert; 'I want to know before evening.'

'Very good.'

Both men sought their rooms.

CHAPTER 13

Putting on Death

MEANWHILE, Annie and her attendant were pushing towards Montego Bay.

High above moved the moon, which now threw into soft relief the hills on the one hand, the gently moving waters on the other. The sky was pale blue, stars thickly studded the luminous vault, and moon and stars gave forth an illumination which, in that clear cold air of the night made possible the perception of objects far away. A murmur came in from the sea and was answered by the whispering breezes from the mountains, and tiny waves were silver where they touched the shore.

Now and then the coastline was obscured by thick clumps of mangrove and by patches of seagrape. The mangrove marked the site of swamps; it grew to a height of several feet, with fleshy, unhealthy-looking leaves of bottle-green. Its roots, gnarled, twisted, lengthy, black, protruded for a foot and more above the oozy soil from which rose a rank unpleasant odour, and looked like thousands of snakes contorting themselves under the shadow of the trees and in the slime. There was something sinister about these mangrove swamps; and there indeed prolificated the dangerous mosquito which could convey to the human body the germs of the dreaded blackwater fever, from which recovery was almost hopeless. But that was not known in those days. If men shunned the mangrove it was mainly because of its appearance and of the difficulty of making way among those protuberant, snaky roots which at any moment might trip up the most careful pedestrian and cause him to plunge headlong into fetid mud.

The road to Montego Bay made rough and tortuous riding. It was full of ruts, and the surface of some of the slabs of stone with which it was strewn was slippery. Along the roadside and among the swamps swarmed myriads of crabs reddish-black in hue, swift on their pointed legs, with claws uplifted in self-defence or menace. They were of small size, but so numerous that they created a distinct sound as they scuttled to hiding or dashed from one spot to another as the riders went by. Annie knew it was quite possible that any moment she might come upon a crocodile which, crawling out of a swamp that edged the road, might stretch itself across the way like a log of wood; but she knew also that the creature would be frightened by the approach of the horses and would hurry away rather than attack. In this part of the country, too, they were not plentiful. Yet she kept an eye on the path before her, since there was no reason why an unnecessary risk should be run, for hers was no crocodile hunt.

When she came to the entrance of the town itself she rode as quietly as possible, giving a signal to her attendant to go slowly. She did not wish to be perceived. She hoped that, even should there be anyone about at that hour, she should escape recognition; nevertheless she knew that the mere presence of a white woman riding through Montego Bay at that hour of the night would awaken considerable curiosity. It would be commented upon the following morning; conjectures would be afloat. It might of course be thought that some belated woman had been pressing on to her home, perhaps the wife of one of the smaller planters; certainly no lady of position. That would render her safe from detection, but she preferred that no living soul should have a glimpse of her going or coming, and on the whole she trusted that no one would.

She trusted rightly. The little town, built upon a sloping, crescent-shaped sweep of land backed by low hills to the south and east, lay in obscurity. There was no lighting save that from the moon and stars, and the moon was now steadily dropping towards the west, and the buildings in the town threw parts of the streets in shadow. All was silent, save for the staccato barking of starveling dogs that wandered about the thoroughfares hunting for food among the garbage and offal that stood exposed in heaps and in open boxes in front of shops and dwellings. Smells arose, assailing the nostrils; the dust lay thick upon the ground, but served to deaden the thud of the horses' hooves. Not a human being was abroad.

On the eminences commanding the town and overlooking the wide bay from which the town derived its name stood the residences of the larger merchants and the urban homes of a few of the neighbouring planters. These too were shrouded in darkness, but Annie gave them not so much as a glance. She directed her horse westward, passing entirely through Montego Bay; presently she had left the town behind her and was riding along a road which cut a sugar estate in two, an estate which began almost on the border of Montego Bay. Here she quickened her pace. Stray cattle might be encountered, but human beings hardly; besides, they would not seek to come near to her or to speculate about her presence there, as would the townspeople. Soon she was passing through a sombre avenue formed by overhanging trees, great trees that grew to a lofty height, with huge branches covered thickly with the heavy foliage of the tropics. Here and there the moonlight streaked through, but thin and wan and ghostly. Fireflies danced among the underbrush: the darkness was irradiated by the swift flashing of thousands of phosphorescent green-gold points of light at one moment, to be rendered denser when, as at a signal, every one faded out as though myriads of tiny lamps had been extinguished by the turning of a switch. Then the trees disappeared and Annie crossed a bridge under which rolled a river, dark-gleaming, and about a mile farther on she pulled up her horse and reconnoitred.

A little while before she had been the subject of discussion on her own estate, and Rider had suggested to his friends her probable origin. By a coincidence her thoughts at this moment ran on Haiti, as she reflected upon what she was about to do. Rider, with the intuition of an educated man who, before his downfall, had studied the history and condition of all the West Indian countries, had almost hit upon the leading circumstances of Annie Palmer's youth. Annie often thought of her youth in the nearby island. Her father had been a merchant there, attracted by the chance of making money under a black king who did not pursue the policy of his predecessor and forbid white people to enter that part of the country over which he ruled. She had known King Henry Christophe, a tyrant, a brute often, but yet a man of outstanding personality, who forced his subjects to work and maintained order with an iron hand. One class, however, though he had made war on them at first, he had never been able to suppress. The priests and the priestesses of the Voodoo defied him in act if not by word, and in lonely valleys and in the depths of dark forests they sacrificed to the great green serpent which symbolized their chief deity, and the sacrifices were sometimes human. She had known a high priestess of this cult. The woman had been no nurse of hers, as Rider had suggested; she had been a woman of position and property in Cape Haitian, a woman who had marched with the armies of Dessalines and Christophe when these set out to free Haiti from the French domination. This woman had been in the habit of bringing the pretty little child some presents and once she had given Annie a beautiful diamond necklace of great value. She seemed to care for the girl; she was childless, and her husband was dead. Annie's parents thought it more advantageous than otherwise that a woman, whose husband had actually been a baron of King Christophe's black Court, should be kindly disposed towards Annie, and consequently towards them. Her friendship was well worth having. Its benefits were seen in the number of the Haitians who patronized the Irish merchant – for he was Irish. Her enmity might have been a thing unpleasant to contend with.

This woman, whose title in northern Haiti was that of baroness, gradually won an ascendancy over Annie. In her way she loved the white girl, though, on principle, she hated the white race, whom she regarded as the natural oppressors of her people. Annie's mind dwelt on her now, even as she scanned the road and the landmarks to right and left. She remembered how the Baroness – she had taken the title seriously when she lived in Haiti – had talked to her about the spirits that wandered about the earth and the air, the spirits who inhabited and animated everything, and how human beings, by determination and practice, and especially by belief and faith, could acquire power over these spirits. The girl had been fascinated. In an atmosphere charged, so to speak, with the supernatural, where white as well as black believed in the occult, in the mysterious, in the traffic of earthly beings with those who were disembodied or of unearthly origin; in a strange, dark land where, among the mountains, in the dead of night, and in spite of the king's decrees, the eerie sound of the voodoo drum could be heard stabbing through the silence and the darkness, it was not surprising that Annie should believe what she was told, especially as the Baroness showed her how the common people worshipped those who called them to the midnight orgies or blasted the disobedient into insanity or death.

Then the Baroness told her that she too had the capacity to do wonderful things, and taught her the secrets of the Voodoo. And Annie came to believe that she possessed the power of a god.

What would have happened to her eventually had she remained in Haiti she could never know. An epidemic of yellow fever had swept both her parents away within a few days. A month after, the old Baroness was also dead. A few white men in Cape Haitian saw that Haiti could be no place for a young unmarried white woman to live in; they suggested Jamaica to her. She had some means, and she was tired of dull and barbarous Cape Haitian. She came to Jamaica, met John Palmer shortly after, but soon found her new home more tedious and dull than ever the old one had been. Had the Baroness been living Annie might have returned to Haiti. The old woman had hinted to her that there was no height to which, in that country, she might not aspire, no power she might not attain. What would have been to others a fatal disability, her blood, her whiteness, would have aided her, with the papalois and mamalois, the priests and priestesses of Haiti, on her side; and with her superior intellect, her strength of will, her fearlessness, her beauty, she would have dominated them. But the Baroness was dead, the sturdy, coal-black female fanatic, and sometimes (it must be added) female fiend, was gone for ever. So Haiti was out of the question, and Annie had no desire to go to England where her mother was born, or Ireland, from whence her father came.

She always felt that in England she would count for but little; there would be no supremacy for her there. In Jamaica there was. Here she could live, almost unfettered, the life she loved, a life of domination and of sensuality. Here she could put to the proof the powers she possessed and of which she was inordinately proud. Tonight she was again about to put them to the proof. These people were quite as fearful, as superstitious, as those of the country of her girlhood. And one of them had dared to defy her. A few days would show everyone who knew of that defiance how temerarious and hopeless it was for any woman to pit herself against Annie Palmer of Rosehall.

She had walked her horse slowly forward while giving free rein to her reminiscences and her thoughts; now, about a quarter of a mile away from the spot where she had halted, she checked her horse again. She was satisfied that she had arrived at her destination. She dismounted and flung her reins to the boy. From him she took a parcel that he had been carrying carefully; then she bade him wait for her and went on her way alone on foot. She had not far to go. Soon she came to a path that led into some small property, a path for which she had looked closely as she walked along.

This narrow way, which ran between rows of heavy-foliaged trees, was as black as a tunnel cut through the bowels of a mountain. Here no friendly fireflies danced with cheerful illumination, here no gleam from the moon could penetrate. All was sombre and still, with a chilling silence. But Annie did not hesitate.

She went slowly, carefully; in that dense darkness sight was of little assistance to her; she had almost to feel her way. But she had learnt the whereabouts of this place meticulously; her information had been precise. She did not think she had failed to find it.

There might be dogs, but she was prepared for them. Not only was she armed with a heavy riding whip, but in the parcel which she carried were bits of meat. No poorly fed mongrel of the countryside would resist such a feast; besides, a peasant's dog would hardly bark at a white man or woman. Nothing disturbed her progress, however; nothing broke the silence of the night. She seemed the only living creature moving about at that moment.

Soon she sensed rather than saw a low three-roomed cottage standing to one side of a little clearing. That was what she sought.

She stole up to the very door of the little house and paused. There was still no sound, no stir, though she knew that behind that door human beings were sleeping.

From the parcel in her hand she now drew forth a queer round object; it was a child's skull smeared with blood. To it was attached, by a piece of wire, a bit of white cardboard. She herself was completely merged in the environing darkness, but her movements were as noiseless as those of a cat. She ran her hands over the lintels of the door and window; her fingers came in contact with a nail; it was something of the sort she had been feeling for. The first part of her task, she knew, would now be easy.

By the same bit of wire with which the little oblong cardboard was attached to the skull, she hung the gruesome object on to the nail: it would be the first thing to strike the eye of anyone emerging from the house in the morning, or approaching it. Then she did a strange thing. Concentrating her gaze upon the door, as though she would pierce with her vision through the solid wood, she stood there tense and erect. Her hands were clenched, her eyes fixed and glaring, as they had been on the night before when that weird, awful, glowing creature had appeared before the horror-struck regard of Ashman and the others at Rosehall. Her rigidity was that of a cataleptic.

One minute, two, three minutes passed, and Annie did not stir.

Of a sudden there came a cry from within the little dwelling, a cry of agony and terror and despair.

Again and again it rose; someone was crying out in mortal fear, in heart-stricken panic.

Annie Palmer heard, and slowly relaxed. She reeled slightly. But a smile of triumph wreathed her lips as she caught the sounds and exclamations of confusion that now broke out in the house; sharp calls and questions succeeding to those terrifying screams that had issued from the lips of a frightened, startled woman within. She stepped back silently, but more quickly than she had entered; she made her way back, sometimes stumbling, sometimes almost running, to where her patient slave stood with the horse; she mounted, struck her steed a sharp blow and went as quickly as she dared along the road, over the bridge, through the town and back to Rosehall. It was in the early hours of the morning that she reached the Great House, and there she repeated her previous instructions to the boy.

'Remember, you are not to say a word about where we went last night; I went for a ride and you accompanied me. Do you hear?'

'Yes, missis,' he agreed abjectly.

'If you disobey – well, you know what to expect!'

He knew. As a matter of fact he had seen nothing that she had done. But that she had been to the place where old Takoo's daughter lived he was well aware, and when a few minutes later an elderly slave woman, who acted as a kind of housekeeper for Mrs Palmer, seized hold of his arm as he was going to bed and asked him whisperingly about his nocturnal mission he told her what he knew. For he was afraid of this woman, who was hand in glove with Takoo, with Takoo who was dreaded by every man and woman on Palmyra and Rosehall. As dreaded as Mrs Palmer, and even more in a peculiar sort of way. For the slaves believed that Takoo could read their minds; he was African, a witch-doctor, and it was madness to try to deceive him. They had often deceived Mrs Palmer, and though she was dangerous she was less so, to them, than the gaunt negro of whom even some white men stood in awe.

Mrs Palmer might whip them cruelly. Takoo could send ghosts to haunt them, could plague them with remorseless evil spirits. Let them gravely offend him and they might end their lives in agony and pass to greater agony in another world.

CHAPTER 14

The Old Hige

'YOU WANT TO GO to Montego Bay?' asked Ashman slowly. 'It is unusual for book-keepers to get off during the day in crop time, but I suppose you can do what you please.'

Robert frowned slightly; he did not like the suggestion that he was a sort of privileged pet.

'Thanks,' he answered shortly.

It was about one o'clock. Burbridge had been as good as his word; very early that morning he had dispatched a boy to where Takoo's daughter lived, beyond Montego Bay, and the youth had learnt that Millicent was staying with her aunt. That had been easy enough to find out, for there were many people at the little place to which he had gone with some made-up story to disguise the real purpose of his visit, a story which he found he was not called upon to tell. Something had happened there the night before and the news of it had been bruited about. There were many free negroes in the neighbourhood; these had left all that they had to do and had assembled in Takoo's yard to offer sympathy. Just what had occurred the boy had not been told.

Of all this Burbridge said nothing to Robert. The young man would find it out for himself, if it concerned him, Burbridge thought.

Robert lost no time in availing himself of Ashman's permission to have the rest of the day. Ashman himself guessed that it was something connected with Millicent that was taking young Rutherford to the Bay; Ashman knew about the leaving of Rosehall by Annie Palmer the night before, knew how late it was when she returned, and had no doubt at all as to where she had been. It was he indeed who, at her command (which fitted in so well with his own desire), had found out whither old Takoo had taken his granddaughter. That some crisis was impending, if it had not yet actually arrived, he was certain. And he thought that it must result, and that quickly, in Robert Rutherford's leaving Rosehall Estate.

Robert himself knew that he was going to find Millicent, to warn her. About what and against whom? He faced the question quite frankly; he realized and admitted that he was taking this girl's part against Annie, realized also that that was what few white men in Jamaica would openly have done. Secretly, yes, many would have done it. But he was not hiding his action, could not in the circumstances do so, as a matter of fact. If the truth must be told, he shrank from the course he was taking. Shrank with every nerve in his body, though his determination held. He told himself that there was nothing else to do. He was convinced that in some sort of way he would be responsible if anything happened to Millicent; he felt he was performing an act of duty; anything like passion, like affection, he did not conceive to be a motive at all. Burbridge took a different view. Burbridge's own opinion, mentioned to no living human being, was that Millicent had won Robert from Annie Palmer, that Annie had realized it, and that these two women, different in colour, in position, in power, in almost everything save a bold and defiant disposition, were embarked on a deadly struggle. Events were moving swiftly to a climax. In a way Burbridge pitied Millicent.

Presently Robert rode out of Rosehall.

At this hour, although it was late December, the sun's rays were sharp, but the heat was tempered and made easily endurable by the wind which blew in freely from the wide, open sea, a sea that glittered and flashed deep blue and green and purple; whose waves, now agitated by the wind, curled and hurled themselves against rock-bound beach or heavy sand, breaking in a welter of fretted white, hissing as the flashing water retreated, to return again and again in its ceaseless intermittent rush and flow.

To Robert's left lay the cultivated fields of cane, a wide expanse of light glittering green backed by the low mountains that rose a little farther beyond. There were people on the road; slaves clad in grey or blue osnaburg, drivers conveying wagon-loads of newly made sugar and of rum to points of embarkation, to the little coves and piers from which estate produce was shipped into the sailing boats (the droghers) that would take it on to Kingston or the Bay. The wagons were drawn by long teams of oxen, at whose side walked men armed with great whips, who kept up a continuous shouting which seemed to be understood by the plodding, patient beasts. Robert rode by these, not perceiving that some of them eyed him surlily, never observing that there was in their demeanour a touch of insolent defiance and that but few of them gave him respectful salutation.

Had he been less absorbed in his own thoughts he could hardly have failed to notice this behaviour. Other white men had remarked it for some time now. He himself had heard Burbridge speak of the change which had come over the slaves in the parish, a change which was attributed to the influence of the missionaries, to a rumour that the people had already been granted freedom but that their new rights were being withheld from them. But he had paid little attention to all this; he had been far too much occupied otherwise. And today, of all days, it would have taken some extraordinary action on the part of all these shouting drivers and trudging men to draw his attention specially to their attitude towards him.

He neared the town, came up to the little fort with the cannon pointing towards its seaward approach, saw the red-coated soldiers about the place, and hurried on. He rode into Montego Bay, through its narrow, dusty streets; it was busy enough at this season, for the Christmas holidays were at hand and trade was brisk. Slaves moved about on their masters' business; by the street corners squatted women, scantily, almost indecently, clad, with bowls and trays heaped with fruit or with sticky cakes made of sugar in front of them. Free negroes went about their pursuits dressed, some of them, in the cast-off clothing once worn by the white people; in this attire figured broad-rimmed tophats and heavy broadcloth overcoats.

It was warm in the town. The buildings were small and dingy. A few vehicles drawn by horses were about, but the men of substance who had come into the town on business were on horseback: owners, overseers and attorneys, and these were not many.

Robert knew the scene well, had observed it often during his week's stay in Montego Bay. It appeared to him more sordid now than ever before. Once it had possessed the interest of novelty; Jamaica was then new to him, a land of promise, of glorious sunshine, laughing people and beckoning adventure. He had now begun to see that below the surface there was much about this life that was drab, unutterably coarse, grimly sinister. He feared, without quite knowing why, that he would shortly come into intimate contact with some of the tragedy that lay implicit in this half-somnolent, sun-suffused tropical life.

A few persons in the town recognized and saluted him, invited him to stay and have a rum punch with them. For hospitality was ever the order of the day in the Bay. He thanked them and declined, not pausing; his goal was elsewhere and he wished to hasten to it, though not so quickly as to cause comment in a little place where curiosity could be so easily awakened. He pushed onwards, left the town, crossed the bridge that Annie Palmer had passed over the night before; after a while he halted and inquired from some people in the road where the old man Takoo's daughter lived. The name, Burbridge had told him, would be well known about here. He found that it was.

Those to whom he spoke eyed him curiously, wondering what a young white man could have to do with Takoo and his people. But they directed him willingly enough; he was to look, about half a mile farther on, for a path on his left hand that led inward to 'a property'; he could not miss it; but did not massa want someone to take him there? That seemed a good suggestion; he agreed to hire a guide. But when he came to the place that he was seeking he paid and dismissed his guide. He wanted no garrulous witnesses to spy upon and talk about him.

In a few seconds he was before the house.

At once it struck him that something unusual was afoot. The space in front of the little dwelling was crowded with people, all of whom looked at him in surprise and with keen, questioning, inquisitive glances. At the threshold of one door of the house a thick smoke was slowly ascending from a pan filled with what looked like herbs and bits of refuse. The stench given off was overpowering and bitter; it was like incense burnt in honour or propitiation of evil powers. Standing over it was the old man who had rescued Millicent from Annie Palmer two nights before. His face was set and brooding. Upon it was stamped terror and a mighty, smouldering anger.

Robert felt embarrassed. He had not expected so many witnesses of his advent. And now that he was there he did not quite know what to say. How to explain why he had come? How to ask for the girl in the presence of all these people?

Takoo saw him, looked at him intently, and seemed to guess why he was there. He waved his arm, and the little crowd drew back. He came up to where Robert sat on his horse; 'You heard already, Squire?' he asked.

'No; I have heard nothing; what is it?' demanded Robert.

'Come inside,' said Takoo laconically.

Robert leaped off his horse and followed the old man. In the room into which he was led, crouched in a chair by the side of a bed, was Millicent. Her head was hidden between her hands, a sound of moaning came from her lips, her body swayed to and fro, the movement of one in mental or physical anguish.

Her grandfather touched her on the shoulder. 'Look up,' he commanded.

She obeyed mechanically. She saw the young man's face bending down with a look of consternation, of questioning, of horror upon it. Her own face was of the colour of ashes, and drawn; she seemed bloodless, and a fear that almost amounted to madness glared out of her eyes.

She uttered a cry and threw out her arms, clinging to Robert's knees. 'Oh, Squire, Squire,' she cried, 'help me, save me, for God's sake save me! Do what you can for me. I am dying.'

'Good God, Millicent!' he cried, 'what is the matter? Why are you like this?

'What is the matter?' he demanded fiercely, turning to the old man. 'Can't you speak?'

'Tell him,' said Takoo to the girl, with a sort of grim quietness.

'Last night, it happened last night,' she whispered.

'Yes? What happened?'

'I was sleeping. I don't know what time it was. But I wake up all of a sudden, for I knew there was something in de room with me; I heard it.

'It was dark, for everywhere was shut up, the window as well as the door. But I heard it. It moved near to me, and then I saw it.' She paused and shuddered convulsively.

'You saw it? But it was dark, Millie,' he reminded her gently, wondering what was the story she had to tell him.

'It was dark but I saw it. It was a woman, Squire; I know that, though the face was all like a white cloud. Her hands was stretched out towards me, and they catch and hold me – caught my throat. I couldn't scream. I wanted to scream an' I couldn't. And I wanted to struggle an' fight, but I couldn't. It was just as if somebody take me strength away. And the woman-thing put her face nearer to me, but not into my face. She bite me here' – Millicent touched a spot between her breasts – 'a sharp, cruel bite – cruel. And she suck me; I don't know how long. Then I scream out, an' she disappear, an' my aunt and her daughter came in. An' we know what it was; it was an Old Hige, an' now nothing can save me. I am dying, O my God! I am dying. An' I am only twenty, Squire, an' I love you so much.'

Robert took both her hands firmly in his. He felt relieved now that he had heard her story.

'Listen, Millicent,' he said quietly. 'I know what is the matter with you. You had a bad nightmare last night; that is all. You were worried and overwrought; you understand? You were worried over what had happened the night before and it preyed upon your mind. So you dreamed this thing, and you have allowed it to terrorize you. If you did not believe in all these foolish superstitions you would have laughed at your dream when you got awake. You will laugh now; there is nothing in it.'

She sobbed quietly, the sobs of despair. Robert looked at the old man by his side. There was no acceptance in Takoo's face of what seemed the right and rational explanation of what had occurred. It came to Robert Rutherford that he was face to face with a terrible problem, an unshakeable conviction in these people's minds.

He drew Millicent gently into a standing posture.

'Now I want you to be sensible,' he said patiently. 'Don't you see that you have had a horrible dream and nothing more? How could a woman, an Old Hige as you call her, come into your room when the door and window were closed? Did you find them open when you got awake? Did anyone?'

The girl shook her head, still sobbing.

'Very well, then, no one could have come in; that's quite evident. Can't you see that you have only been imagining that something evil has happened to you?'

'Look here,' whispered Millicent; 'tell me yourself what you see.'

She opened her bodice. Two firm rounded breasts were displayed. In the little hollow flanked by the soft promontories was a blistered space, about the size of a shilling. Purple against the golden brown of the glossy skin it stood out; and the skin was almost broken. It looked as though it had been caused by a blow which, a trifle harder, would have drawn blood.

Robert gazed at the mark with astonishment in his eyes, with a sense of sickness in his stomach. But he rallied his common sense. This might have been caused by some perfectly simple and natural means – must have been. Its discovery by Millicent, coupled with her nightmare, had made her give to it a significance that had no basis on fact.

'Millicent, boils and blisters are very common,' he urged. 'This is only one of them. You have a dream and a blister, and you put the two together and make a fuss about it. Nonsense! I will go to the Bay for a doctor for you and he will have you right in half an hour. But if you go on moping and mourning as you have been doing, you will certainly make yourself seriously ill. Have you sent for a doctor?' he asked Takoo.

'A white doctor can't do anything for her, massa,' replied the old man heavily. 'What she say is true. Old Hige come here last night an' suck her blood. We may save her, but it won't be by doctor's medicine.'

Millicent had sunk into her seat again. Once more her arms were clinging about Robert's knees. It was as if she felt that in him was some support, some help. She clung to him as to a last pillar of refuge.

He placed a hand upon her bowed head. An awful fear possessed him. He remembered that ride of Annie Palmer's out of Rosehall last night, and the strange creature which, on the night before that, even white men had seen. This girl's sickness and despair might well be some devil's work.

'What is this Old Hige she is talking about?' he asked Takoo. 'Is it a sort of ghost, a fiend, some wretched African belief? Why do you people believe such horrible things?' A gust of anger (born of fear and a sense of helplessness) swept through him. 'Why the hell do you all think such frightful, beastly things? You all live in hell with your degraded imaginations;

there is nothing clean and healthy about your minds. Your souls are blacker than ever your skins could be. Don't you see, you old fool, that you are torturing your granddaughter by encouraging her to believe the rank folly that seems like meat and drink to you? By God, if I had the power I would flog half to death any man that talked nonsense about Old Higes and the rest in the presence of children! Look before you now and see what your teaching has done!'

'If anybody else was to call me old fool, massa,' said Takoo quietly, 'he would see before long whether him or me was the fool. But I understand you. I know how you feel, young massa, an' I am grateful to you for it. You are a good man. I won't forget you.'

'I don't care a damn whether you forget me or not! What are you going to do to rid your granddaughter of her foolish fear? What can I do? Can't you suggest something?'

'I doing all I can just now,' said Takoo, 'an' I will do the utmost if Mrs Palmer drive me to it.'

'It is she, I know it is she!' broke in Millicent wildly. 'I didn't see her face when she or her spirit come into the room, but I feel it was she. She was here, sucking all me blood; she is an Old Hige, a witch, a devil. She want to kill me because she want you for her own self.'

'What is this Old Hige?' again asked Robert, with a note of resignation in his voice. There seemed to be no use arguing against so profound a belief.

Takoo told him in a few words, speaking as one who had no doubts whatever, but rather intimate knowledge and personal experience. An Old Hige was a woman with the power to divest herself of her skin, and to render herself invisible. She sought out people whose blood she desired, babies as a rule, and sucked them to death. A grown person could not so easily and quickly be deprived of his or her blood; but to show that Millicent's death, a death by occult means, had been determined upon, Takoo added, an obeah spell, a curse, had also been put upon her the night before. The proof of it was there.

He went outside and came back with a child's skull and a bit of white cardboard. There was no other human being in those premises (except Robert) who would have dared to handle those objects.

Takoo pointed to the bit of cardboard. Sketched upon its white surface was a coffin, and in the coffin lay a shrouded girl. The face was unmistakeable. It was Millicent's.

Takoo spoke slowly and with emphasis. 'Mrs Palmer ride out of Rosehall last night. Where to? She came here. When I heard it today – for I know everything dat take place in Rosehall an' Palmyra – I came straight for dis place; I know something bad had happened. The first thing I saw, massa, was this skull and piece of board, and though I was afraid – for I know more than you about dese things – I take them down. Then Millicent tell me what she see and feel last night. And I know the worst.'

'But you can't believe—'

Takoo's voice rose abruptly passionately; his self-control, never very strong at any time, had given way. 'I believe, I know that that dam' white woman, that witch, that Old Hige was here last night, an' that she was in dis room sucking me gran'child blood! She was here; she come to commit murder – it is not the first time she done that. But, so help me God, it is going to be the last. If I can't save Millie's life, I will revenge her!'

But for his overwhelming, overpowering anger, Takoo would not have ventured to speak like this. He was uttering terrible threats against a white woman who, however much she might be shunned by her own class, could claim the protection of the law against a well-known obeahman, one who was watched by the authorities, who had long wanted to get enough evidence against him to send him to prison or to the gallows. But now he was crazed with grief, maddened by wrath also, and was reckless. Perhaps, too, he knew well the young man would not breathe to anyone else a word that he said. Black and white, old and young, master and ex-slave, they had this one enduring, mighty bond in common: sympathy for the suffering girl before them, heart-sorrow for her predicament.

Others had heard Takoo's vehement words. The people outside had gradually been drawing nearer to the house while the colloquy inside proceeded. Their exclamations now came sharply to the ear. Wails and lamentations, and curses. Some of the women were on the verge of hysteria, some of them already raved as though demented.

Robert saw that this atmosphere, super-charged with superstition and excitement as it was, must do Millicent an immense amount of harm. The air of the room in which she sat, too, was close, and fetid with the odour of burning bush and sweat-saturated garments. It sickened him.

'Won't you send some of those people outside away?' he suggested to Takoo. 'I want to take Millicent into the open air for a while. It will do her good.'

Takoo bowed his head and went outside; he returned in a few moments to say that the visitors had gone, though as a matter of fact they had only withdrawn out of the yard into the road, standing ready to return as soon as they might.

Only two women remained: Millicent's aunt and her daughter.

'Can't you walk, Millie?' Robert's question really affirmed that she could if she wanted to.

She rose with his help, staggering a little; it was clear she believed that she could move only with great difficulty. Her fixed belief that her blood had been sucked and she was doomed had sapped her will, and her body reacted sympathetically to her extraordinary obsession.

Robert led her outside, impatiently kicking out of his path the pan of smoking bush. He guessed its purpose. It was all so puerile, almost obscene, he swiftly thought, and yet he was far from disbelieving that there might be something in these strange, degrading superstitions. Annie Palmer had openly proclaimed her knowledge of the existence of wicked spirits, of their prowling presence on the earth. And these people would say that she ought to know, since she had traffic with them. Besides, did he himself utterly disbelieve in them? In his heart of hearts he knew that he did not.

He motioned to one of the two women, Millicent's relatives, to bring a chair; this he placed under a spreading mango tree, the thick foliage of which afforded a welcome shade. He asked for another chair, had it put close to the first one, seated Millicent and then sat down himself. Here in the sunlight he noticed, startled, that her pallor was more deathlike than it had appeared in the darkened room. It as just as though she had indeed been deprived of blood, as if her veins had been drained. And there were dark circles round her eyes.

She looked very pathetic, this girl, who, a couple of days before, had been so full of vitality, so confident in her strength, so upright and virile in her bearing. A poignant pang of pity shot through him; he felt stirred by something of the same rage that had possessed the old African and had caused him to utter wild and dangerous words. It came to him that something must be done, and quickly, to rid this girl of her conviction of approaching death; otherwise she might die of sheer terror.

He had heard of something of the sort happening in other countries. Fear could kill.

'Millicent,' he said, holding her right hand in his and fixing his regard firmly on hers, 'I am going to help you. Do you understand me? It does not matter what has afflicted you: I am going to help you to get rid of it.'

'How?' she asked, while tears of gratitude filled her eyes.

'Well, in the first place, you were christened, weren't you? And you are a Christian?'

She nodded her head, murmuring 'yes'.

'That being so, you must believe that God can aid you, can restore you to health, that He is more powerful than all the Higes or fiends in the world, don't you?'

Again, she said yes, but there seemed no great force of conviction behind her agreement.

'Well, then, I am going to ask the rector of this parish, today, to pray for you, and' – in his groping for assistance he remembered Rider, the broken clergyman who was, nevertheless, as he understood it, still a clergyman, and a man of real kindness of heart, despite his fallen estate – 'and I am going also to ask another parson to pray for you; a man who knows Mrs Palmer, and is not afraid of her. And I am going to send you a doctor. If you believe in God you cannot believe that the Devil is stronger than God, can you? And if you make up your mind to get well, you will. You see it all, don't you?'

Even while he spoke it seemed to him queer, and even mawkish, that he should talk of religion, and prayer, and parsons, he who had never done anything of the sort before, and who would have shuddered to think of himself as doing it. But a human life, at least a human being's reason, might be at stake. And if it were Annie who had, somehow, brought the girl to this pass, all the power of religion as well as of human agencies might be needed to save Millicent.

'You will promise me to do your best to get well?' he asked her.

'Yes, I promise; I will try; but,' she wailed, 'don't you know dat she will harm you too if she know you come to see me and try to help me? She hate me, and she going to hate you too. She's like that.'

'I don't care a fig for her hate. I will face her or anyone else. I want and am determined to help you, Millie; you may depend on that.'

A glad look lit up Millicent's dejected countenance, then it faded away and her head dropped once more. She was weeping again. Watching her, Robert had himself to struggle to keep tears from his eyes.

'Squire,' she said softly, 'I promise you I will try, but I don't think you save me. I know how I feel last night, an' how I feel now.' She seized his hand with sudden force. 'Oh, my God,' she cried, 'I wonder if I will ever see you again.'

He could stand this no longer. He rose abruptly, and beckoned to Takoo, telling him briefly what he intended to do in the matter of the doctor. 'You must let me know how she gets on,' he said, 'and if you want money you can have all that is necessary. You will keep her here?'

No, she was going to be removed that day. But Takoo promised that he would let the young squire know where she was later on. He had not yet made up his mind where he would take her to; he had to be very secretive. He did not dare let her future whereabouts be known.

'Not that de Old Hige will come again like she did last night,' he said, 'for we will be watching; but she might do something else.'

'I wonder how much of this is sense and how much nonsense,' said Robert sadly.

'Mr Ashman an' Mr Rider saw the Horse two nights ago,' said Takoo slowly; 'saw it plain. I saw it before Mrs Palmer last husband die. Young massa, there is plenty of things you don't know, that is why you disbelieve. You can send de doctor, but not later than seven o'clock. After that him won't find any of us here.'

'I will see you again shortly, Millie,' said Robert; 'meantime, believe you are going to get well.'

He took her hand in his. 'Promise me that you will try,' he said.

She was loath to let go his hand. 'I don't believe I will ever see you again,' she wailed, and as he moved away her heavy, despairing sobs seemed like blows falling upon his heart.

CHAPTER 15

Robert Intervenes

ROBERT GOT BACK to Rosehall in time to meet the other two book-keepers together; they had finished dinner, not having waited for him. His meal was being kept warm by Psyche, who had been relieved from all extraneous duties to act as cook for the three men. But he refused to have anything to eat just then, he was far too anxious to face food: later on, he said, he would eat something.

Burbridge would be off presently to his night work, but there was still some time for talk; and Robert wanted to consult with these two, partly because he wished their opinion and advice, partly because he felt the need of someone to whom he could speak openly as to a friend.

He told them where he had been that afternoon, though both of them already knew, and just what he had seen and heard.

'It is inexplicable to me,' he said, 'how these people can believe all these weird, horrible things, and yet I saw the mark on Millicent's bosom myself, and there can be no doubt that she believes what she says.'

There was silence for a couple of minutes when he ceased. Burbridge broke it.

'Who is to say that the girl isn't right, Rutherford? Queer things happen everywhere. You don't know that there are not evil spirits plaguing men and women; the Bible tells us that there are. I never laugh at what these people say. Perhaps they know more about certain things than we do.'

'Then you actually believe that this girl is being haunted, haunted to death?' asked Robert, 'and that Annie Palmer is the prime cause of it?'

'I don't know who is the cause of it,' said Burbridge dourly; 'we mustn't be too free with names. But I have seen people on the estates die from ghost-haunting, and I have seen some go mad. It isn't anything to scoff at, I can tell you.'

'What is to be done?' Robert put the question tensely.

'Whatever is to be done will be done by old Takoo; you may rest assured of that. He told you, didn't he, that your doctor could do no good? But he is a sort of doctor himself, where these things are concerned. Perhaps he himself has put ghosts – death – on people before now, so he knows how to handle such a situation. Maybe this is the retribution that has come upon him. For what he has done his beloved granddaughter suffers today. He'll feel that.'

'Then all I have to say is that that is damned injustice!' broke out Robert harshly. 'But you think that Takoo may cure Millicent?'

'He may be able to; he'll have a try at it, anyhow. I wouldn't worry much about it – yet,' added Burbridge kindly, for he saw that the young man was distressed. 'After all, Millie wasn't anything to you; she hadn't really become your "housekeeper", had she?'

Robert gave no answer, Burbridge continued: 'Whatever there is to be done for her, Takoo will do it; you may rest assured of that. And it won't suit you, Rutherford, to mix yourself up too much with this business.'

'And yet perhaps,' said Rider, speaking for the first time, 'unless Rutherford does interest himself in it the girl will die.'

'What do you mean?' asked both the other men at once.

'You both believe that Mrs Palmer has had something to do with Millicent's sickness,' Rider went on, but with lowered voice. 'You don't know how she has acted, but you look upon her as the real cause of this trouble, and I have no doubt that you are right. Well, I am wondering whether Takoo, however powerful an obeahman he may be, can succeed if he acts alone against Mrs Palmer's will and influence; but if we could bring her in as a sort of kindly or forgiving agency, something might be done. Takoo might ask her for help, but is she likely to heed him? Rutherford might ask her; we all know that she – that she has a liking for him. She may do something for him – at a price. That is just possible. She might be content if, say, the girl went to the other end of the island, though she may think Jamaica too small for herself and a coloured, free young lady who dared to defy her and to charge her with murder. She is terribly vain; her vanity has been outraged by Millicent's presumption, and forgiveness comes hard to a woman like Mrs Palmer; indeed, she doesn't forgive, though she may not insist upon revenge. But her intervention may be Millicent's only hope. Do you think it worth your while to appeal for it, Rutherford? You couldn't harm the girl any more than she is harmed already, anyway; for if she believes she is going to die, you may take it from me that she will die.'

Robert and Burbridge shuddered. Rider, sot though he was, was sober enough now, and he was speaking with a quiet certitude that carried terrible conviction to the minds of his two companions. And no one could doubt that he was sympathetic.

'Then you are satisfied that Millicent is really haunted?' asked Robert. 'You believe what these people on the estates believe? Is it all true, then?'

'I have told you what I saw the other night with my own eyes, haven't I?'

'Yes; you were very clear about that, though—'

'No; I was quite sober; I haven't touched a drink for nearly a month. It was not, either, a case of my imagination being affected by the imagination of the negroes. Remember, Ashman indicated that he saw it also, and Mrs Palmer spoke as if it were a fact. You have, therefore, the testimony of three white people, all of them presumably sober. And now you bring us this tale of an Old Hige, which is only the Vampire of other countries, Rutherford, the Vampire which is human and which lives on blood.'

He stopped as though to think; his auditors waiting breathlessly on him, for he seemed to have some explanation of this miserable mystery to suggest.

'We may rest assured that, whatever else she did last night, Annie Palmer did not take off her skin and pass through wood in order to get at this girl. That sort of belief is sheer nonsense. Yet Millicent saw, or felt something – a presence – in her room with her, and there is a peculiar, suggestive bruise on her chest. And there is the child's skull that was hung up outside of her room, which must have been put where it was found, and also a sketch of her lying in her coffin. The skull and the sketch are pure obeah – witchcraft mummery; they are meant to terrify, to complete the work of the so-called Old Hige. They are Millicent's signed death warrant so to speak. A real Vampire, a real Old Hige, supposing that such a thing existed, would not need to employ them. The blood-sucking would be enough.'

'The people about here,' interrupted Burbridge, 'believe that you can keep an Old Hige away if you know she is likely to come at you. Takoo is doing that now.'

'Yes; but they didn't know last night that our lady of the Great House would be on the prowl; and if she were powerful enough to pass through locked doors and fastened windows she would have been sufficiently powerful to kill the girl outright. She must have known that she was not going to reach Millicent with her hands and teeth when she took care to prepare the skull and sketch. Besides, would she have run the risk of being found in the room? Even as it is, if it can be proved that it was she who put that skull and sketch where they were found, she could be indicted for practising obeah. But she is not a fool. She knows that while a white woman may be suspected of murder, no jury would really believe that she practised obeah. That would be thought highly unlikely.'

'Then,' said Robert bluntly, 'you conclude that she sent a ghost into the room to Millicent; some damned wretched creature from the Pit like the one you yourself saw here the other night? She is a witch, then, as well as a murderess – for I have never felt sure she wasn't a murderess ever since I heard the story about her, although I have not wanted to give it any credence. Indeed, I should still think it a lie but for this last thing that is happening.'

'Yes,' said Rider slowly, 'I believe that she sent something to prey upon Millicent's mind; but what was it? I too saw something three nights ago. But what was it?'

'The Three-footed Horse, the Horse from Hell,' said Burbridge bluntly.

'That's what it looked like. Isn't that what Mrs Palmer intended that it should look like?'

'You mean—?' Robert paused, glimpsing a little what Rider had in his mind, but not quite able to express it.

'You heard of Mesmer when in England, or when on the Continent, Rutherford?'

'Yes, a little; not much. I wasn't interested.'

'Mesmer claimed extraordinary powers and did some extraordinary things in France in his time – before and after the Revolution. He could certainly influence the minds of people: they say he "mesmerized" them. I have heard of the same kind of thing being done in India, where the workers of magic cause you to see all sorts of queer and impossible phenomena. If they can do that, why should not other people – a very few perhaps, but still some – be able to do it also? The power may be purely mental, not supernatural at all.'

'I see,' breathed Robert, but Burbridge looked puzzled. The talk was a little above him.

'I have been a clergyman, even if a damned poor one,' Rider went on, with a rueful smile, 'and I was taught to believe that there is a Devil and his angels whose work is to torture mankind and cause them to lose their souls. And the Witch of Endor, you remember, brought the Prophet Samuel up out of his grave. There is Scriptural warrant for believing in witches and in human ability to use and control the spirits. There are plenty of people in England today who believe in witches. There are more on the Continent. But I am not naturally superstitious. Annie Palmer may have a power which is of the mind, not of hell.'

'But such power is of hell!' asseverated Robert passionately. 'What else is it? For what purpose is it used? Or it may be that she employs her own spirit. Millicent said something about Mrs Palmer's spirit, not her body, being in the room with her last night. Surely that suggests hellish power.'

'In a way you are right,' continued Rider quietly, 'but what I mean is that perhaps she causes people to see things she herself thinks of; it is a vision of her mind that she projects into space, now in the form of a spectral horse, now in the form of a shadowy vampire. Mark you, I don't say she doesn't herself imagine that she calls up these shapes from hell, or from the grave. Quite probably she does. She herself may not be able to explain her own powers, and as she is more likely to pray to the Devil than to God she would believe, and gladly believe, that she has influence over the world of evil. A woman like that would be intensely proud of her power – puffed up – and what better food for vanity than a conviction that even devils obey her? Going, Burbridge?'

'Yes, I have got to be off now. But listen: I can trust you fellows, and I tell you now, quite frankly, that I believe that damned woman up there is in league with hell. She is a witch, and as soon as I can get another job I am out of Rosehall. I have had enough of it!'

He jammed his hat on his head and marched away. Rider looked at him with a smile. 'His nerve is going,' he said, 'and yet Burbridge would face a dozen riotous slaves without hesitation. He may have to face more than that, too, very shortly. There is going to be trouble on these estates before long, Rutherford; everything points to that.'

'The sooner it comes the better!' cried Robert. 'It seems to me that only fire and blood can wipe out some of the iniquity that festers here.'

'Maybe; but I hope I shall not be considered part of that iniquity,' smiled Mr Rider.

He became grave again instantly.

'You see now, don't you, why I said that it may be necessary for you to concern yourself further with this strange affair of Millicent's? If she has been bewitched or "influenced" by Mrs Palmer, how on earth can poor Takoo's medicine or incantations help her? I believe that our imperious little mistress has caused the girl to believe that an Old Hige is sucking her and that she is doomed to die within a few days. It would not be difficult to get Millicent to believe that; all her life she has been surrounded by superstition; she herself is convinced that her grandfather controls ghosts and can work wonders. She knows that Mrs Palmer is her enemy; only Mrs Palmer, then, can induce her to believe that she is no longer bewitched. Millicent's obsession is so strong that a blister has appeared on the spot where she imagines the Old Hige sucked her. The girl's own mind is working on her body; that is how I understand the matter. So I think that only Mrs Palmer can bring her to believe that she will get well. Mrs Palmer may undertake to do this if you beg her to, but she will demand a price for the service. And it will be damned awkward for you to ask the favour. I rather like the girl though; I knew her slightly before I came here, and I knew her grandfather – the white one. He died not so long ago, and he was fond of her in his way; he did a good deal for her – and for me, so far as he could. He was kind to me. I should like to think I could do something he would be thankful for....' Rider's voice died out as though he were indulging in some secret reminiscence.

With elbows planted on knees, with his face buried in his hands, Robert pondered over what the other man had said. Rider was assured that Millicent's life was at stake, and was suggesting that perhaps it might be saved, but in one way only. He, Robert, must use what influence he possessed with a woman whom, he now saw so clearly, he had come to suspect and even to detest, though but a few days ago he would have said he loved her.

He raised his head. 'I don't know if I shall succeed in getting Mrs Palmer to let this poor girl alone, Rider,' he said, 'but I will try. I feel that I am in some way responsible for her predicament. If I had not come here, if I had not engaged her services, above all, if … if she had not been with me in this place that night – and it was I who made her remain – she would not be in this awful condition. I must help her if I can. I will speak to Annie about her, but I am not hopeful.'

'You can but do your best,' said Rider kindly.

'When do you think I should see Mrs Palmer?'

'As soon as possible,' answered Rider gravely. 'Millicent spoke only the truth when she told you she was dying.'

Robert shivered, then rose abruptly, and went into his room. He emerged with a hat and cloak, for it had begun to rain slightly. Dark clouds had swept across and obscured the sky while they had been talking, the night had grown chill and eerie, a moaning wind came in from the sea. It was as if the dark spirit that brooded over Rosehall was affecting even the material world.

He called for his horse, and one of the boys brought it round to him after a little while. He mounted and rode away.

When he got to the Great House it seemed plunged in darkness, but he knew that there might be lights and people awake to the rear of it, in spite of the hour. His rap at the great front doors convinced him he was right in his conjecture; the doors were soon opened by Annie herself. She did not seem surprised to see him.

'Come in, Robert,' she said, 'and take off your cloak. You must be tired after your long ride to Montego Bay and back.'

'You know I went to Montego Bay?' he asked.

'Why, certainly, Ashman told me. I know you went to see Millicent too; I needn't say who told me that; it is immaterial. Well?'

She had led the way into the dining-room as she spoke; she seated herself now in one of the chairs and motioned him to another close by. The candelabrum was placed on the table by which he sat. It brightly illuminated her face and hair and bosom. Her bodice, he noticed, was cut very low, revealing most of her bosom.

Her eyes were fixed on his and the light in them was soft. Her lips were slightly parted. Not a strong and dominating, but a weak and helpless woman she appeared.

Again it struck him, as it always did, that she was a wonderfully beautiful woman. Now that he was in her presence he wondered once more if the things said about her could be true, though his reason clamoured a warning. The fascination of her was strong tonight; she seemed to exert all her power of allure and appeal. Looking at him in the warm yellow light of the wax candles, she saw the trouble in his face, guessed the surge of emotions in his mind. He was still possessed with desire for her. Whatever the stern purpose with which he had come there that night he might yet be rendered as plastic as clay in the potter's hands.

With a quick movement she bent forward and placed her hand on his.

'Are you still thinking badly of me, Robert?' she murmured.

His impulse was to take her in his arms. A wild impulse which he fought to conquer. Her arm lengthened, it crept up to his shoulder. 'Do you think I am the murderess, the witch, that that young woman called me, Robert? Do you hate me? Do you believe that I have injured her? Oh, I know what you have been told; there were many people in Takoo's yard to hear. He said I was an Old Hige, didn't he, and had bewitched his grandchild? And you believed it? Your belief in my guilt is my reward for loving you, isn't it, Robert?' Before he could guess what she would be at she had flung herself on her knees before him. 'Because I love you I must suffer,' she moaned. 'And yet you told me that you loved me!'

He stooped and lifted her up; without quite realizing what he did he placed her on his knees and put his arms around her. Her own arms were thrown about his neck and her lips were pressed on his. Then she whispered: 'So in spite of all, you do love me a little still!'

'No one can help loving you, Annie,' he cried: again he was under the dominance of her will, her beauty, her personality. 'You are very lovely, very adorable; but' – he forced himself to say it – 'very terrible also.'

'Terrible?'

'Yes. This poor young woman – everybody believes you are the reason why she is suffering, dying, and that is awful. It is a crime, if true.'

'Do you believe it is true?' she asked, modulating her voice to a cooing whisper. 'Do you believe it is true?'

He remembered what Rider had said to him; he must not allow himself to forget what had brought him here.

'I don't believe that you are a witch, Annie, or any of that sort of nonsense,' he protested, 'but I am sure that you possess strange powers, and I know you dislike Millicent. What at any rate is true is that she believes that you have everything to do with her illness, that you have doomed her to death; and I think that only you can rid her mind of that strange belief, and I am asking you to do it.'

He paused; she made no reply, and he continued:

'Don't you see that if you don't do what you can you will be responsible for her death just as much as if you killed her with your own hands? And already they say—'

'That I am a murderess. Oh, yes, I know. *She* said so in your hearing; she – a woman like that, Robert, tried to paint me black in your eyes. And because she is sick from fright you come to me to ask me to help her to get a stupid idea out of her mind.' She laughed. 'How generous, or how foolish, you must think me!'

He lifted her, gently but firmly, and put her back on her own chair. That laugh had jarred upon him. There was a merciless timbre in it.

She saw she had made a false move; she asked quietly, with almost perceptible self-repression: 'What do you want me to do?'

'You know,' he said haltingly, 'what she believes.'

'Yes, I have heard.'

'Can you rid her mind of that idea, cause her to become convinced that she is mistaken, that she will get well?'

'Why do you think I can do this? Who suggested that I could?'

He would not answer; to do so would be to give away Rider, and he felt that she was seeking for information.

'Do you, too, imagine that I put this woman in the condition she is in?' she insisted, 'and that I can take her out of it?'

Bluntly he answered, 'Yes.' For a picture of Millicent weeping had risen before him, and Annie's fascination had suddenly failed.

She stiffened, anger gleaming from her eyes. 'Then I am a very dangerous person,' she exclaimed, 'and greatly to be feared.'

Her anger inspired him with a similar emotion.

'That is so,' he answered as sharply, 'but I do not fear you, Annie.'

'Your woman does!'

'That is an admission that she has reason to fear you.'

'It is an admission of nothing! You have come here to quarrel with me on her account; putting her against me! Do you understand that that is an insult?'

'Then you refuse to help her?'

She studied his face for some moments, and again her attitude changed. Again she became soft and clinging.

'Robert, if you want me to help her, of course I shall; but you have misunderstood me much. How have I been able to injure her? It is her own guilty mind, and her own beliefs, that have afflicted her. I left Rosehall two nights ago, yes, but it is only an assumption that I went to Takoo's place. There was someone with me, a boy from this estate. Let me call him and you can ask him where I went; he was with me all the time. Can I not leave Rosehall without people thinking, and you above all, that it is to commit a crime? Good God! Have you no faith in me whatever, Robert?'

He made no suggestion that the lad should be summoned; she knew he would not. That would have shown brutally that he disbelieved her. Not that she was afraid of any interrogation, for the boy had been carefully trained as to what he was to say and would not have dared to add a word of his own.

'I hate the woman,' she continued, 'but is not that natural? Remember, she was with you when I came to your house; she had been in your arms. And you, just the night before that, had been in mine. What woman could easily tolerate that, if she really loved you? That girl was trying to take you away from me; you know that. And she defied and cursed and abused me before your face – *she*. Then fear came upon her; she believes I am a witch. I have told you before that we have to rule these people by fear, and I, a woman, must encourage their foolish ideas if I am to hold my own amongst them. Don't you ever think of my position here, in spite of all that I have said to you? And now you come to tell me of my strange powers, and to ask me to help her! I answer that I will try for your sake, but how I am to know that I shall succeed? I cannot control her mind; I know nothing about what diseases she may be suffering from; I only know that she has tried to injure me. But because you ask it I will do my best for her. How shall I do it: send her a message, bid them to bring her to see me – for you would hardly expect me to go to her, would you?'

He saw the difficulty. 'I can make no suggestion,' he said. 'I must leave it to you to find a way.'

'Very well. I will send to Takoo and ask him to come to me; I promise you that I will try my best. I can do no more. Are you satisfied?'

He was grateful. She had spoken with a great show of sincerity; there was an appeal to him in her voice, in her look. 'When will you do this, Annie?' he inquired.

'Tomorrow. You may depend upon it that there will be no unnecessary delay. And if I succeed – what happens to me, Robert; what are you going to do with this girl?'

'Nothing.' He was emphatic. 'I don't think she will want to remain in this neighbourhood.'

'And you – are you going to remain with me at Rosehall?'

She perceived his hesitation, knew that he wished to speak the truth, did not believe that he spoke the truth when he answered, heavily, 'Of course.' She felt, as she had done before, that he was slipping away from her; though she still fascinated him when he was in her presence and she appealed to his chivalry and his desire. She realized that the one man she had ever loved was being wrenched from her by circumstances stronger than herself.

'You don't want to,' she said bitterly.

He tried to deny this, did deny it, and she let him go on with his protestations for a while.

Then she rose and came and stood before him, lifted his head towards her with her hands and bent her face towards his. 'I have promised to do what I can for this girl,' she said; 'are you not satisfied? You are all the world to me; would you leave me now?'

'I will remain, Annie,' he replied, helpless. For the life of him he could say nothing else.

'Stay up here with me tonight, and go on staying,' she pleaded; 'whatever happens, let us love one another. You can do what you like with me, Robert, and you are the only man of whom that has ever been true.'

'I will stay at Rosehall, but not with you tonight,' he urged. 'I am weary and worried; I have been living the devil of a life since I have been here. It seems as though I have been at it for months, not merely weeks.'

'Sweetheart, stay! I want you, I want you ever so much! Don't leave me in my loneliness tonight, for I am very unhappy! Tell me that you will stay!'

She was on his knees and pressing close to him, her arms about his neck, her face against his, and the pleading note in her voice. All her great power of allurement seemed alive and intent upon his surrender. He spoke no word in reply. But she knew that again she had won her way with him.

CHAPTER 16

Annie's Promise

AT ABOUT NINE O'CLOCK the next morning Robert was at his work in the cane-fields. His face was drawn, his brow dark with anger and self-loathing. He had weakly yielded to the blandishments of Annie after having made up his mind to break away from her, and he hated himself in consequence. Yet he kept saying to himself that only by doing what she wished at present could he help the unfortunate young woman who believed herself to be on the point of death. He remembered that Rider had said, on the night before, that for any assistance for Millicent for which he might ask Annie Palmer he would have to pay a price.

The price would have seemed nothing a week before; indeed it would have been a privilege. But now he knew too much. Annie startled even while attracting him. He wished to get away from her; today he was thinking of England with an almost overpowering nostalgia. He had had enough of Jamaica. Yet, only a few hours before, he had promised this woman to remain with her, and now he felt that he must break that promise, come what might. It is true that on her side she had pledged herself to help Millicent, and so rid him of his feeling of self-reproach. And if she kept her word would he not be morally obliged to keep his?

He was afraid of her: he admitted that to himself quite frankly. He was as courageous as most other men who were accounted brave. But all these dark powers of the mind, which Rider was convinced were possessed by Mrs Palmer, and all these darker uses that she made of them, seemed to him to be not dangerous only but loathly. There was something unclean about them, and consequently about her. She was still young, she had had three husbands, and all of them had died violent deaths. Love could turn to hatred. Her vanity, wounded through any rejection of her by him, a rejection in the spirit if not in actual fact, would arouse the worst devils in her heart. She would know what he felt; he sensed that she had followed pretty closely the various changes of his mind the night before. She would feel scorned, spurned, and then might come to her the irresistible temptation to show him that he could not treat her lightly and escape. Yes; he admitted that he was afraid of her, as seemed most or all of those who had come into close contact with her. That perhaps accounted for her escape up to now from the consequences of her acts; that and the unsettled condition of the country and the difficulty there must be in collecting trustworthy evidence against her, who was as wily as she was bold.

He noticed that Ashman openly scowled at him this morning. Ashman knew where he had been last night, and raged at the failure of his hopes and plans to alienate him from Annie Palmer. Millicent had gone, and Ashman had heard, for he had sought the information, of Millicent's plight; he concluded that Millicent would shortly disappear from the scene and Robert would reign at Rosehall; last night, he argued, there must have been a complete reconciliation between Rutherford and Annie Palmer. Burbridge also, Robert observed, had spoken to him nervously this morning; Burbridge, who had been so very outspoken on the previous night. It was not that Burbridge actually believed that his words would be reported to Mrs Palmer, though, in the jealousy that sometimes raged among the minor employees of an estate, anyone was quite capable of mean treachery towards another. But Burbridge knew that a woman might eventually wheedle out of a man the very secrets of his mind. He cursed himself for having been so brutally frank, for having at last denounced so openly a woman whom he detested and feared.

But Rider's demeanour had not been at all different. Perhaps Rider knew that Robert had done his best; perhaps Rider had guessed what would happen. Anyhow, there had been no restraint about him when he had greeted Robert an hour or so before.

And now it was Rider who came up to him, cantering smartly on his horse. 'Ashman has sent me to summon you, Rutherford,' he said quietly, when he drew up at the young man's side. 'An important message has come from Montego Bay, and all the white men on the estate are wanted up at the Great House. Burbridge already knows. Let's ride along together. These fellows' – he indicated the field labourers – 'may go on working for a few minutes without our eye on them.'

They rode off, Rider making no allusion to anything that had previously passed between them, and Robert, though wishing to do so, not knowing exactly how to open the subject that was uppermost in his mind.

In the dining-room of the Great House, where they were told that Mrs Palmer was awaiting them, they found Ashman, Burbridge, the chief mechanic and the chief carpenter, both young Scotsmen who usually kept to themselves and who, though their status did not seem to imply it, were much better paid than the book-keepers. There was a stranger there also, a man of middle-age, who had come in about fifteen minutes before.

Mrs Palmer opened the conversation. Rider keeping himself in the background, watched her closely. He could not but admire her coolness, her matter-of-fact attitude. Everybody there knew, with the exception of the stranger, that she had made one of her book-keepers her lover, but that did not in the least embarrass her. What they knew and what they felt was a matter to which she seemed to give no attention at all.

'I have got a message from the magistrates in Montego Bay,' she began, in her clear, carrying voice, 'that the slaves of this parish have made up their minds not to work after New Year's Day. They believe that their freedom has been granted to them from that day, and it is feared that there may be trouble.'

'Yes,' broke in the stranger, who was a planting attorney and connected with the local militia, 'and the slaves have already heard that Sunday next is to be counted by us as one of the three days' holiday they are allowed at Christmas time. We have heard that they will refuse to accept that decision.'

'Refuse!' Mrs Palmer laughed a little scornfully.

'I think they mean it,' said the man, 'but of course we must not give in to them. These infernal ministers and missionaries are the curse of Jamaica. They are giving us any amount of trouble and may cause bloodshed. But there you are. We have got to face this insubordination and put an end to it. We can only do it if we stand together.'

'Sunday is Christmas,' said Ashman; 'and today is Friday. I don't see why we should give these people from Sunday to Wednesday night to go idle and get drunk; I have already made mine to understand that they will have to be at work on Wednesday morning. That's fixed, and they know better than to grumble about it to my face. I have known for some time that there have been palavers and plottings all around; I have surprised one on Palmyra myself. But there won't be much trouble here or on Palmyra, I fancy.'

'No,' said Mrs Palmer quietly; 'we have put the fear of God – or of the Devil – into their hearts. We know how to manage our people on these properties, Mr Hancock.'

'So I have been told,' replied Hancock, a little dryly. 'Well, there isn't one proprietor or attorney we have sounded who does not agree that we must include Sunday as one of the Christmas holidays. Considering it is Christmas Day, and that the law is that we must give three days including Christmas Day, we are well within our rights. I believe that the parsons want Sunday to be spent in prayer, and the lazy brutes we have want to pray the first day and debauch the next three. We won't have it, that's all! But we think it would be a good thing for all the white men on the estates to be prepared for any emergency; that is why we are sending round to them. You now understand what the situation is.'

'And we'll have it well in hand, never fear,' added Ashman. 'Have you sent to Spanish Town to let the Governor know what may happen in these parts?'

'No; we don't think that is necessary; in fact, we think we'd better not. The Government, Mr Ashman, is secretly with these missionaries and slaves – we are in a devil of a position when it comes to getting justice and our rights, I can tell you. The Government backs up the negroes whenever it can; this Governor seems to have been sent out to do nothing but that. We'll never get fair play from him any more than from the English Government; so we have to do what we can for ourselves. But there's a good lot of fight left in us still!'

'I for one,' said Mrs Palmer coldly, 'am prepared to make no concessions at all. The better you treat these people, the worse they are. If you give way on one point, they expect you to give way on all. They will be at work on Wednesday morning on Rosehall and Palmyra, whatever happens; I shall myself see to that.'

'See also that the white men here are armed on Tuesday,' insisted Mr Hancock, 'that is why I asked to see them myself; and, of course, any of the chief negroes you can trust.'

The conference was over; Mr Hancock rose to say good-bye. He would visit some other properties during the rest of the day. He was doing this as a duty and as a labour of love. He believed that the estate proprietors and attorneys were being treated with the gravest injustice for the sake of slaves who, so far as he could see, had nothing in the world to complain of. The unfortunate owners had all Mr Hancock's sympathy. He was virtuously proud of being able to do something for them, his own class.

The men were dismissed; but Annie gave Robert a signal to linger behind. When the others had ridden away she said to him:

'You see now, I need your presence in the Great House. You wouldn't like to leave me unprotected, would you?'

'No,' he answered quite truthfully, for if a woman needed protection he would not hesitate in affording her what he could of it. 'But you suggested only a while ago that there was no danger here.'

'It would not do to confess any fear,' she retorted readily, 'and there may be no real danger. But how can I be certain? If I am alone in this house and the slaves were to get out of hand suddenly, what would happen to me? There should be someone here with me, at this time especially. You will remove your things up here today?'

He shook his head. 'That is impossible, Annie. That is the one thing I cannot do.'

She looked at him long and searchingly. 'Very well,' was all that she said.

Before leaving he asked her, endeavouring to speak casually: 'You have sent for Takoo as you said you would?'

'This morning. Two messengers went, one to his daughter's house and one to his own. I'll let you know if he is coming to see me.'

'Thank you, Annie,' he said, with real appreciation, and left feeling far more kindly disposed towards her than he had been an hour before.

He did not believe that she ran any risk; she had indicated as much. But he did not realize she had divined that, whatever had been the reason of his objection to living at the Great House before, it was now his reluctance to be constantly with her. Perhaps if she had begged and cajoled him again, as she had done last night, he might have yielded; he did not find it easy to resist a woman's imploring. But Annie Palmer had her upsurgings of pride, and now she was bitterly angry. She was more used to being sued than suing.

On going back to his work he met Rider, and paused for a few words. He now said what he had been wanting to say to Rider. 'I got her to promise to help Millicent,' he remarked, 'but I don't think she is altogether pleased with me, Rider. I don't seem able to say or do the right thing all the time.'

'None of us are,' said Rider sententiously, 'but I am sure you have done your best. Leave it there, Rutherford. We are likely to have our hands pretty full with other things during the next week or so. Our lives may be in jeopardy, for all we know.'

'You seriously think it is as bad as that?'

'I do; we are in for serious trouble.'

'It may do good,' said Robert grimly; 'it may end a lot of things.' Rider knew that he was thinking of himself and his relations with Annie; he was entangled and did not quite know how to break out of the net.

It rained again that night, and Robert kept to his quarters. The next day, Christmas Eve, not much work was done on the estate. The slaves had become excited, and no expostulations or threats could move them to continuous labour; the spirit of the season affected them, as well as some secret understanding of momentous events that were to come to pass. But the spirit of the season affected the white men on the estate also; it was Christmas Eve, and those who were from the Old Country were thinking of how it would be just then in England and in Scotland; little given as they were to day-dreaming, their minds went back to their homes and to the past, and for the time they ceased to be mere cogs in the machinery of a sugar estate. During the late afternoon Robert caught a glimpse of Annie on horseback; she was riding about the property. She passed fairly near to him but seemed oblivious of his presence. He concluded that she was still displeased with his last refusal to come to live at the Great House. He wondered if she had yet heard from Takoo. He thought it likely that she had not.

For he too had heard nothing from Takoo. That the old man had removed Millicent he knew; Rider had told him; Rider had heard this from Burbridge. The latter had been spoken to by Rider, who had made a point of assuring him that Robert would never betray his friends. When night had fallen on Christmas Eve, therefore, the three men forgathered in their quarters talking of trivialities. Then, somewhat to Robert's surprise, Burbridge mentioned that he had again heard that afternoon about Millicent; Psyche had told him.

'Where is she?' asked Robert.

'That I don't know; I don't think Psyche knows, or she would have mentioned it to me. She has been commanded by Takoo to some sort of ceremony they are having for Millicent; Psyche says they are going to try to take off the haunting, to lay the ghost that is killing the girl. Psyche was ordered not to say where this is to take place, but I got it out of her. These people have secret meetings on the estates, where they carry on all sorts of strange practices, some of which are horrible. There is to be one of them tomorrow night.'

'Where?' asked Rider.

Burbridge named the spot. 'Psyche is a relative of Millicent's, and of course will go. Tomorrow is a holiday, anyway, and the gathering is to be on Palmyra. I am not supposed to know; if I knew officially I might have to report it. But during these Christmas holidays the slaves have freedom and even licence; it has been so for generations. It would be madness to try and interfere with them now.'

'You know,' observed Robert, 'it appears to me that you are as much afraid of these people as they are of you?'

'Of course, we are,' said Rider; 'it has been a case of fear on both sides. Fear is in the very texture of the mind of all the white people here; fear and boredom, and sometimes disgust. That is why so many of us drink, friend Rutherford.'

'I should like to see this exorcism, or whatever you may call it,' said Robert suddenly; 'it is strange that Takoo has not communicated with me.'

'You forget,' Rider reminded him, 'that he probably knows that you spent Thursday night at the Great House, after you had left his place near Montego Bay. He may have misunderstood that. Even if he did not, he may think it wisest to keep Millicent's whereabouts as secret as possible for the present, though this *myal* or exorcism ceremony of his tomorrow night is too big an affair to be kept entirely secret.'

'But Annie promised me she would send for Takoo and do what she could for the girl,' mused Robert. 'I wonder if she has done it. If she has, why should it be necessary to have this African exorcism?'

'Has Mrs Palmer kept her word, I wonder?' muttered Rider.

'You think she hasn't?' asked Robert; 'but I believed she would do that at least. She left me no reason whatever to doubt that she would.'

'And if you asked her she might say that she tried, but that Takoo would not come to her,' Rider explained. 'How can we ever be certain as to what she will or won't do? We can only hope she will keep her word. Besides,' he added judicially, 'she may actually have sent for Takoo and he may have refused to obey her summons. He would be naturally suspicious, you know. He knows her, too, in some respects, far better than any of us do. Probably he has refused.'

They were silent for a little while, Robert recalling to his mind how carefully Annie had avoided even looking at him that afternoon. He recalled also that long and searching look she had given him yesterday when he bluntly refused, with finality in voice and manner, to take up his abode at the Great House. His heart sank. Could she have abandoned Millicent to her fate, after all? Then indeed the girl's chances of life might be slight, in spite of all that others might do to aid her.

Mr Rider seemed to guess something of what was passing in his mind. He placed a hand on Robert's knee. 'You have done all you could,' he said, 'and now we must leave the rest to Providence. Excuse my sanctimonious language; one can never wholly escape the influence of one's profession. You want to go to this exorcism, Rutherford?'

'I would like to, yes, if I could do so without being seen. I suppose the people would object to my presence?'

'They would, unless you consented to take part in the ceremony.'

'And that is—?'

'It is a thing no white man in Jamaica could do and retain his self-respect and the respect of any other white man,' said Rider decisively. 'You would become one of them, don't you understand, a devil worshipper or something very much like that. Not that many white men don't worship the Devil; I think he is the prevailing deity out here. But they don't do it along with negro slaves, dancing and moaning, contorting themselves and grovelling in all sorts of open abominations. There are different orders of devil worship. Mine is drink. But the obeah order – phew!'

'Is Annie Palmer any better than an obeahwoman?' demanded Robert with savage contempt: he had begun to suspect that she had tricked him.

'No; but she works in her own way, and that is the difference.'

'Yet you think I can see this ceremony?'

'If you are cautious. I will go with you; we may be able to hide ourselves and watch; at any rate we can try. Will you go with us, Burbridge?'

'No, my friend,' replied Burbridge. 'I am not even supposed to know about what is going to take place, and to witness it without trying to stop it would condemn me in the eyes of every proprietor in Jamaica. Your position is different from mine.'

'True,' laughed Mr Rider a little bitterly. 'I am at best but a temporary hand, and no one regards me as a responsible being. In another week I shall probably be at the drink again. And Rutherford can leave soon – as I am sure he has decided to do – and he'll be all the better for it. Well, as I don't count I can take risks, and in any case I know that my time on Rosehall is rapidly drawing to an end. Our lives may be rapidly drawing to an end also,' he added.

'We'll go tomorrow, then,' said Robert. 'That is decided.'

There came a rap at the door. A boy handed a note to Robert. It was from Annie. 'I have not been able to find Takoo,' it ran; 'he seems to be keeping out of sight.'

CHAPTER 17

The Arrangement

CHRISTMAS DAY dawned cool and bright, the wind coming in briskly from the sea which, stirred and fretted by it, flashed and sparkled in a glory of green and purple and broke in noisy billows upon the shore. The burnished surfaces of long green leaves, narrow spears of the cane plants, and of swaying fronds of palms, reflected back the sunlight, so that the whole earth seemed bathed in splendour and steeped in flaming light.

There was brightness everywhere; every object was suffused with it. In the hollows of the hills which formed the background to the land- and sea-scape in the midst of which was Rosehall, masses of mist had rolled and ascended and floated about an hour before, shrouding the view and spreading like a soft wide cloud; but soon this mist had melted away before the triumphant progress of the sun which had swiftly transformed the opal and faint pink of the morning sky into a dazzling blue. The tang of the salt sea was in the air, poinsettia trees and other flowering plants flamed red in the sunshine in which they rejoiced. And though noises broke the stillness, noises shrill and piercing, dominant, insistent, they were not those of labour but had a special implication of their own.

For this morning no horn or conchshell sounded its far-carrying melancholy note to summon the slaves to their daily task. No crack of driver's whip or harsh command was heard. In the pastures the cattle stood idle, from the chimneys of the boiling-house arose no smoke. Banked were the fires today, and banked would they remain for some three days. In the negro village on the estate men and women wandered about at will. Their time was theirs to do with entirely what they wished.

The Christmas holidays had come, the three days of grace which were given to the people by law, to pass in frolic and in merry-making, or in complete rest.

Even as Rutherford gazed from his room upon the scene outside, striving hard to realize that this was Christmas, he caught sight of a crowd of people who came towards the book-keepers' quarters, singing and dancing. Burbridge joined him, and together they waited to see what would happen.

At sight of the white men the crowd raised a cheer and came hurrying onwards. Arrived, they stood displayed as a variety of figures, some utterly ludicrous, others rather tastefully attired in garments of variegated colours, and every one of them as cheerfully vociferous as if none had a care in the world. Two of them had got themselves up as animals. One was garbed in a dried cow's skin, with the horns towering upon his head and the tail sticking out behind; he leaped and bellowed as though he were a bull in pain, though probably he intended to impersonate a bull in ecstasy. Another one had rigged himself up as a horse, with mane and head complete, and he capered about upon his two legs neighing merrily, whirling round and round, and kicking out with feet that were quite human and bare. Some of the performers wore masks, hideous things, devil faces, with grinning teeth, elongated noses, and other fantastic appurtenances. But there were also a number of young girls, clothed all in red, with their robes trimmed with lace, and with flaunting feathers in their beaver hats, and these were headed by a leader, or Queen, who took herself very seriously indeed and gave commands to her subjects of a day with quick, imperious voice. Robert knew that in these red girls he saw a Jamaica 'Set', and that other 'Sets', Reds and Blues respectively, would be dancing about the towns of Jamaica during the next couple of days. These girls before him, Burbridge said, would be going down to Montego Bay tomorrow to take part in the promenading there and to uphold the honour of the Reds against the Blues, with as much zeal (Robert imagined) as did the rival factions in the ancient Roman circus. The Red Set represented the soldiers of the King, the Blues stood for the sailors, and between the two there was a mighty rivalry. The Rosehall people were Reds; just why, they themselves did not know. It had been so for years, and so, therefore, it must continue to be.

The red-clothed girls were now dancing quite gracefully for the amusement of the white men, and when Mr Rider came up, as he did presently, they hailed him as 'parson', hesitated as if in doubt as to how he would take their gyrations on a Sunday, and then went on with redoubled vigour when they noticed that he neither looked nor spoke disapproval. From the estate village opposite came the throbbing of drums, and there too the festivities were in full progress. True, it was Sunday, and the missionaries in this parish had sought to impress upon the people that Christmas Day, falling as it did upon the first day of the week, should be spent decorously, in prayer and in thanksgiving for the great deliverance which the Lord was about to work for his faithful followers. But the spirit of Christmas had seized upon these people, and, anyhow, missionaries had never been encouraged to visit Rosehall. Consequently the musicians pounded their drums with energy, shrill pipes emitted weird sounds, human bulls and horses, and Red Set girls, and shuffling couples, moved and whirled to the tunes given forth, and shouted, screamed, jested and laughed, and enjoyed themselves immensely.

In the village the cooking fires were already alight. There was to be a feast that day. And yet everyone knew that Christmas was not celebrated on Rosehall as it ought to be and as it was on other estates. The custom was that, in the Christmas holidays, the owners or their attorneys should give a great dinner to all the slaves, a dinner consisting of roast meat, and cakes and rum and other delicacies. He should throw open the Great House to his people, and in the big drawing-room they should be allowed to dance the whole Christmas night away. More, he too was expected to dance with them, he and the other white men on the estate. There was always a wild fraternization on this particular occasion: all differences were ignored, all caste distinctions set aside. It was the rule, and though this year there were not many estates in St James where this rule was being observed, it had always been done, and in other parts of the island the custom was still held in respect. But Rosehall was different. It had long been so. Mrs Palmer had not had her people up to the Great House since the death of her first husband; since then there had been no special Christmas feast for them; she had not put herself out in any way to make this her day of rejoicing with them.

This ignoring of an established West Indian custom had affected her white employees also; she held them, even at Christmas time, at arm's length. Mr Ashman might have prevented this to a certain extent; had he chosen to carry out the rule of Christmas kindliness and consideration, Annie Palmer would not have prevented him. So long as she herself was not directly inconvenienced it would not have mattered to her what was done; it was not the extra expenditure that influenced her to indifference and neglect. But Ashman himself was indifferent; he knew he was not liked by white or black on the property and did not see why he should put himself to any trouble to facilitate them when he was not directly instructed by the mistress to do so. Two days before Christmas he had distributed to each of the slaves the few yards of cloth for dress which the law demanded should be given once a year. And the few pounds of salted fish, and the straw hat, to each, and the needles and the thread: all these had been handed out. But the law said nothing about a Christmas dance and a Christmas feast, though public opinion, white public opinion, held that they formed part of the rights, or at least the privileges, of all the bond people.

So, this Christmas, the chief mechanic and the chief carpenter of Rosehall (who superintended the work done in their respective lines on Palmyra estate also) had gone off to Montego Bay for the day and Mr Ashman would dine alone, for he had not been bidden as in times past to the Great House for Christmas cheer. The dancing crowd had come from Ashman's house, where they had gone to wish him a merry Christmas, to which he had made some sort of response. He had risen to the occasion otherwise and donated to them sundry bottles of liquor and a ham, and he had given them a few pieces of money. He might despise or dislike them, but he did not relish the idea that they should regard him as 'a stingy backra', a parsimonious white man. Here was the joint in his armour. They could pierce his pride and his vanity here. And they knew it.

Now they were come to do the honours to the book-keepers and to reap their reward. Of course, they should first have gone up to the Great House with their greeting and their dance, but Mrs Palmer did not care to be disturbed early on any morning, unless she had given the word to be called betimes. And the dancers and musicians felt that she cared little about this annual function of theirs. It would take place outside the Great House later on, however, and she would come out on the porch and watch their antics, and she would make the presents that were expected of her. For even Annie Palmer, indifferent to so much else, could not have brought herself to refuse these people the gratuity which the Christmas dancing drew from every other white planter in the country. She might neglect the annual ball, punish them severely for ordinary misdemeanours, terrify them, do things in their sight which others might wish to hide from them. But she would not let them go from her presence on Christmas Day without a gift. There are certain acts that no one can dare to be guilty of and escape self-contempt. No one can completely rise above the influence of one's time and its implicit obligations.

Rider had little to give to these merry-makers, but what he had he knew must be offered freely. Burbridge was in not much better case. But the financial difficulties of the situation were solved by Robert who, when he thought they had seen enough of the dancing and heard quite a sufficiency of cacophony, threw a handful of silver among the crowd. This caused on the instant a wild scramble, in which the horse and the bull joined, these incontinently flinging off their disguises so as the better to snatch at the rolling coins. It was a fairly large sum that Robert flung to them, more than they would get from any other single source. When, after much jostling, pushing, swearing and screaming every coin had been picked up, and the crowd, with a loud 'Merry Christmas, massa' and 'God bless you, massa,' had pirouetted away, the three men went inside to drink the egg-punch, the flip of beaten egg and rum, with nutmeg, which was the regular Christmas morning draught and which Psyche had prepared steaming hot, prior to the preparation of the coffee.

But Rider would not have any rum in his flip. And the other two did not press him to make an exception of this Christmas wassail.

Burbridge had invited Robert and Rider to share pot luck with him today. Dinner would be eaten at one o'clock. Psyche had claimed, not without reason, to be able to prepare a plum pudding.

When the dinner hour drew nigh they met on the veranda as usual, and began talking about the Rosehall Christmas and the festival's celebration elsewhere in the island. To Robert it seemed a miracle that a people known to be discontented, and said to be on the eve of a demonstration, should yet seem happy as had the slaves of the estate that morning; their conduct, in view of what was imagined about their intentions, did not appear to him to be reasonable.

It was Rider who pointed out to him that these slaves believed implicitly that sufficient to the day would be the evil thereof; meantime they took what came to them. 'They may be frenzied rebels tomorrow,' he said, 'but today is today, so they dance and enjoy themselves. I don't know but they are right.'

Just then Psyche announced in a triumphant tone of voice that dinner was ready, the Christmas feast that was to be eaten hours earlier than the dinner of any ordinary day.

They sat down to it, though Robert felt no inclination for festive repasts. He had to be of the company, however, if for no other reason than that he had insisted upon furnishing for it some madeira for which he had sent to Montego Bay on the Christmas Eve.

Psyche's mother had been a cook, and Psyche had inherited a genius for cooking. More important perhaps than this inheritance, she had been taught by her mother to cook, and her abilities in this respect was one reason why Burbridge always felt that in her he possessed a treasure. Ordinarily she had no opportunity of displaying her skill, but on rare occasions like this Psyche was able to do herself justice, and today she had done herself more than justice. She gave them little oysters picked up with peppered vinegar. She served fish seasoned with slices of onions and rich butter sauce; her roast beef was tender and juicy and of noble flavour; her roasted guinea hen was done to perfection. And her plum pudding, with hot rum-and-butter sauce, was the real Jamaican plum pudding, black with fruit and flavoured with good old rum. On the table were rum and madeira, the rum tempered with cool coconut water, which at this time of day was better than lime-juice and sugar.

Mr Rider's eyes glowed with appreciation as the feast proceeded, and when Robert, thoughtlessly, asked him to have some wine his eyes snapped and he was about to accept. Then, with great effort, he mastered his impulse. 'Better not, Rutherford,' he said. 'The time is coming, I am afraid, when I shall not be able to refuse, and I don't feel like refusing even now. But if I touch the stuff today I may be done for during the next couple of weeks, or longer. I may go on drinking as long as there is anything to drink, and there is plenty here. Still, one glass mightn't hurt me perhaps – eh, what do you say? But no, better not. I want to see tonight what is going to happen: you know what I mean. I am afraid that if I once taste that wine—'

'Very good,' said Robert hastily; 'and I, too, don't think I should have anything to drink. Fact is, I have been taking far too much since I have been here. There hasn't passed a day when I haven't drunk something strong, and lots of it some days. I drink too much.'

'We all do,' said Burbridge, 'that is the custom here; and today being Christmas, I am not prepared to abstain. I have not been abstaining. If it were not for that wretched woman up at the House we should be able to enjoy our Christmas as we should. She is the bane of our lives!'

'Just as all roads lead to Rome,' smiled Rider, 'so do all Burbridge's remarks now tend towards Mrs Palmer, in an uncomplimentary fashion. But he is right; strange as it is, we are all undoubtedly affected this Christmas Day by her actions.'

Robert nodded his head in gloomy acquiescence. This turn of the conversation expressed his own mood. This could not be a merry Christmas party for any man with humane impulses and feelings. And though he had just said he didn't think he should take any liquor, he mechanically stretched out his hand for some wine, and continued to drink during dinner.

He knew that Burbridge was not allowing anything to disturb him; Burbridge had long since grown hardened to sights and sounds and actions that must have shocked and disgusted him once upon a time. But Rider was different; periodical drunkard though he was, his heart remained tender, not in a maudlin but in a real and true sense, and he had a gentleman's instinct for fair play and generosity. As for himself, Robert realized now that he had come to have a genuine liking for the unfortunate young woman who had so quaintly and boldly, without meaning to be forward, insisted upon installing herself as his housekeeper. That, he felt with genuine sorrow, was scarcely a crime to be punished almost with madness and perhaps by actual death. She was naïve, foolish maybe, impetuous and reckless. Something of a savage. But bad and corrupt – no, he knew she was not that.

The meal ended quietly. Yet Psyche was, on the whole, well satisfied, for if Massa Rutherford was silent and showed but a poor appetite, Psyche knew the reason, and as Millicent was her cousin, she felt that this loss of appetite was a fitting tribute to the condition of a member of her family.

Dinner over, the men again repaired to their veranda, where Burbridge tilted his chair against the wall, placed his feet against the railing, and very soon fell asleep. Rider and Robert were less somnolent, yet they too felt lethargic, depressed, burdened each by his own weight of thought, and not perhaps unaffected by the early Christmas meal. There were occasions when the meaning of his fallen estate came to Rider with a peculiar poignancy; today he felt his position with a more than exquisitely unpleasant keenness. Yet, he said to himself, it might actually have been worse. He knew he was helping young Rutherford, and he might be able to aid Millicent also: that was possible. So he was not quite useless, not utterly an outcast. And maybe, he thought, some day he might be able to give up the drink altogether; just as he could refuse it today, so he might be able to refuse it altogether in the future. But in his heart of hearts he doubted his strength.

When the thirst came upon him it was fierce and raging, not to be suppressed. He would believe sometimes that he had the craving under control at last, and would begin to plume himself upon that, when, suddenly, he was gripped by it and then would sell his shirt for a drink. Many such experiences had rendered him cynical about his resolutions; yet every now and then he would make such resolutions. Even while gravely doubting, he half believed, and at the root of this belief was hope. Today it came into his mind that perhaps, if he could get back to England, he might be able to open another and better chapter of his life. He thought of Robert; he too, if he remained in Jamaica, might become, if not an outcast (for he had means), at any rate a poor specimen of a man; he had seen such things. Robert would have a good career at home. It was better that he should return as quickly as possible. Even supposing that this girl, Millicent, whose paternal grandfather had been a gentleman and a man of authority in the country, should recover, that would actually not be for Rutherford's good, unless he resolutely refused to remain in Jamaica. A lifelong liaison with the girl, and children, and drink, and no real obligation to work (which might mean more drink and other liaisons), what was there in all this save the deterioration of a young fellow who had fine instincts and was a gentleman? In the tropics some men throve; those were the men of stern fibre or of a sort of brutal hardness. These tropics, with their large servile population and small aristocracy of proprietors who lived in a world of the narrowest mental and moral horizons – what a horror they actually were! If they did not become physically the white man's grave, they formed for him as deadly a spiritual sepulchre. It was death anyway.

'Why don't you go back home, Rutherford?' he asked, apparently apropos of nothing, turning to watch how the young man would take his suggestion.

'That is exactly what I was thinking of,' replied Robert, somewhat surprised. 'It is as if you had read my thoughts.'

'I am glad to hear it,' said Rider. 'This is hardly the sort of place for you. If you go to Barbados later on, you know, you will go as the head, and then conditions will be different. But here—!'

'I don't think Barbados will ever see me,' asseverated the younger man; 'I have had enough of all of this "eternal sunshine and happy, laughing people". I can almost hear some of them laughing from here, they scream so loud. And yet it would not take much to make them cut all our throats, if what you yourself believe is true.'

'It is true,' said Rider, nodding his head decisively.

'Well, that's just it. These slave tropics may look and sound mighty fine on the surface, but they are nastily dangerous underneath. Yes; I have come to the determination that they don't suit me. But neither do they suit you, Rider.'

'I know that,' answered the other simply; 'I found that out long ago.'

'Then why didn't you leave?'

'I suppose I drifted along till it was too late. I had nothing to return to, you see; I feared that if I went back to England there would no longer be a place there that I could make for myself. Once here, I was in a sort of prison. Turn me out into the free world again, and I should be at my wits' end. It was all cowardice and weakness, of course; and something worse. The life here, for a man like me, was infinitely easier than it could be in England. My duties were light, my pay was sufficient to keep me, and I could do what I pleased to a great extent without being called to account for it. I liked the life, at first; I didn't realize what it was leading me to. I liked the drink; I didn't grasp that it was making me a drunkard. When I did, I was down. And here am I. But you – as Burbridge is always saying – with you it is quite different.'

'I am going,' said Robert resolutely; 'I have been coming to that conclusion, and I have decided within the last ten minutes. But I think you are wrong about yourself. You could go back – now. And now is the best time to go.'

'I cannot walk upon the wild waves, my dear boy, and sea captains do not give passages for nothing. And if I sent the hat round the results would be trifling, and I should suffer the shame of having begged in vain. Not that Englishmen are not sent home by their friends; they are. But I have no friends, and my few acquaintances would believe (and could not be blamed for believing) that I had merely fallen back upon a quite unoriginal method of raising drinks.'

He spoke flippantly to disguise the seriousness of his feeling.

'I have thought of that,' said Robert; 'I wouldn't have mentioned the matter if I hadn't. But you can get the money for your expenses without any difficulty. I can advance it to you.'

Rider looked at him with a peculiar expression on his face.

'Advance?' he said. 'You really mean that you will *give* me the money.'

'I couldn't offer a man like you money,' returned Robert, somewhat embarrassed; 'but once you were in England it would not be difficult for you to repay it.'

'You are offering it to me in the nicest way you can think of,' said Rider quietly. 'You mean that if I can repay it I may; if I can't, you won't mind that. It's deuced decent of you, Rutherford, and I thank you with all my heart.'

'Then you will go?'

'Gladly. That is—'

'What?'

'If my resolution holds. If I don't go back so badly to the drink before we can start, that I won't be able to do the little things necessary and take myself to the ship.'

'That will be all right,' said Robert. 'We'll go together, and even if you are drunk I will carry you on board. I am strong enough to do that literally, you know.' He smiled as he spoke, but Rider knew he was in earnest.

'Good. It is agreed then. I might almost say that your coming to Jamaica was providentially designed in my interests, Rutherford; I should see a miracle in this thing if I were not disposed to be sceptical about any modern miracle. By Jove! To think that I might actually see the Old Country again! Might? I am going to! This is farewell to Jamaica for me.'

He fell to silence, thinking over this wonderful, unexpected stroke of good fortune. It was almost too good to be true.

Robert rose. 'I am going over yonder,' said he, pointing in the direction of the negro village, 'to see how those folk are enjoying themselves. They seem to be having high jinks.'

'And you had better get a couple of hours' sleep when you come back,' advised his companion. 'We may be up all night.'

Robert nodded and went off on foot, leaving Rider to think over alone the new prospect that he opened out before him. Rider knew it was through a feeling of delicacy that Rutherford had left him to himself.

CHAPTER 18

The Exorcism

THE THROBBING OF DISTANT DRUMS came to their ears; it waxed and waned, rolled and staccatoed, seemed to die away, and then began again.

Other like sounds came to their hearing, from south and east and west, but Rider and Robert Rutherford pushed steadily on in the direction of this particular faint muttering and rumbling sound from the south, for Rider had carefully inquired his way and knew that he was right in persisting in his course.

'The other drummings are for dances,' he explained; 'it may be Sunday night, but the people are making merry, though perhaps not so much so as they would have done a few years back. You could easily be misled by all these contradictory noises, but I know the way. I fancy that where we are going has been often used before for some startling ceremonies.'

They were both on foot. Horses might have betrayed their presence once they had arrived; indeed they might have been observed long before they could arrive. But Rider hoped that, by keeping within the shadow of the trees, they would not attract any attention. Many persons were moving about tonight, and it would not be strange if two white men should be seen abroad, so long as they were not noticed when close to the site of the projected exorcism.

The moon had risen. It was growing full-orbed. Preoccupied with his own affairs as he was, Robert had yet watched it night after night as it had increased in size and splendour, as it had grown from a slender sickle attended by one lustrous star, brightening in the west as the sun went down and then suddenly flashing into radiance with the swift dramatic coming of the tropical darkness, until it had become a globe of silver sailing serenely among the lesser lights which paled and disappeared as it pursued its progress to the sea. He had seen it bathe the looming hills and fields of cane in a soft argent glow, had seen the answering glimmer from the metallic inner surface of the multitudinous leaves, and had, unconsciously, been touched and moved by the beauty of the scene, so unlike anything he had ever known before. Tonight, however, he gazed at the moon with somewhat different feelings. It was like a lantern set up for the illumination of the earth, and they did not want to be seen. They were shunning observation. Darkness would be their kindest friend tonight. But even as he thought, a mass of cloud, materializing swiftly out of the shining blue, floated across the face of the moon and everything grew crepuscular, sombre, as though a dark shroud had been flung across the world. Presently the moon struggled out from behind the shadow, but now Robert noticed that here and there in the sky were other small banks of drifting cloud.

'Looks as if it were going to rain,' he said to Rider.

'It is quite likely it may rain later on; there has been a feel of it in the air for hours. Clouds are gathering. Even if it doesn't rain we shall have spells of darkness soon,' Rider answered.

'I am hoping for that. I am wondering what would happen to us if these obeah people caught us spying on them.'

'They wouldn't harm us physically tonight, unless they were ready for an instant outbreak, which is not probable,' said Rider. 'But they would scatter; they would never allow us to see them breaking the law. Besides, they are keenly alive to ridicule, to contemptuous laughter: that is the one thing that these people shrink from. They may think we are foolhardy to flout ghosts and devils, yet when we laugh at them for their belief in such things they have an unpleasant feeling that they look like children or simpletons, and they are not happy. So they hide their faith and their curious cults from the eyes of the white man, though when a manifestation of these cults takes the form of a little poison in one's morning coffee, the African's religion becomes a very serious matter.'

'And they do poison?' asked Robert, thinking of what he had heard about old Takoo.

'Now and then, but only the desperate and really dangerous characters. The majority are safe enough to trust that way. When you consider their condition, and that they have set their hearts for years on becoming free, the wonder is that they have never attempted to wipe us out wholesale. You could hardly blame them if they did.'

They had now left Rosehall; they had ascended the low hills behind that estate, and were making their way carefully very near to where the principal cultivations of the bondspeople were; they had followed a trail made and used mainly by the slaves who had their plantations among these hills. The custom of the country, now reinforced by law, was that each slave should cultivate a small piece of his owner's land for his own family's sustenance. At least one half-day a fortnight, and more commonly a half-day a week, was allowed him for this purpose. The lands thus set aside were situated at some distance from that part of the estate farmed for the proprietor's benefit and were usually among the surrounding eminences which could not economically be put under cane, or of which the soil was poor. Here, of a Saturday afternoon, would be found crowds of the people, hoeing the ground, weeding at the roots of the growing crops, digging holes for the planting of the yam or the potato in its season, making provision, in short, against anything like famine. Thus they in reality supported themselves by their labour, and here, as in every other rank of human society, differences made themselves plainly apparent.

For some of these people only worked as much as was necessary to ensure that they should have what foodstuffs they would need, while others took particular pains to get the most that they could out of the not very fertile soil. The latter wrestled with the earth and from it drew, not only sustenance but some degree of wealth. There were thousands of free blacks all over the country; there had been for decades. These had purchased their freedom with money gained by selling the surplus of their products, the yield of their little fields. Everything that they produced was theirs by custom and the force of public opinion; long since it had been found that if this were not to be so there would be very little effort put forth by the slaves on these plots of land. The price of a slave had steadily risen in the last twenty or thirty years, and still men and women bought their freedom by hard work and thrift. Takoo had done so some forty years ago. And Takoo, by what he made out of lands that he had since acquired by cash purchase, and even more by what he had been paid by awestruck people who went to him covertly for aid against dark supernatural powers (or for means to bring those powers to do their will), had accumulated what was for him and those in his position a respectable fortune. Most of what he had he intended for Millicent. He had said so openly. He had determined that she should be respected by all of her class and those below it, looked up to as a young woman of wealth, regarded as a superior, treated with deference. He had succeeded in this aim; he was proud of his success because he was proud of her. But in the last few days his pride had given place to a horrible fear. And tonight he would know whether he had toiled all these years to good purpose or in vain.

The moon shining out brightly just when they were passing by a clearing, Rider with a gesture drew Robert's eyes to some peculiar objects hung on trees here and there among the little plantations. Tiny bags were a few of these, others again were miniature bundles tied with dried tendrils or with string; one or two were the skulls of animals, cats they seemed.

'Protective charms,' he explained. 'There are thieves everywhere, and these cultivations are left for days together with no one near them. They would be entirely at the mercy of predatory persons but for such obeah charms. There is hardly a man within a radius of twenty miles who would venture here by day or night to rob these provision grounds. He would believe that the magic inherent in the charms would work him harm. He might even think that a special ghost, perhaps a relative of the owner, haunted the particular ground he had robbed, and then his state would be almost as bad as Millicent's and he would have to pay some obeahman heavily to take the ghost off him. His plight would be worse if it were the spirit of a child that was plaguing him; child ghosts seem to be particularly vicious.' Rider laughed, but somewhat sadly. 'You may from this gather an idea of the difficulties which a practising parson has to contend with in this country. The irony of it is that some of them hardly ever guess what is going on under their very noses.'

Thrum, thrum, drrrrrummm; thrum, thrum, drrrrrummm; the noise was nearer now. They had left the slave cultivations and were going through a wood. These two men were not accustomed to walking in the tropics, but the night was cool and excitement held them; they were conscious of no fatigue. The umbrageous trees reached high above their heads, their branches swishing gently as the wind went through them. Sometimes they thought they heard a movement near at hand, as though some heavy body were stealing parallel to them at no distance to speak of. It might be imagination, they argued, since the negroes would move about in groups on a night like this, and would certainly be talking among themselves. But whatever it was, these sounds were weird and thrilling. It came to Robert's mind that they might almost have been the rustling of the shrouds of the dead who had risen from their graves to assist at a ritual whereby a struggle was to be conducted against the powers of darkness.

'Slow now, and be careful that our voices are not heard.' Rider's admonition was whispered, and peering in front of him Robert could see a gleam between the tree trunks; noticed too that the gleam came from some open space beyond, and heard a wailing chant that mingled with the beating of the drums.

They stole forward quietly, until they must stop or shortly reveal their presence. Their point of vantage was good. Trees shielded them, and they stood in shadow. About twenty yards away a concourse of people crouched upon the ground, form-ing a rude circle, and within this circle blazed a great fire which hissed and crackled and threw fierce sparks upwards and brought into fiery relief the strained, staring faces of the men and women from whose lips streamed forth an eerie, curious sound. Bodies swayed to right and left in unison with the rhythm of that chant, and the drum-throbs marked the cadences of the hymn of exorcism. It was nothing that even Rider had ever heard before, no Christian words or air; it was something that had come out of Africa and was remembered still. There were people in the swaying crowd who had been born in Africa, and in their minds and emotions they had travelled back to that dark continent tonight and were worshipping again some sinister deity with power and will to harm, one to be propitiated with sacrifice and who would not be turned aside from his designs by mere appeals and prayers for mercy.

It was nearly midnight. For over an hour must this chant have continued; for over an hour must these people have squatted there on the bare, damp earth, watching the roaring flames, singing, singing in that low monotonous voice, and waiting for what was to happen. A shudder passed through Robert; to his surprise he found that he too was slightly moving his body to the rhythm of the sound. Rider had himself better in hand, but the hypnotic influence of the scene did not leave him entirely unaffected. It had an appeal to the more primitive emotions. It stirred up something in the depths of one's being. He could understand how devotees in pagan lands were moved at times almost to madness by the call and compulsion of their strange and horrible religions.

The roll and throb of the drums went on. Suddenly a wild burst of laughter rent the air and a young woman in the first row of the crowd pitched forward on her face, crying and laughing convulsively, twitching her limbs as in a fit. Hysterics had seized her, her nerves had given way; probably this was the first time she had participated in such an orgy, probably she knew Millicent and was filled with fear for herself, for who could be free from danger? But no one took any notice of her; only the tempo of the chant quickened, there was a note of exultation in it now. There were to be wonderful manifestations tonight, and the spirits of the older hierophants rejoiced and revelled in the anticipation of what was to come. Not often did they dare to practise thus the ritual of an obscene faith, the magic of Old Africa. The law forbade it, and the masters struck at it with an iron hand.

To one side of the fire was a bench, parallel to the right of the two hidden men, but just now it was unoccupied. Robert scanned the crowd keenly for some glimpse of Millicent and her grandfather; they were nowhere to be seen. He noticed, however, that at the farther opposite curve of the circle of human beings the crowd was not packed closely together. One could walk to and fro there without much difficulty. Behind it was a dense darkness created by the trees. Somewhere there, he concluded, Millicent was waiting.

It was midnight. No stroke of bell announced the hour; yet he knew it must be so, for at that instant, at a signal from a woman clothed in white, the chanting ceased. There was a deathly silence, a silence broken only by the crackling and spluttering of blazing wood. Then, where the people crouched sparsely, a lane was rapidly made, and from among the sheltering trees came a girl, walking with stiff, short steps, and a tall, gaunt man behind her. He himself was followed by a youth who bore something in his arms.

From the waist down Millicent was wrapped in a robe of purest white. The upper part of her body was bare, her breasts and arms were exposed completely. Her hair was covered, also with white, and where the blister had appeared on her chest was marked with white. Takoo was clothed from head to foot in flaming red, robed as a high priest of Sassabonsum or some other potent god of the African forests. In this robe of office he loomed taller than Robert or Rider had ever seen him before, and there was dignity in his gait and a gloomy earnestness in his gaze that seemed to inspire that crouching, silent audience with awe. Millicent had been given her instructions; she skirted the fire, reached the bench, and quietly sat down upon it. Her grandfather placed himself directly behind her. The boy who followed him stood by his side, and now it was seen that what he carried was a snow-white kid.

As the little group took up its position the chanting recommenced. But now it was louder, quicker, frenzied; now it was a passionate invocation, and the fire leaped higher as more fuel was thrown upon it, and the swaying people became wildly agitated fanatics, sweat pouring from their bodies, foam flecking the lips of not a few. Louder and louder rose the voices; and when the sound had reached its fullest volume, its wildest crescendo, the voice of Takoo thundered out some words, and in the midst of all that tempest of sound it seemed he could be heard. His tones dominated the others as did his stature, and the wild look in his eyes, and the sweeping gestures he was now making with his arm. But the gaze of Robert and Rider was fixed on the unhappy girl who sat staring into the fire, hardly conscious of what was proceeding around her, pale in that leaping light, with lines of fatigue and terror stamped upon her face. She looked as though she it was who would be the sacrifice to be offered up that night.

Robert turned sick, clutched Rider's arm. He whispered: 'This is awful, Rider, it should be stopped. That girl will die of exposure if nothing else; and it is all so vilely heathenish. I cannot look on any more.'

'You dare not interfere,' whispered Rider quickly. 'It would spoil all that they are trying to do, and it is very real to them. If anything happened now through us, they would say that we had robbed Millicent of her one chance of life.'

'But this, this—!'

'Do you want to go?'

Robert did not answer, but fixed his eyes again on the scene before him. He found that he did not want to leave.

He saw Takoo plunge his right hand into the fold of his robe and withdraw it. His left hand he held over Millicent's head; he seemed to be sprinkling her with some powder. More than once he repeated this movement, every member of that crowd, save only the young woman who still lay prostrate upon the ground, watching him with intent eyes. Again his voice rose in that thunderous chant, and at a signal from him the others ceased their singing and only he continued; he was a man born to command, his look showed that, and his imperious dominating voice.

Such a man must have been Christophe, King of Haiti, the slave who rose to the governance of the north of Haiti, and who had died by his own hand but a few years before, when at last, stricken and helpless, he knew that the people he had ruled were marching against him with death in their hearts. But here Takoo could rule only by stealth and through fear of his supernatural gifts. And tonight he was calling upon his gods for personal aid, for succour; he was a suppliant and he knew that he might be striving against powers that were mightier than he.

He ceased. Silence fell again, intenser, more breathless than before. It was as though everyone held his breath. The moment of sacrifice had come.

With his left hand Takoo slowly took the kid from the boy, and the little creature bleated pitifully. He grasped it by the head, holding it over Millicent, while it kicked swiftly in a vain effort to free itself. From beneath his robe he had drawn a long, shining knife and this he waved in a sort of ritual for a moment or two. Then, with a swift movement, he thrust it into the animal's throat.

The blood spurted in a hot stream upon the body of the girl and a hoarse cry burst from the people. Deftly the old man laved Millicent with the gushing blood, and now there was no rhythm in the sounds that came from the lips of that crowd, but fierce, delirious howls and shouts, ejaculations of frenzy, a wild medley of cries. And Takoo was shouting too, at the full range of his sonorous voice he was charging the evil things that had taken possession of Millicent to leave her, to depart forever, to be banished from her neighbourhood everlastingly. He had sacrificed, the victory was his, he proclaimed triumphantly; his power was greater than that of anyone who had brought his granddaughter to this state: the battle was won and the girl was free.

And then, startlingly incongruous at such a gathering, a new cry rose upon the air and was heard above the shouting. It came from the voices of a dozen people who had leapt to their feet, and the word cried aloud was 'O Christ!'

For the first time since these people had assembled the name of Christ was uttered. It was shrieked out in an agony and spasm of fear. Men and women who had sprung upright were pointing in one direction with outstretched arms. Their motion attracted universal attention and from Robert's lips also came that same exclamation – 'O Christ!'

For there, about the spot whence Millicent and the witch doctor had emerged into the light, stood the grotesque figure of a mighty, ill-shapen bull, twice the natural size of any creature that these people had ever seen, and about its neck hung a chain that glowed as though it were of fire, and its eyes were like balls of fire as they rolled menacingly in the hideous head. The brute pawed the ground slowly as it stared at the gibbering crowd, it was as though it were about to advance upon them. But they waited for no more. It all happened in a moment or two. Everyone was on his or her feet. Through the trees they all rushed, screaming; vainly, Takoo, for a brief instant, sought to stay them; they did not heed him, did not even see or hear him; their one thought, their only impulse, was to flee to safety. And as they fled Robert heard the words, 'Rolling Calf!' And still the monster stood there, though already it seemed to be vanishing.

Millicent had been lifted in Takoo's arms as soon as the old man realized that there was nothing to be gained by waiting. Fear was in his face also, though affection and pride would have impelled him to front even that devil that glared at him with eyes of fire; but he knew he was powerless alone. Millicent had to be conveyed away; at this spot there was imminent danger. With the girl in his arms the old man disappeared among the trees. Then Rider and Robert saw that there was nothing whatever there: the huge bull had also gone.

'Great God! What is the meaning of this?' cried Robert, though even in his agitation he remembered to subdue his voice. 'Rider, what does this mean? What was that devil? I could not have thought it possible; did these devil worshippers bring it out of the Pit?'

Rider smiled, a grim and mirthless smile. 'You heard what they said,' he whispered cautiously. 'It was what they call a Rolling Calf, an evil spirit or devil that is supposed to take the form of a gigantic bull. Even to see it is dangerous. To be attacked by it is certain death.'

'We have been in touch with hell tonight,' said Robert bitterly; 'it is all about us.'

'Hell is about us wherever we are,' rejoined Rider; 'but don't raise your voice. I believe that the chief devil is very close to us now.'

'That brute?' asked Robert quickly.

'No; that woman. The brute that we all saw, Robert, was, believe me, a figment of the imagination. It had no existence outside of the bad brain of the wickedest witch in this country. Don't you understand? Ssh! I thought so!'

Rider grasped Robert's arm to steady him. Into the now deserted space, where the fire still burnt brightly, stepped a slight figure clothed all in black and like a man. They knew it at once. There was no mistaking it.

Annie Palmer walked over to where Millicent had been sitting and looked down upon the dead body of the kid, which the crowd had been too startled to take away. Then she cast her eyes slowly round her, standing still for a minute, as though to listen for any sound that might indicate some watcher in the woods. She heard nothing. The men, holding their breath as they looked, saw her kick contemptuously the kid's carcass that lay at her feet; then she laughed. The utmost contempt was expressed in that peal of laughter, contempt and a consciousness of triumph. She turned and went the way she had come.

'She rode here; she must have left her horse out yonder,' said Rider, when he judged that she had done some distance. 'You see, I was right. She conjured up that vision to frighten the people and to terrorize that poor girl still further. Poor Millicent! I think this is the end of her now.'

'Good God! Is she dead?'

'That I don't know; but she might have seen that terrifying spectacle; everybody did. She knew it was not expected: so there could have been only one conclusion for her: it was sent to prove that she had not escaped, that everything her grandfather had done was so much time and effort wasted. Mrs Palmer must have heard of this exorcism; she has probably been having Takoo watched. And she knew when to come here too; she must have waited until she felt sure that everybody was here who was to attend: then she rode over and took her own time to strike. She has perhaps killed Millicent just as though she had stuck a knife into her. But killing doesn't come strange to her.'

'And she promised me to help!' exclaimed Robert.

'And deliberately broke her word. I always thought that possible. She suspected that, even if you had nothing more to do with Millicent, you would not remain with her. She was right there, too; but I also fancy she thought that if Millicent got better you would take up with her again. Annie doesn't believe in anyone. So she had taken no chances; and now she will lie to you. That's how the matter stands, to my thinking.'

'Rider, we must help Millicent.'

'If I could I would, gladly; but what are we to do?'

'I want to find out where they went tonight; if Takoo is convinced he has failed he may now be willing to try what a doctor can do. Psyche must find out where he is, and I am going to take this matter up with Annie. We have not failed yet.'

It had started to rain. Steadily the dark clouds overhead had gained in volume and depth; during the last half-hour the moon had shone but fitfully; then only pallid gleams had struggled through the veils of vapour; now the light had gone and every distant star was blotted out, and from the velvet black above came pattering down the heralds of the deluge to follow.

The rain fell slightly at first; a minute later it rushed earthwards in great splashing drops and buried everything around in pitchy, moving, almost palpable blackness. There was no seeing the path three feet ahead. But Rider knew the country, and so knew how to find himself about it at any hour of the night and day, though he had come this way but once before, and that but a couple of hours ago. They were drenched before they left the shelter of the wood; as they toiled over the hills on the other side of which lay Rosehall, they realized that they could not possibly get wetter than they were; but still they pressed on at as rapid a pace as the now slippery ground and the murk would allow, for they feared the chill and the paralysing fever which so often followed a wetting in these tropics. The walk was silent; they were too much occupied with the difficulties of their passage to attempt to talk; besides which, they would have had to shout in that roaring vertical torrent. Then, just as they reached the Rosehall boundary, the rain ceased as though it had been shut off by the turning of a faucet; ceased entirely; and the clouds, rapidly thinning, began to fade away into the ether; the blue sky shone bravely out once more, and the moon rode brilliant and bathed all heaven and earth with silver.

The transformation was complete, miraculously swift. Every object now stood out with distinctness, and wherever there was a declivity streams of water were rushing downward, muddy, brawling, while from the sea there swept landwards a delicious wind which, however, the sodden men could not appreciate since it struck coldness to their very bones and made them shiver. Robert plodded on, no longer now interested in phenomenona which, at some other time, he would not have failed to admire. Then something that Rider murmured caught his ear and sent a thought through his brain.

'After light darkness, and after darkness light,' said Rider. 'The light triumphs.'

'Yes, and it may be an omen, Rider,' commented the younger man. 'It seems so to me!'

'One comes to believe in omens in countries like this,' Rider agreed. 'We are always, consciously or otherwise, seeking for a sign.'

'It may be one,' insisted Robert, catching at any straw of hope and comfort.

'We part here,' said Rider; 'your way is before you, and I had better hurry to my den and get out of these clothes. Don't neglect to strip immediately you get inside and rub yourself down dry. Perhaps you had better swallow a mouthful of rum too; it will help to keep off the fever. Rum is a medicine when you are not so used to it that it can do nothing but fuddle your wits.'

Rider added that he would be with Robert as early as possible in the morning and went his way. Robert hurried on to his room, followed the advice of his friend, and then flung himself on his bed.

Wide-eyed he went over the incidents of the night. Again and again he said to himself that, if Rider was right, if that monstrous creature with the eyes of fire that he had seen had been merely the effect of Annie Palmer's will, then indeed she herself was a devil. And he was resolved to fight that devil. It was not only with an old superstitious African negro that Annie Palmer should have now to deal.

CHAPTER 19

Are You Not Afraid?

JAGGED NERVES and a physical frame taxed by the experiences of the previous night, notwithstanding, Robert abided by his resolution when, after but a couple of hours' sleep, he rose, shaved, bathed, and changed his clothes that same morning, for it was morning when he had thrown himself on his bed to think. At nine o'clock Rider made his appearance, and Robert informed him briefly what he intended to do. Rider did not look hopeful, but made no attempt to argue. He had some knowledge of human nature; he felt certain that it was better that the young man should be allowed to follow his own mind just now, whatever came of it.

At about ten o'clock Robert was at the Great House asking for Mrs Palmer. He was informed that she was still in bed, but would be down presently. He waited in the drawing-room for nearly half an hour, when she came in, clothed daintily in white, and if she was paler than usual she seemed otherwise no worse for her adventure of the night before.

'Have you come to wish me a merry Christmas the day after?' she inquired, taking a seat near to him. 'Or to what am I to attribute this visit?'

She was very calm, very collected, even formal; he gained an impression that she knew it was on no pacific mission he had come. He had an impression that she knew something of that reason and was prepared to have the matter out with him.

'No,' he said slowly, 'it is not to wish you a merry Christmas. You had a strange Christmas, but hardly a merry one. I know that.'

'Yes?'

'Yes. You made me a promise and broke it. You pledged me your word that you would try to rid that girl's mind of her obsession, and instead of that you increased it. You have lied to me, Annie, and quite probably you have killed a human being. That was your work last night. I can't conceive how it could have been merry work even for you; it was devilish work. I know all about it.'

'Indeed?'

'Yes. I saw you last night; I was there, just as you were there. You did not imagine that, did not expect it, did you? You thought you would tell me that you had done your best, and that I, being a fool, would believe you. But I know you now. There isn't a word of truth in you.'

She sat very still, clenching and unclenching her hands, her lips set tight, her eyes wide with rage. Then, to his great surprise, instead of rising and driving him from her presence, she began to laugh. There was contempt in her laugh. He always seemed to catch that contemptuous note these days.

'So you were at the negro ceremony for taking off ghosts, and you saw me there too, and you say that I have killed this slut of yours! What a clever soul you are at making deductions. I didn't see you, but what is to hinder me from saying that *you* have killed this girl? What did you see me do more than you did? Why, my dear man, I didn't even arrive until the people had all run away. If you were there you surely must know that.

I had a right to be there; that orgy was against the law. It was my duty to prevent or stop it. I suppose you know that.'

'I am not such a fool as you think,' he retorted sharply. 'That bull—'

'Well, that bull,' she prompted.

'Was your work. It was intended to increase Millicent's terror, to rob her of her last hope of freedom from the haunting of which she believes herself a victim.'

'Who told you that? For you did not arrive at that conclusion by yourself, did you? Who is this new "friend" of mine that puts ideas into your head, ideas which you are quite incapable of originating?'

He did not reply. She went on. 'Perhaps I can guess. Ashman tells me that you are very friendly now with Rider, and Mr Rider is a man who, when he is not drunk, believes he knows a lot. He goes at the end of this year; he would go today but that the law compels us to keep the full complement of white men required on the estate at a troublous time like this. Was Rider with you last night, Robert? Tell me what he thought of the result of his former years of preaching to the negroes: that was hardly a Christian service, was it?' She laughed again. 'And they seemed to have called up a ghost. Well, I believe in ghosts, and all these sacrifices must be efficacious in raising them. Are you going to hold me responsible for the meeting last night?'

'I hold you responsible for Millicent's condition,' he cried, 'and I have no doubt that you went to her aunt's house last Tuesday night to obeah her – that is the right word, and I am not going to beat about the bush any longer. You were seen to leave this place, a thing you had not done for many months. I saw you myself, and you had a boy with you. That boy is still here. Obeah, even if practised by a white woman, is against the law, and this time it means the life of a free fellow-creature.

Unless by this evening Millicent is on the way to recovery, Mrs Palmer, I am going to the magistrates of Montego Bay to lay a charge against you. And I shall go further. I shall urge that an inquiry be made into the death of your husbands. Takoo helped you there, I have heard it said, but Takoo is old; he loves his granddaughter, and if she dies he may think it worth while to turn king's evidence; he can plead fear and intimidation, and they are not likely to do anything to him if it can be shown – as I have no doubt it can be – that you were the actual murderess. Besides, I understand that two of the murders were committed by yourself alone. You will be placed in the dock charged with murder and with practising obeah with intent to cause death. Once you are arrested, the slaves here, whom you terrorize, will turn against you. Evidence will be found. You see what you have to expect, don't you? Now, will you agree to stop your evil work while there is time?'

Such a speech, spoken too in a grim and resolute manner, which left no doubt whatever that it was meant, Annie had never heard the like of in her life. Here was a charge deliberately brought against her by a white man, and for the first time she was told that men in authority in Montego Bay would hear it also, and she knew that if they did they might feel compelled to take some action. She looked long at Robert. Was this he who, but a couple of weeks before, was kissing her lips passionately, protesting her undying love for her, almost her slave? Panic seized her. Was her beauty waning, then, her power over men disappearing? For that would be the ultimate calamity! Or was it that this boy really loved the mulatto girl who had dared to become her rival? Her vanity would not admit that her beauty was less potent than before. This surely was another instance of a white man being bewitched by a native harpy, who, quite probably, wielded influence of a dangerous character through her grandfather's agency. Annie firmly believed in such influences.

It was clear. Here was a threat and challenge, and if she yielded Millicent must be victorious. The girl would have Robert; she had no doubt of that. He might say no, might believe what he said, but he was not as steadfast as he thought he was, and Millicent would have him in the end and be able to mock at Annie Palmer. And she, Annie Palmer, she would never give him up; he must be hers or— Better he were dead than the lover of a nigger girl! If she must go without him, so must every other woman – Millicent or any other.

She bent over, so that she seemed to huddle up on the sofa, and her eyes were fixed on the floor. She had tried persuasion, appeal, fascination. She had other and different weapons. Would they assist her? At least they could be tried. They must be, for her situation was desperate.

'I love you and you have threatened me,' she said softly. 'You have charged me with murder, and have promised to denounce me to the magistrates. Are you not afraid?'

'Afraid of what?'

'Of me.'

'No; you cannot harm me. I am not a superstitious Jamaica woman.'

'You are not. But you saw what the others saw last night, didn't you? And you believe that I called it up from its natural dwelling-place. You are right; I did, I sent it there on purpose; it obeyed my will. And you, white man though you are, educated man though you are, you too saw it and trembled, and had I decreed that it should appear in your own room at dead of night, it would have been there, Robert Rutherford. It will be there tonight if I will it.'

He laughed harshly. 'I know too much to take you seriously,' he said. 'Your spectral bulls and horses are nothing real; merely something you think up, and it seems that you must be on the spot before they can be seen. They are visions to frighten negroes and children. Tell what you have said to your slaves and not to me: you cannot frighten me.'

'No? One of my husbands said as much to me once. He is dead.'

'You killed him.'

'Let us agree that that is so. I can kill others, Mr Rutherford.'

'Only if they are in your power; but, remember, I am not. And perhaps the men you killed were never sufficiently on their guard. You are a woman, Mrs Palmer, and I hate to speak as I do to you, but it must be done. You know I mean what I say. If a change for the better has not taken place in that young woman's condition by this evening, tomorrow I go to the authorities with my story.'

She sprang up, standing close to him with flashing eyes and trembling lips.

'Go!' she cried. 'This comes of loving you, worshipping you, giving myself to you, offering to you everything I possess. Go! Tell your story. You will have cause to do so, for your woman dies! Do you hear? She dies! And God Himself could not save her. Tell your story and see what comes of it. The magistrates have trouble enough just now with threats of a slave rebellion in this parish. They will have plenty of time to attend to you! They will ask you for evidence, and you will produce a well-known obeahman whose granddaughter you have made your mistress and who you will say was bewitched by me through jealousy. A fine tale that will make, especially when told by a white man against a white woman. You fool! All evidence against me is buried these many years in my husbands' graves, and if you, a stranger here, or Rider, a drunken unfrocked clergyman, were to accuse me of obeah you would merely become the laughing stock of the country. The white people here still have some regard for their own class and reputation; they will know how to take your charges.'

'We'll see, Mrs Palmer. So you will do nothing for Millicent?'

'Go!'

'That is your last word?'

'Do you wish me to call some slaves to put you out of this house?'

'I wish I had never seen you,' he cried bitterly.

'And I – I hate the very day I saw you! Only a mean coward would have dared talk to me, a woman, as you have done. Only something less than a man would have left me for a thing such as you have selected. And if it will hurt you more to know that you are the real cause of her death, I tell you so now. Had you had nothing to do with her she could have lived until she withered so far as I was concerned. But even while you were pretending to love me, pretending that you were mine only, you had her with you, chattered to her about me, mixed my name in filthy conversations with her! Forgive that? What do you imagine I am? Forgive! I have only just begun; I am by no means near the end yet. Think of that when you go to her funeral!'

She was raging now; he wondered if she were quite sane. She had let herself go – her fury was uncontrollable. She took no care to keep her voice in restraint; she was storming. He caught up his hat hurriedly and strode out of the room. He rushed down the front steps, threw himself upon his horse, and rode away.

Chapter 20

The Die is Cast

A MOMENT AFTER, Annie was on the portico, every nerve tensed, despair in her heart. She saw the recklessness with which he dashed off towards his own quarters, read in that dare-devil pace his resolve to carry out his threat, to put everything at venture in his determination to punish her. He was lost to her; he had become a danger to her; and she was far from not realizing what that danger meant. There had been too many rumours and suspicions about her; to a white man of his family and position – for he would keep nothing secret now, and would be vouched for by the rector of Montego Bay – the authorities would be obliged to listen. True, they would pay little attention to what he might say about Millicent. But he would speak of her dead husbands, demand why no investigation had been made into those three successive deaths. And there was always Takoo, and there were one or two others on the estate who knew something, perhaps too much. Yes; she was in real danger. And it was coming from a source from which she could never possibly have expected it.

She must take some action. Frustrated passion, injured vanity, a wild longing for vengeance all urged her to it, as well as the instinct of self-preservation. She must act and at once.

Every hour was precious now. Besides, a man who had insulted her so, and for a native girl, ought not to escape unpunished.

She went to the rear of the house, called a boy, and ordered him to run over to Mr Ashman's and bid him come to her immediately. If Mr Ashman were not at home the boy must find out where he was and bring him.

Ashman was soon with her. He had seen from a window of his room that Robert had ridden up to the Great House: had watched for some time and had noticed Robert dash away later on at a speed which suggested that some unpleasant scene had occurred between him and Annie. Ashman knew that he had been sent for because he was badly needed.

Annie wasted no time in preliminaries or equivocations. She came to the point at once; told her overseer with what she had been threatened, and how she had ordered Robert Rutherford out of her presence, never to return. She spoke quietly and coherently enough, but with the suppressed fury of a scorned woman who, to her face, had been told some damning truths.

'He can make it dangerous for me, John, and you know I have no friends in this country – except you. What am I to do?'

'So you have found out that I am your only friend, Annie? And you turn to me after the young man whom you thrust me aside for, and insulted me for, is about to try to get you on the gallows for the sake of a brown girl! What do you expect me to do?'

'I expect you to behave like a man, and not like a child,' she answered with some asperity. 'To begin to fling things in my teeth, especially just now, is not a very chivalrous action. Will you help me or not?'

He was a little overawed by her downright mood and felt that this was no time for recriminations. She was in a desperate temper and a desperate plight; she might do something terribly risky on her own account without thinking clearly about the consequences.

'I will help you to the best of my ability,' he replied with decision; 'but at the moment I don't see what we are to do.'

'He might want to see me on a gallows, John, as you have said, but you don't, do you?'

'God forbid!' exclaimed the usually impious John Ashman; 'I have always loved you far more than he ever could, Annie.'

'If you are to continue to love me, John, if there is to be anything left of me to love, he must be prevented from carrying his lying tales to the magistrates. Remember, any sort of evidence might be considered enough to sacrifice me on.'

'I don't think it would,' he said, and in this was honest; 'but of course we don't want any trouble, or open scandal, though it may be some time before any of us here will have time to think of purely personal matters. The slaves—'

'How do you think he can be stopped?'

He shook his head. 'I can't think, Annie. Unless you can help this girl.'

'Impossible. What can I do? Send to tell her that I am going to save her? She would not believe it. Takoo would not believe it. They both would say that I was setting a trap for them to hinder them from doing what they can on their own account. And I don't want to do it either; I wouldn't do it if I could. It would be like your going on your knees to beg forgiveness of a slave that had thrashed you in public. Could you tolerate the thought of that?'

The set of John Ashman's jaw as she asked the question was answer sufficient. He knit his brows in an effort to think.

'John,' she whispered, 'this whole parish is in an unsettled state, isn't it?'

'Worse at this moment than it was two days ago,' he admitted. 'I have been hearing some stories this morning. They won't turn out to work on Wednesday, and I doubt if they will at all until they are forced. There may be plenty of fighting all over the country in another day or two.'

'And white men will be killed?'

'That is very likely,' he answered soberly.

'So if this Robert Rutherford was killed…?'

'Annie!'

'Why not?' she asked, speaking very low. 'It may be his life or mine!'

'I couldn't do it,' he replied positively. 'I hate the man; but I could not do it. I am only an overseer; I would be found out; it would be my life for his.'

'I am not asking you to risk anything, but I think you would not like to see me in a court-room answering that man's accusations, and perhaps, afterwards, on the gallows. Don't you think of that?'

'It wouldn't come to that,' he said; not wishing to face the ultimate hideous possibility, and feeling uncomfortable under the repetition of that ominous word 'gallows'.

'It might; it probably would. See here; you have men under you who are pretty hard characters, haven't you? And there will be trouble all around. If any of these men – you know what I mean, don't you? No one would see him if he were careful, and you could find ways and means to help and protect him. Money would be no object …'

He sat very quietly for quite a long while, thinking. He saw her plan. It was feasible, and need involve no risk for him. Yet, hard as he was, he did not like the idea of dooming a young white man to death. This seemed murder, and he shuddered at murder. The killing of a slave would not have appeared to him to be at all in a similar category.

'Have you any plans?' she asked at length.

'I don't like it, Annie,' he confessed; 'yet you must be protected. There is a man on this estate whom Rutherford has treated nastily ever since the first day he came; Rutherford kicked him, you remember, when he was going to punish Mary, and since then has shown that he has no use for him. I know he hates Rutherford, and he would stop at nothing. I expect he is planning some sort of mischief here now, but he is afraid of me. If he got his freedom and some money—'

'He can have both. How can it be arranged?'

'You would have to give him a receipt for a sum of money which he will say he paid you for his "free papers" a couple of weeks ago, the papers to be given to him in January next. That would be quite in order, and it would show he had arranged to buy his freedom some time ago. Afterwards, you could give him twenty pounds. That would be enough.'

'Promise him thirty when he has – you know. And give him ten at once, with the receipt you speak of. It's worth it. You can depend on him?'

'I am sure I can.' Again Ashman paused to think heavily.

He resumed. 'Today is Monday, and Rutherford can do nothing before Wednesday, for all the offices in the Bay are closed. On Wednesday he probably will leave for the Bay; but, anyway, our man can watch him and follow him wherever he goes. Pompey has been a hunter of wild hogs for a long time,' added Ashman grimly. 'He is a splendid "shot".'

A little shiver went through Annie; in a flash of imagination she pictured a malignant negro crouched behind a boulder or a clump of cane at some lonely spot by the wayside, heard a shot ring out, saw Robert pitch headlong from his horse and the slayer slinking away to refuge. No slave would track him now, none would interfere on behalf of a white man. This shot indeed might be considered their first blow for freedom, the signal that was to plunge the whole parish in blood.

She shivered, for the man fallen stricken from his horse was one whom she had loved, whom, in her mad, perverted way, she loved still. But it was his life or hers, and if he lived and Millicent lived – for she could not be sure that Millicent would die, for all her terror: if he lived and Millicent lived, he would be to this woman what he had been to her.

The thought hardened her heart.

'I am doing everything for you, Annie,' said John Ashman significantly as he rose to go.

'Your reward is myself, John,' she said with a bitter smile of self-pity, and he wondered what his ultimate recompense would be if in the future he offended her or she wearied of him.

When Ashman took his departure Annie remained where she was, sitting very still, listening to voices in her brain that had begun to speak with insistent distinctness. It was as if she were a stranger that these voices spoke to; she heard them from the outside, as it were. The die was cast, they said; Robert Rutherford was doomed. He would die, for the murderer would not miss; hate as well as cupidity would nerve his arm and direct his aim. Robert would die. And what after that? She loved him, she desired him passionately; in spite of the insults he had put upon her, of the indifference he now showed for her, she wanted him. And if he died she would never see him again; death was the one irremovable obstacle in anyone's path.

He would not act if Millicent lived, and even if the girl lived, might she, Annie, not be able to win him back again? Was that altogether impossible? Without knowing that she did so she shook her head; she could not forgive Millicent; and even were she inclined to do so, that woman's case was beyond her intervention now. She could set agencies of harm in motion; she could not control their effect. Perhaps if she had not interfered last night there would have been a chance; now everything was beyond her power, and what was to be must be. There was still just a possibility that Millicent might recover, and Robert would not move until he knew the worst. But if the girl recovered! Annie's whole being revolted at the ignominy of having to watch, or even to imagine, Millicent's flaunting triumph.

She thought she might be able to endure the successful rivalry of a woman of her own class, or even of her own race; the humiliation would not then be so complete. But she knew that that test would never be offered to her in this country. The white women were few, most of them were but ordinary looking; she knew she was considered to be the most beautiful woman in all Jamaica; she had nothing to fear from any other white woman. Nearly all of them had rivals among the coloured girls, but accepted the situation and so brought about no open rupture with their husbands. But she had no legal claim on Robert, and in any circumstances could tolerate no pretender to his affections. He must be hers only. Other white women might compromise with the existing conditions and make a sacrifice for some sort of external peace. She sneered at them: such pitiful weakness moved her to contempt. What a man like Ashman did could not matter to her; if she ceased to care for anyone his actions no longer concerned her. But if she still loved him she would yield nothing to those who challenged her hold; the struggle must continue to the end.

So the die was cast; she would not countermand the order she had given to Ashman. Indeed, he would hold her in utter contempt if she did; he would look upon her as a timorous, hesitant, lovesick fool, she whom he had always regarded as a strong, imperious, self-reliant woman. She could never submit to such a degradation. She would despise herself. She would despise herself for having allowed herself to be despised.

But the future? Again the voices in her brain asked her questions, and they were about her future. What would life hold in store for her when Robert was gone? Was she to remain here, alone with a bore whom, recently, she had been able just to tolerate but no more? Was Ashman to be her master, sharing a terrible secret with her, insisting upon being her lover? That too would be a humiliation unspeakable, a long-drawn-out torture; she did not see herself enduring it; she would not.

But Ashman would be on his guard. He cared for her, yes; she knew that; he cared because he could not help it; but he distrusted her and would not fail to watch her closely. She felt she would never be able to get rid of him, save by open dismissal, and then he might try to subdue her will by threats of exposure. That was a contingency which would have to be dealt with should it ever arise; worse by far would be the having to endure this man week after week, month after month, year after year. And hating him more and more. And longing for the one great love of her life, for the man whom she herself had just sentenced to his death.

She did not think that she could live through the future without Robert. She was no longer very young, and she wanted no man save him. She had known the awful agony of a boredom almost without relief in the months before Robert's coming; it would be much worse in the years to come, a nightmare black and hideous as hell. Think as hard as she could she saw no way of escape. She had built a prison about her. Its impalpable wall would hold her faster than could walls of iron and stone.

A faint hope flickered through her brain; she uttered it aloud, as though in answer to the voices which were painting her future in the blackest hues. Something might happen to turn the whole course of events. The hired assassin might be hindered from carrying out his design at the last moment almost. Robert might shrink, when it came to the point, from denouncing her, even though Millicent should be dead. If these things happened – and life was full of such out-of-the-ordinary incidents – all might yet be well. She could defy Ashman then. Indeed, with Robert alive and Millicent dead, he would be submissive enough.

It was this slender hope, this possibility, that she clung to for a while; but this mood soon passed. Again she was plunged into despair. She walked to the sideboard (laden with the silver which her first husband had collected with such pride), and poured out for herself a glass of madeira, which she drank slowly. The wine heated her blood and brain; she felt stronger in will and in purpose. She had never been intoxicated in her life; but during the last year or so she had taken to wine as some sort of refuge from the ennui that had plagued her. She had no illusions about drinking. She knew that, strong-willed though she was, she might pass the limit of safety in drinking, might steadily drift into a habit of semi-intoxication, and would in her loneliness be all the more likely to do so than other women. She knew how drinking caught hold of and completely captured thousands of men, and some women too, in this country. They went to it for forgetfulness and solace. Often they found it a master and a terrible tyrant.

But there was no help for it. She must silence the doubts and the questionings in her mind, doubts and questionings the like of which had never tormented her before. She must stifle them, or her will might be weakened and she might become a very fool, not knowing what to do, not standing resolute as she had always done, and so winning her own admiration. She had set her course, had laid her plan; if she of her own will altered them now she might find herself in an awful predicament. If chance or fate chose to intervene, that she could not prevent. But of her own volition, of her own action, to act now so as to give Robert Rutherford every opportunity of bringing her to open disgrace, which would be worse than death to a woman of her spirit, and which might even send him to the arms of that daring, mulatto wretch if she happened by some miracle to recover – that would be madness on her part. Then indeed should she deserve any horror that might befall her. She cried aloud that she could face anything but that.

Deliberately she poured herself out another glass of the wine. She knew that she would not cease to turn to it for aid until this whole crisis was passed. She knew that she must not allow herself to think much about Robert, for then the poignant grief which gnawed at her heart might master her. She gazed with staring eyes into the glass she held in her hand. For the first time in her life she needed extraneous aid to steel her to her purpose.

CHAPTER 21

Rider and Millicent

IN THE AFTERNOON of that same day, at about five o'clock, Robert and Rider called at the house of a well-known doctor in Montego Bay and asked him to accompany them a little distance to see a girl who was dying of superstitious fear. It was not the same man whom Robert had previously asked to see Millicent. They explained the circumstances briefly, not mentioning Mrs Palmer's name. The girl, they said, believed she had been bewitched and was obviously in a dangerous condition. Did the doctor think he could help?

He was sceptical. He had come across such cases in his career, but he had never known much help derived from a regular practitioner. These people simply refused to eat, hardly slept; they were convinced that their death was approaching and it was almost impossible to rid their mind of the conviction. But he would go and see what could be done. That could do no harm.

So they went on to the house of Takoo's daughter, entered the yard and saw a number of people standing about, as on the first occasion when Robert had visited the place.

It was dark by now, the early dusk of the December day had fallen and already lights were gleaming in the little house. But in spite of the obscurity the visitors observed that the people were hostile, for murmurs arose as they reined in their horses and dismounted, and no one seemed inclined to give them way.

Rider had been told of Robert's intentions. He knew that his friend was about to do something that most men would have avoided. He did not believe it would be easy, if indeed possible, to bring home a charge of murder against Annie Palmer, and he reflected that the long wait would prevent Robert from returning home as early as he had hoped. He was going too, and he wished to go quickly; he did not wish to tarry in this country one day longer than was absolutely necessary. But Robert's mind was made up, he was not to be argued with; he was in revolt against his weakness and vacillation of the last three weeks, he was moved to the depths, determined to do something that should redeem him in his own eyes. Rider understood all this. He acquiesced in what was said to him, even if he thought the plan rather futile.

He had been asked and had agreed to go with the young man to this place this evening, when Robert had learnt from Psyche that Millicent had again been taken there. He feared the worst.

And in Rider's mind was a feeling that Annie Palmer, who had been told of Robert's intentions, would not be idle in the meantime, could not afford to be. Rider felt that serious trouble was impending, trouble in which he would be a mere spectator. For beyond a very circumscribed limit he could not help at all. He had no power, no influence, no reputation even. And to warn Robert now would be worse than useless; Robert would proceed upon the path mapped out by himself in spite of all expostulation or argument.

The three white men ignored the hostile murmurings and attitude of the assembled negroes. The doctor took precedence, led the way to the door of the room which Robert indicated, rapped, and, on a woman coming to the entrance, mentioned who he was and asked if they would allow him to see the sick person.

The woman retired, returning in a few moments with Takoo. The old man, even in that obscurity, looked bowed and greatly aged. Gone was all the power and dignity with which he had seemed clothed the night before when, as the high priest of some mysterious cult, he had dominated a multitude of credulous fanatics. He now looked like an old, broken negro, with all the energy gone out of him, But at once he recognized who the gentlemen standing there were, and he quickly came out to meet them.

It was at Robert that he glanced, questioningly.

'I have brought a doctor to see your granddaughter,' said Robert kindly. 'The last time, when the other doctor came, you had removed.'

'It's no use, massa,' groaned the old man heavily. 'Millie dying!'

'You had better let me see her,' said the doctor briskly; 'quite possibly you are mistaken. Where is she?'

Takoo motioned to the door; the doctor passed in, leaving the rest of them standing.

Rider addressed old Takoo.

'Last night,' he began, 'you tried to take off what you believe to be a ghost that is haunting Millicent – oh, yes, we know all about it: we were there though you did not see us.'

'You there!' exclaimed the old man. 'Then you saw de spirit that—'

'We saw everything. And we want you and Millie to understand that it was nothing real; only something imagined ... by someone else who caused you to see it. Can you follow me? That person first pictured the Bull in her mind and had power enough to make it appear to all of us also. But the thing itself wasn't real; it was only a vision. Do you think we could get Millicent to understand that?'

'Understand what, massa? If a woman have power to make you see such a thing, what can you do against her? And it *was* real. Massa, Rolling-Calf *is* real. And it appear just when I was taking off the sucking spirit from Millie, Mrs Palmer's spirit!'

Rider looked at the old man hopelessly, he spoke with such absolute certitude. Nothing could root out of his mind beliefs that were now a part of its texture. Rider made a despairing gesture.

Robert, however, resolved to see what his persuasion might effect.

'You know Mr Rider and I would like to save Millicent, don't you?' he asked Takoo.

'Yes, Squire, but you can't. I fail; you must fail too. And now you will have to look after yourself.'

He said nothing more, nor did they; they could only await the doctor's verdict. Presently the doctor issued from the room. He drew the white men slightly aside. 'It is as I feared,' he said, 'the girl is beyond all argument and beyond all treatment. She has had a terrible shock; her heart is failing. It was never strong, though she might have lived for years and years had nothing much occurred to distress her.'

The two men knew what this meant, yet the question came from Robert: 'Is she dying?'

'I don't think she will live through the night.'

Though Robert had been expecting to hear something of the sort the actual words came as though they were a blow. It seemed so horrible, this swift passing from life to death of a girl who but a few days ago seemed so free from danger and serious care. This was tragedy in one of its most awful forms, for behind it loomed the sinister figures of what anywhere would be considered as malignant and deadly witchcraft.

Takoo came up now. 'I know what the doctor say,' he remarked; 'he couldn't say different. You want to take leave of me poor child before she go, massa?'

'Let me see her for a little while first, will you?' suddenly said Rider, before Robert could answer. 'She is conscious now, I gather. I had better see her; I won't be long.'

He spoke with quiet, authoritative insistence, as one who had a right to the interview he requested. He seemed to take it for granted that he would not be refused, for he waited for no answer.

He passed into the room. The other men, almost automatically, drew nearer to it. The people in the yard came nearer also, moved by curiosity.

They heard a murmur of voices within, Rider speaking and Millicent replying weakly, and then they heard Rider alone. They caught the words, 'Yea, though I walk through the valley of the shadow of death I will fear no evil, for Thou art with me'; they heard other words, they knew that this man, without a church, a drunkard, one even thought to care nothing for the religion in which he had been bred and of which he had been a confessor, was striving to bring some consolation to the last moments of an unhappy fellow-creature. He was the minister of souls once more, and perhaps never so sincerely before as now. This death-bed touched his heart, every sentiment of purity in him vibrated to the appeal of a scene than which he had known none more piteous. Here was a duty, sacred, solemn, and he knelt and offered up his prayers with a sincerity of which there could be no doubt. He alone, at this moment, might soothe the tortured spirit that was so soon to leave this world.

The waiting, angry crowd heard and were impressed. An influence superior to their own surly, snarling temper dominated them. There were women there who, the night before, had swayed and writhed their bodies to the compulsion of a weird, heathen rhythm; now some of them sank upon their knees and sobbed softly, murmuring the name of Jesus. And men stood with bowed heads and respectful demeanour, who last night had looked with bloodshot eyes at the slaughter and sacrifice of an animal to some but half-apprehended evil deity. It was a strange spectacle, for all that crowd was silently praying in unison with the voice inside the room, and overhead the stars came out and pricked with light the enveloping darkness, and the wind sighed through the trees. Then the voice ceased, and after a couple of minutes Rider issued forth, a strange, sad look upon his face, and beckoned to Robert.

The young man stepped into the room, where only one woman stood beside the bed on which lay Millicent. He went quietly to the bedside and touched her hand lightly; she looked up at him and smiled.

'I know you would come,' she said faintly.

He found no words to reply, could not trust himself to speak.

'Take care of yourself,' she whispered again; 'take care, Squire. You promise?'

He bowed his head and patted her arm, and there was silence for a little while.

When at length he bent over she appeared to be sleeping; her strength had given out. He turned and tiptoed out of the room.

There was nothing more to do, nothing to stay for. The doctor was anxious to be gone. Robert knew that for the last time he had seen Millicent's face, had taken final farewell of a victim of strange and atrocious superstitions. He mounted his horse and, with his two companions, turned to go.

Takoo came up to him. 'I will never fo'get all this, Squire,' he said, 'whatever happen.'

Without a word the white men rode off, and in Montego Bay the doctor left them, regretting that he had been of no slightest use. He parted respectfully from Rider, too, who, on the way to Takoo's place, he had hardly noticed, knowing much about him as a man who had fallen below the esteem of his class. The two friends went on, their destination Rosehall; tomorrow Robert would inform Ashman that, no matter what the consequences, he would not be back at his work on Wednesday. He briefly told Rider of his resolve and Rider said that he too would endeavour to leave, especially since it was only too probable that on that day the slaves would remain idle, and it might even be that the white people on the estates would be forced to flee into Montego Bay. 'The rumours are coming thick and fast now,' he added, but did not interest his companion.

Early on the following morning news came by special bearer to Psyche. Millicent had died in her sleep during the night.

CHAPTER 22

In the Dark of the Night

'SO YOU WANT to leave Rosehall?' said Mr Ashman; 'when do you plan to go?'

'Tomorrow morning,' returned Robert.

'Very well; you can go. You haven't been of very much use here at best. I will send you what wages are due to you a little later.'

'The wages you can keep; your impertinent remarks you had better keep to yourself also, or you will be sorry for them.'

'Hell! Sorry, I?' Ashman exploded. 'But I am not going to quarrel with you, young man; you're not worth it. Well, sir, what are *you* waiting for?' This to Rider.

'I should like to leave, too, Mr Ashman, tomorrow morning.'

'You have not my permission, Mr Rider. This estate will be short-handed and you must remain for a little while yet. But you can go at the end of the week, if you like,' he added contemptuously. 'I suppose you want to follow your friend.'

'That has nothing to do with the matter,' said Rider with some dignity. 'You must know by this, that the slaves are not likely to come out to work tomorrow, so there will be no use for me here.'

'If you were a man, there would be. We may want four or five white men here to keep the people in order in case they begin to attempt any foolishness, but I suppose you wouldn't be any use for that. But you can't leave in the morning unless you want to be prosecuted. I'll tell you what, though,' he said, as a thought seemed to strike him, 'I'll let you go during the day sometime, if nothing happens here. Rutherford can leave as early as he wants to, and the sooner the better. I want his room fixed up. Next time I take good care that we don't employ fal-de-la young men and deserters on this estate.'

The two men walked away without answering, and Ashman looked after them with a scowl. So Mr Rutherford would be leaving early the next morning, before daybreak probably, to have a cool ride into Montego Bay. He was done with the estate. He wished to be soon in the town to begin his criminal prosecution, or accusation, or whatever he might choose to call it: he would waste no time. But perhaps he would never reach Montego Bay.

No; it would never have done to let Rider go along with him, though the sooner Mr Rider was off the premises the better. He had kept too sober. He too might be inclined to make trouble.

The day wore on. Psyche had received permission from Burbridge to go to her cousin's funeral, which was to be that afternoon, and she had set off betimes to trudge the twelve miles of distance she had to cover. Burbridge joined his friends at lunch-time, but no one had much of a lunch. Burbridge had been informed by a book-keeper on the neighbouring estate that there would be difficulty with the people next day. He had cleaned and oiled his gun. He knew that Ashman and the two Scotsmen would also be prepared. Rider and Rutherford were leaving.

But four white men, who could depend upon two or three black headmen (who would also be armed) should be enough to put down any ordinary demonstration. If anything more serious threatened, the white people would be compelled to withdraw to the town and leave matters to the militia.

They had little to say to one another today. Burbridge knew better than to dwell on the death of the girl, Rider avoided the topic with a natural sensitiveness, Robert did not mention it. What now filled his mind, occupied his thoughts to the exclusion of almost anything else, was the duty before him, the duty of bringing to justice the most dangerous woman in all the West Indies, a woman who might be insane but who in any age and country would be accounted a criminal. He tried to think of the matter impersonally. He spoke to himself about justice, not vengeance. But the memory of a wan face and faint voice, a voice whose last words were an appeal to him to take care of himself, was uppermost in his mind. He was thinking less of pure justice than he desired to believe.

The night came dark and squally, though there was no rain; and by seven the darkness was dense. He could not sleep, he was restless, the minutes seemed long, and it would be hours before morning came. Rider, he had noticed vaguely, was very restless, too; he attributed this to the emotional disturbances they had both experienced yesterday, and to the approaching end of their connection with this accursed place. He was right as to his belief that Rider had passed through what was, for him, an exhausting spiritual phase of emotion; his whole past had, as it were, come back to him, with his sudden assumption of sacerdotal office and authority; he had been profoundly shaken; his whole being had been disturbed. And now, suddenly, as it usually did, the craving for drink had come upon him, his body felt dry, burnt out; there was a feverish thirst in every fibre of it. Yet he resisted it as he had not done for years. In spite of the craving he had not touched a drop of rum that day. But it shook and tortured him, and he hoped and prayed that his resolution would last until he could be back in the town and preparing for his departure from the country. Rider felt that if he left Rosehall and had something to occupy his mind amid different surroundings, with a new future beckoning to him, he might be able successfully to withstand the terrible temptation.

At about ten o'clock he came to Robert, coming on foot, and found the young man seated on the veranda. Burbridge was in his own room.

'I walked over; I couldn't sleep,' he explained. 'I thought you wouldn't be sleeping either.'

'I can't.'

'No. And I marked the drums particularly tonight. There are more of them than I have ever heard before and they are not all for dancing, I imagine. Do you notice how they seem to come from every quarter?'

He paused, while the air seemed to throb with the sound of the drumming, some of it very faint and far away, travelling for miles through the atmosphere, which at that moment was still.

Mechanically Robert listened to the staccato beats, the low rumblings, that sounded through the surrounding darkness.

'Some are drums of the dance, and some of religious ceremonies, perhaps; but some, I fancy, are war drums,' said Rider. 'There are big palavers tonight.'

'Shall we take a walk?' suggested Robert. 'We both don't want to sleep. Let us wander about a bit.'

This suggestion fitted in with Rider's restless mood as well as with Robert's. The latter clapped on his hat and they started out.

They had no particular objective, and unless they wished to entangle themselves in the cane-fields they must either go north towards the main road and the sea, or south towards the hills. The path southward was that which led to the Great House, which was in darkness, a thicker black in the midst of the blackness of the night. They could not be seen if they came near to it and skirted it; so they turned their steps in that direction.

Robert felt impelled by a necessity for audible self-criticism. 'I have made a nice hash of my life in Jamaica, Rider,' he said, as they went on.

'Most of us do,' replied the other man grimly: 'I think I have said that before. But you appear to have done so much less than most others. You have caught yourself up in time.'

'Circumstances have stopped me. I did not know myself. I had all sorts of high hopes and resolutions. I was going to learn a lot while enjoying myself; I was going to have a fine time and yet become a competent planter. I was going to make my old man proud of me; show my strength and determination, and all that. But I hadn't been here a day before I was making love to a woman I knew nothing about, and I hadn't been here a week before I was philandering with one of the native girls, and drinking lots of Jamaica rum, and neglecting my work, and beginning to ruin my constitution. And now one woman hates me like poison and threatens me, and the other is dead, through me. A lovely record in less than a month!'

Rider made no comment.

'I suppose,' continued Robert bitterly, 'I am only a rash, impulsive fool, after all, not the paragon I imagined myself to be.'

'You are not more rash or impulsive than most other people, I fancy,' said Rider soothingly. 'Nine out of every ten young men from the Old Country fall by the way in Jamaica if they begin low down. That was your mistake, and yet the idea behind it was excellent. Well, there is nothing to be gained now by dwelling on mistakes; you had better let the dead past bury its dead. You are a young man and your future is still in the making.'

'It will certainly have to be much different from the present.'

'In a way,' said Rider, wishing to stop Robert from too much self-accusation, 'you have even been more unfortunate than the majority of men who have come out to Jamaica. You fell in immediately with a sort of Lucrezia Borgia. Annie Palmer has lived out of her time; she should have been born in the fourteenth or fifteenth century; with her will and ability she, woman though she is, might have made a great name for herself, and her iniquities might have counted as venial offences even if husband-killing were included among them. But here she was, and you met her, and she fascinated and encouraged you, made open love to you. I wonder how many young men could have resisted that temptation. I can't think of one.'

'And even now,' said Robert suddenly, 'I feel sorry for her. Terribly sorry. I have made up my mind what to do, for she is dangerous and will always be so. But it is not pleasant to think that I, who loved her – and she has said she loves me, too – should be the one to accuse her. The more I think of it, the more the thought harasses me. I have felt more than once today as if I were about to be a betrayer: a man who has eaten a woman's bread and salt and then goes about to hand her over to – it may be death.'

'I had a feeling that you would be thinking something of the sort,' said Rider, a trifle dryly. 'Don't you think you might take a week or so to consider calmly your steps? Nothing is to be lost by that.'

Robert shook his head resolutely. 'The blood of a murdered woman cries out of the ground for justice,' he said.

'The quotation is not quite correct, but I might cap it with another: "Vengeance is mine, saith the Lord, I will repay."'

'Would you have me let her go free, to do what she wills with other people?' cried Robert.

'I would have you do nothing you do not wish to do, my friend. You yourself are having your doubts now as to the best course to follow, and I should be sorry if you did anything now, however right it might seem, or be, with which you should reproach yourself later on. I cannot advise you, but you yourself have said that you both have been lovers.'

'I wonder,' said Robert, as though he were thinking aloud, 'if she is quite sane?'

'Pride, and the life she has led, and the power she has had over her slaves, may have unhinged her brain,' Rider commented; 'that is quite possible. Inordinate vanity and fierce passions, in surroundings like these, may have unbalanced her, or insanity may be her heritage. Or traffic with evil things in Haiti may have affected her brain. We cannot know. Perhaps it is only charitable to think so.'

'But what a splendid asylum for a mad woman?' exclaimed Robert, looking up, for they had come within less than a stone's throw of Annie Palmer's home.

It was all in darkness. Its façade towered above them as they halted on the upward slope to gaze upon it; it stood out dark against the pitchy background of the night, with all its blatant assertions of opulence and power. It had been built to set forth the riches and pride of its first possessor; money had been lavished upon it, not merely for comfort, but by way of emphasis. Even to a headstrong and proud plantocracy it was intended as a sort of challenge from one of its members who wished to be considered as the first among his peers. And now it housed one woman only, and she shunned by her class and shunning them, more self-assertive than had been any of her predecessors, and one who had carried her love for power and domination to lengths of which they had never dared to dream.

Instinctively they walked soft-footed. They had no wish to draw attention to themselves, though as the mistress must have been sleeping then, and the servants had probably retired, there was no danger of their being seen or heard. The wind, too, was blowing fitfully, and the night was black. Heavy clouds drifted across the sky. Ordinary sounds would not penetrate into the Great House at that hour, nor could casual eyes observe them.

They turned quietly to their right, following a path which would lead them to the rear of the property, towards which they planned to walk until they were tired. Pursuing this course they would pass the servants' quarters and the kitchen at the left wing of the house. They had ceased to talk; in a minute or two they found themselves on a gentle slope which they proposed to climb, and on their left hand, some seven feet above the level of the ground on which they stood, rose the paved platform (up to which some steps led) which formed part of the back veranda of the main building.

Here too everything was in darkness.

But it seemed to them both that the darkness was moving, or rather that something moved in it. It was not curiosity alone that caused them to halt as though one man, and peer fixedly through the gloom towards that raised stone platform. There was some suggestion there of presences, something like whispers floated on the air; as their eyes became more accustomed to the scene at which they stared they perceived without any doubt that figures were outlined dimly there, human figures, and even while they stood with muscles tensed and all sorts of surmises in their minds the shadowy figures seemed to dissolve or fade away and then they vanished entirely.

Robert clutched Rider by the arm. 'What on earth can that mean?' he whispered, having in mind the malign apparition he had seen on Christmas Night in the woods that led to Palmyra.

'They look like human beings, and they have gone into the Great House,' whispered Rider in reply. 'My God what can that mean?'

A scream, sharp, piercing, agonized, stabbed through the sombre air, then ceased abruptly as though smothered. A light broke out in the room which Robert knew to be Annie's, a light shining dimly through the glass panes of the closed windows.

'It is her voice,' exclaimed Robert, 'and, and—'

'Come!' commanded Rider. 'Those men were slaves. I understand now.'

They leapt up the steps that led to the platform; then, Robert now leading the way, ran to the little sloping structure which he had noticed on the night when Annie had shown him over the house. The opening which that contrivance covered formed the back ingress to the cellars of the house: a short flight of brick steps, a vaulted passage, brought you into the cellars, which were paved with rubble. But Robert knew also that, to the left, was a little door, usually locked, which led by a sort of ladder, or narrow wooden steps, to the hall above in which began the grand stairway which was the pride of Rosehall. Anyone who negotiated that cellar door would be able to gain the topmost story without any difficulty whatever.

He led Rider, for he knew the way. Down the outer steps, then through the low vaulted passage they went as rapidly as the thick blackness would allow; they reached the small door in the cellar – it was open! Evidently the key had been purloined from Annie, in whose possession it usually was. In a few seconds the friends reached the hall above, were leaping up the stairway, had gained the upper story. There they found that they had hurled themselves into the midst of a number of men who, surprised at their sudden and unexpected appearance, and frightened desperately by it, made no effort to hold them back as they rushed through an open door into Annie's room.

Her candelabrum was lighted. It dimly showed a group of blacks some armed with machetes, with wild rolling eyes and menacing demeanour; it showed a slim, white figure clothed in a night-robe, grasped by two powerful men, one of whom had his broad hand placed firmly over her mouth. Her eyes were aglare with terror, for the man whose hand had stifled her screams was Takoo. And in Takoo's face was the unpitying exultation of a savage.

Before they could reach her Robert and Rider found their path barred by some six men, four of whom seized them, while the two others lifted their machetes as though to cut them down. The men outside had now rushed in, ready to give assistance: they had grasped the fact that these were the only two white men attempting a rescue. Robert, with his immense strength, and in his sudden fury, was equal to any two of his captors, but there were many to grasp and overpower him. Rider was like a child in the hands of one man. A smell of rum pervaded the room. Evidently these people had been supplied with drink before being brought by Takoo on their murderous enterprise.

The old witch doctor shouted to his followers an order that they were not to harm the two white men. But he added immediately, 'Don't allow them to make any noise.' Rider began to speak immediately, in a quiet voice, for he did not wish his words to be smothered. Robert desisted from his efforts to break loose, efforts which were useless and which would only have prevented Rider from being heard.

'Think of what you are doing, Takoo,' implored Rider. 'If you harm Mrs Palmer you will get yourself into serious trouble, you and your men. Do you want to be hanged?'

'Who deserve hanging most?' Takoo volleyed back to him; 'me or she? She kill Millicent an' you know it. Who will punish her if I don't? I pass sentence on her tonight over the grave of me dead gran'daughter,' he continued passionately. 'I sentence her to death, as chief an' leader of the people of St James. You talk about me an' dese men being hanged, Mr Rider? Is it the white men who have to look for themself now, for we are all free from tonight – every slave in Jamaica is free – and we taking to the mountains to fight until the damn slave-owners here acknowledge our freedom. It come from England an' they keeping it back. Very well, we will take it ourself, even if some of us have to die for it. I expec' to die, but dese men with me will live free for ever. And before I die dis woman will; she will go before me. No power from hell or heaven can save her!'

'But man, she is a woman, and you are all strong men. Surely you have some mercy in your hearts?' panted Robert.

Annie looked at him with eyes in which gratitude and a wild appeal for aid were mingled. From him help must come if from any source that night. She trusted to him only.

That he himself had intended to report her to the authorities of Montego Bay as a murderess was forgotten by both of them. There seemed nothing incongruous in this effort of his to save her, in this mute supplication of hers to him. It revolted him to see her in the rude grasp of these slaves, handled brutally by people who, a few hours ago, would not have dared to look her impudently in the face. She was a white woman, she was Roschall's mistress, she was beautiful, she was of his own race and a member of the ruling, dominant class. For these men to terrorize her, to dare to threaten her with death, was soul-sickening, revolting, incredible. It had to be prevented! They should not murder her while he had strength sufficient to fight against them. What she was did not matter now. Outraged pride of race animated him; he was a white man struggling for the life of a white woman. And he felt, vaguely, wildly, that he loved her still. If needs be he was prepared to give his life for hers.

Rider, even at that moment, realized that Robert was acting in defiance of his resolution to bring Annie Palmer to justice if that could be done. And Rider knew that if Annie were saved that night Robert would never utter a word against her to anyone who could track her to her doom.

And what Robert, burningly raged against – the indignity, the enormity, of this besetting of a white woman by her slaves, this impending hideous execution or murder of her by them, Rider also felt to the full. The very idea was monstrous, atrocious. It mattered nothing what she had done, it was not for these men rudely to handle her and slay her. It was the duty of every white man on the estate to stand by her in this deadly hour of peril. Alas, the others were out of hearing. And they two were matched against twenty.

'Mercy?' repeated Takoo, almost mechanically, in answer to Robert's cry. 'She didn't have no mercy on anybody, Squire.'

Robert stiffened himself for the fight he perceived to be inevitable, but Rider stayed him with a look.

Rider recognized that further pleading would be in vain. Yet something must be done. An idea flashed into his mind.

'Remember,' he said impressively to Takoo, 'this lady has command over powers and spirits that are greater than you.

Touch her, injure her, and your life will be miserable for ever: yours, and the life of every man here, both now and hereafter. Do you realize what you are risking, Takoo?'

Even as he spoke he tried to convey his inner meaning to Annie Palmer. His eyes were fixed on hers, trying to telegraph his message to her brain. And she grasped it. He saw a responsive flash of comprehension pass over her face, and her gaze became fixed. If only she could conjure up, at this moment, in this apartment, some nebulous image that these people had pictured and talked about again and again, believing firmly in its malign death-dealing influence, she was safe. They would fly howling from the room. Even Takoo's nerves might not be proof against such a terrible test; and if he should stand his ground, Robert alone would be more than a match for him.

But Rider had conveyed his idea to another mind also. Takoo saw his men start, observed that on the instant they were apprehensive, half drunk though he had made them. Sober, they never would have faced Mrs Palmer, even with him as leader; even now the warning of Rider had struck a chill through them and dread was already beginning to master them. Takoo glanced at the woman whose mouth he still covered with his palm. He saw her gaze grow steady, staring, as if she were concentrating her mind and will upon one overwhelming purpose. She was calling her spirits to her aid. In another minute she might defeat him. Suddenly he shifted his hand from her face to her throat: a half-stifled scream, and the old savage was throttling her with all the strength of his hardened muscles.

A thunderous curse from Robert, a cry of protest from Rider, but the slaves held them fast. Robert went down amongst a heap of them; Rider soon gave over the impotent struggle, exhausted. It was over in a very little while. The woman's eyes protruded horribly from the sockets, her tongue hung out limply. The contortions of her body subsided into a spasmodic twitching, then the corpse rested heavy and inert. Annie had died as one of her husbands had, in the same way and by the same hand.

For a moment or two there was silence, the silence of a horrible tragedy. Then:

'We could kill both of you, Squire, if we want,' Takoo said. 'But both of you are kind. We may have to fight you tomorrow, but for Millie's sake you can go tonight.' He turned to his men. 'Let us throw this woman's body through the window, like them throw Jezebel of old, for she was another Jezebel.'

'Takoo,' broke in Rider, 'for God's sake don't do that. She is dead. Leave her alone now.'

'Very well, Squire. Come, we going to the hills.' He spoke to his men and they went out with him, leaving the white men behind.

The sounds of their footsteps died away. The corpse, half flung on the bed, looked so pitiful, and withal so awful, that Rider threw a sheet over it. 'What an end,' he muttered to himself.

With his face buried in his hands, Robert was sobbing.

'We must rouse Ashman and the others, Rutherford,' said Rider. 'Let us go down.'

They went down by the way they had come, and now they found the yard in a state of excitement and agitation. The house servants were up and chattering volubly. What had occurred? What was amiss? Why had Takoo forced them to stay in their rooms, with two or three men armed with machetes to compel their obedience? Where was the missis? The white men vouchsafed no reply; but Rider noticed that an elderly black woman, the chief of the servants, said very little, and guessed that she knew all. Even in the Great House Takoo had had his followers. Annie had watched others, or had had them watched, and had sought to terrify them. And all this time she had herself been watched, and her movements had been faithfully reported to the terrible obeahman, and efforts to terrify her had been made. If they had failed it was because of her superior mentality and her contempt for the poor, futile tricks that illiterate slaves had tried to play upon her. Of one thing she had never dreamed – a direct assault upon her. It was that which had taken her unawares, with such sinister and tragic consequences.

'Both of us cannot leave here at the same time,' said Robert; 'will you go to Ashman?'

Rider nodded and set off. Robert remained behind, not permitting any of the slaves to enter the house.

'This is the work of you and your kind,' he muttered. 'There must be no further insults for her.'

One or two of the younger women began to whimper. Fear gripped them, and they cowered in the presence of such an overwhelming occurrence as they would in the midst of a hurricane.

In a short space of time new-comers were on the scene. Ashman and the two Scotsmen had not waited for their horses, but on hearing from Rider of the tragedy at the Great House had rushed thither on foot. All three men carried guns. The crisis was on at last, and they came prepared.

Followed by Robert and the others, Ashman strode up to the room where Annie's body lay; he drew back the sheet and gazed dumbly at the staring eyes and protruding tongue as though unable to credit the testimony of his sight. Then he stopped and lifted the corpse, and pressed his fingers on the eyelids in an effort to close them: failing, he covered up the face, walked to a window, threw it open, and in a harsh voice, menacing with suppressed feeling, he ordered some of the women below to come up.

He was a man of action; he knew what had to be done. He gave sharp orders to the women; the mistress would be buried in the morning; it would be impossible to delay her burial longer. 'And, by God,' he said, 'if I find one man or woman disobeying what I say, in the slightest degree, I will shoot you on the spot and shoot to kill. This is a rebellion, is it? Well, you will learn how I deal with rebellion.'

They left the room, with the women in it already going about their allotted duty.

'I will stay here during the night,' said Ashman, 'and these gentlemen with me'; he indicated the master mechanic and artisan. 'Those beasts may return to set fire to the house; if they do—' he broke off significantly. He was clearly not afraid of that crowd. 'What will you do?' he asked Robert, to whom, now, he showed no animosity.

'I am going,' said Robert, 'I have had enough of it. Unless you want my services? I don't think Takoo will come back, but if you think he will I can stay.'

'You needn't, Mr Rutherford. Your friend Rider has not come back; he seems to be badly upset. But you had better send Burbridge to me. I can deal with this situation.'

Robert, for the first and last time in his life, held out his hand to Ashman, who took it without hesitation. Ashman was seated in a chair placed in the back entrance hall whence the grand stairway led upwards. As Robert passed through the rear doors, knowing he would never enter them again, he saw Ashman's head lowered on his chest.

Ashman was mourning for Annie Palmer.

CHAPTER 23

One Taken, the Other Left

ON THE VERANDA of the book-keepers' quarters Robert found Burbridge up and ready to go off to the Great House. Psyche was awake and crying, through sheer excitement and fright. Some of the boys of the estate were standing about, realizing that a terrible thing had happened and not knowing what to do.

'Where is Rider?' asked Robert, and was told that Rider was in his room.

He threw the door open and saw the ex-parson with a bottle half-filled with rum on the table beside him. Rider was sitting down, one arm resting on the table, the other within reach of a glass in which a dark red liquor gleamed. He must have consumed already at least half a pint of rum. And he had not finished drinking yet.

But he was not drunk. It took more than the amount of liquor he had swallowed to make poor Rider drunk. He seemed on his way to drunkenness, however; he had yielded to his old temptation: previous abstinence, unwonted excitement, and then the culminating horrors of that night had been too much for his nerves and resolution.

'Couldn't keep away any longer, Rutherford,' he muttered. 'I should have gone mad if I hadn't had a drink.'

Robert nodded his head in comprehension, and reached out for a glass himself. He too felt a sudden craving for a stimulant of some kind.

Burbridge came to the door. 'I suppose I shall be up there till morning,' he said, 'and so I may not see you before you leave, Rutherford. But perhaps you won't go as you intended?'

'There is no need for me to stay,' answered Robert, with a gesture of distaste. 'I won't even wait until morning. Ashman says he does not want me, so I am going tonight.'

'A few hours would make no difference; it may be dangerous on the road tonight. I believe the slaves are out everywhere; a rebellion has begun.'

'I'll take the risk, Burbridge. Especially as Ashman says he does not need my assistance here.'

Robert considered a moment. Then: 'As things are, can't Rider come with me?' he added.

'That's not for me to say,' Burbridge replied. 'Everything is different now that Mrs Palmer is dead, and I don't suppose Ashman would mind if Rider went with you – I don't know. But Rider himself must decide.'

'You had better come, Rider,' urged Robert, 'and leave all this.' He indicated the rapidly emptying rum bottle.

'I couldn't now,' Rider protested. 'I must steady myself first. I feel – God alone knows how I feel. Besides, I haven't a horse like you.'

'Burbridge could lend you one.'

'I daren't,' said Burbridge.

'Very well; I'll go on to the Bay tonight on foot,' said Robert decisively; 'it is only ten miles away and the night is cool. Rider can use my horse.'

'Couldn't hear of such a thing, old man,' protested Rider a trifle thickly. 'I will walk it over myself tomorrow, if I am in a fit condition.'

'You couldn't walk,' said Robert sadly, 'I'll tell you what I'll do. I'll leave my grey for you, and you can ride her over. The walk will do me good. Start early, Rider; get away from here as soon as you can. Do try and meet me in the morning.'

Rider rose, looking very pale and limp in the feeble light that burnt in a tin lamp on the table. 'I'll meet you tomorrow, old fellow, alive or dead. You have been a good friend to me; the best I have had. God bless you.'

He grasped Robert warmly by the hand, and Burbridge also clasped the young man's hand with a sympathetic pressure. Burbridge did not pretend to be upset by Annie's fate; it left him unmoved. But he knew that Robert could hardly feel about her as he did, in spite of all, he had been her lover. And he had witnessed her awful end.

In this way Robert Rutherford took leave of Rosehall, where, in some three weeks, he had passed through experiences that most men's lives did not compass in a generation. He was glad of the movement, the activity, which this long trudge to the Bay compelled him to; he gave but little thought to the possible dangers of the road, though he knew that the slaves were out. But as he went on he saw broad sheets of fire grow against the hills to the south, and beyond them the sky was illuminated here and there by a pale glare for which there was but one explanation. On many of the estates the revolting slaves were giving the cane-fields to the flames.

Montego Bay was vastly agitated. The uprising of the slaves had come at last, but most persons were surprised at it, though the portents had been plain for anyone to see. The militia was mustering; the fort at the land entrance to the town, which commanded the highway that led by the northern shore to the capital, was put in a better state of readiness than it had been, for it was thought that the rebels might march on Montego Bay itself, though sagacious persons knew that this would be utterly unlike the tactics of the slaves. Robert had reached the town while still it was dark and before it had awakened to the gravity of the situation. He had gone to a small lodging-house, where he had slept upon a sofa. It was now nine o'clock, and he was waiting for Rider. He himself had met with no interference on his walk. Indeed, he had passed no one on that long tramp to Montego Bay.

It was about ten o'clock when a rumour took its way to him. Something had happened; a white man had been brought in, dead it was believed, by a party of white people who, with slaves that had remained faithful to them, had fled by the northern shore road that morning into Montego Bay. More out of curiosity than from any other cause, for by this time he had concluded that Rider had been too drunk to leave Rosehall estate as he had planned, Robert went over to where the body of this white man was laid out. Before he got into the house he knew the truth.

The party coming along the road, some time after daybreak, had found the corpse lying in the way, a bullet hole through the heart. Farther on they had come upon a grey horse, rider-less, evidently connected with the dead man; they had caught the reins and brought in the horse, using it as a means of conveying its erstwhile rider. The man must have been shot dead immediately, said the doctor who had been summoned; he was one of the first victims of the war that had begun. There was nothing to do about it. No one knew who his slayer was. No one would ever know.

They buried Rider that afternoon. The rector officiated, and Robert was the chief, perhaps the only mourner. He felt as though life had grown more sombre with this taking off of a man who had been the enemy of no one except himself, who had been kindly, cultured, understanding, but had become a slave to circumstances and a derelict in a land where human life and happiness were held so cheap. Robert wished bitterly that he had waited until dawn before leaving Rosehall, for then Rider and himself might have made the exodus together, and, he said to himself, Rider would in all probability have escaped. That was true. What he never guessed was that the bullet which struck Rider down had been intended for him and would have been fired.

But when Ashman, Burbridge and the two Scotsmen came post haste into Montego Bay that evening, after having fought against a revolt on Rosehall and been compelled to witness the burning of the fields, Ashman knew just how Rider had come by his death. On parting from Robert Rutherford the night before, when Annie Palmer lay a corpse in the upper story of the Great House, Ashman had forgotten the plot he had helped prepare against the young man. Not that Robert's death would have mattered anything to him, but he had nothing to gain by it after Annie was gone and would not have wished it to happen then. As it was, it was Rider who had become the victim. And Ashman had always had a sort of regard for Rider.

Well, he was finished with now, and there were other things to do.

Ashman had buried Annie Palmer in the morning at Rosehall: some slaves had been compelled to dig her grave, on a lonely spot on the estate, under the pointed rifles of the white men. She had had fairly decent burial. And that afternoon the bondsmen had risen and applied the torch to the luscious reeds, rich with juice, which burnt so readily.

The call now was for men to put down the rebellion. Robert offered his services, Ashman went with his men into the mountains to fight the rebels; troops poured in from Spanish Town, the island's capital and seat of government; in a few weeks it was all over. In a tavern in Montego Bay Robert heard Ashman talking one evening. They had nodded to one another, but had shown no inclination for further intercourse. Perhaps, however, what Ashman said he intended particularly for Robert's ears.

He was relating some of his experiences during the recent tracking down of the revolted slaves. 'I knew Takoo at sight, and I dodged about the trees to come near to him. He knew I was trying to get at him, too, and he was trying for me. But I shot the old devil, and I am glad it was my hand that did it. I would have preferred, though, to have strangled him exactly as he strangled Mrs Palmer. I would have choked the life out of him slowly, the old black dog! He's got off far too easily.'

So that was Takoo's end.

Only Mr McIntyre, the rector, was at the waterfront to say good-bye to Robert when, in the February of that year, he took his seat in the boat which was to bear him out into the stream to the ship whose destination was England.

'Do you think you will ever come back to the West Indies?' asked the old parson, by way of saying something.

'Never,' was the reply.